Beaton Back

Alan Searle

Text copyright© Alan Searle
All Rights Reserved
ISBN-13: 978-1517792558

To Jeri

1

He arrived, after a four-hour United Airlines flight, at Boston's Logan Airport and took the water taxi to Rowe's Wharf. He carried his shoulder bag to reception in the archway of the upscale Boston Harbor Hotel. He wore what he had been told to wear – a dark suit and tie with a white shirt. Its damp collar was grabbing his neck in the humid mid-afternoon of a warm, early-spring day.

He'd also been told how to behave. He was to tip generously, but not recklessly; say little, but answer all questions and order room service. If asked, he was there on business. What business? He was to say he was an executive for Logi-Cal Software, a computer company out of San Francisco. He was Reginald Smith, attending a meeting in town, and the software was for monitoring inventory changes in grocery stores. If anyone asked him any more details he was to say he was just a salesman.

No one asked. He thought about taking the stairs and walking to his room with his single bag. He was fit, tanned, and not overweight, but if you stayed in a suite at the Boston Harbor someone was supposed to carry your luggage. He thought a ten-dollar tip was appropriate – not enough to encourage obsequiousness, but adequate for the bell-boy to pocket and not mention it to any of his colleagues. Perhaps a twenty would be appropriate for room service. He didn't have to worry. He'd been given five hundred for incidental expenses. He did wonder if your average software salesman would be staying where he now stood, in the Harbor View Center Suite, overlooking the waterway and its activities, but the hotel was known for its discretion. He'd looked both up online. Logi-Cal Software actually existed, and the Boston Harbor Hotel had five stars to its credit. He checked his Timex watch and wondered if he should have had a Rolex to fit his image. He'd examined the Rolexes in the display cases the last time he was delayed in the transit lounge at Heathrow Airport. He'd come away amazed anyone would spend the equivalent of the average annual American family-of-four income on a watch. And it still just told the time, or he wondered, was he missing something – did it say something about who you were? If it did it, was one more reason not to buy one.

His Timex told him he still had another three hours before the meeting in his room. He had time for a swim, a shower, and a meal.

This was how it usually went. He arrived with plenty of time, opened his bags, left them in the room and went for a walk or a swim as instructed.

They were getting better, and if he hadn't left his underwear just so, he wouldn't have noticed. It was easy to reposition the clothing on top so no one could detect anything had been moved, but they hadn't thought to replace the underwear exactly where he'd placed them. He sighed and wondered why, after all this time, they didn't trust him.

He smiled. They were right to not trust him.

At 6:45 there was a knock on his door. It was room service.

"But I just finished my meal," he said, a little surprised when he opened the door.

"Sir, these are the items you ordered earlier to be delivered to your suite before seven. Am I correct?" She said with a forced smile. She was about his age, mid forties, a little heavy, with over-dyed, burnt orange curls protruding from the sides of her hotel uniform hat. She gave the impression of tired efficiency. She cocked her head dismissively, and advanced with the service trolley.

"Of course, please come in," he replied, covering his ignorance, moving aside, and feeling he had no choice but to admit her. "Oh, and please take these away with you," he said, trying to regain some initiative, and indicating the remains of the meal he had just finished.

"Of course, sir," she said, without looking at him, and began to empty the contents of her trolley onto the table and remove the plates from his recent meal.

He glanced at the items he had apparently ordered. He couldn't recall seeing some of the food now on his table on the room-service menu, but this was the Boston Harbor.

Clearly, someone had clout.

She finished and turned to face him. He offered her two twenties. She took them without a word, turned and left with her trolley, closing the door behind her.

He returned to the table to see what he had apparently ordered. He noted the year on the bottle of Clos de Vougeot and smiled. It was the year when he had turned thirty and when he had been released from prison. It had been a very good year for him; he wondered if it had been for the wine too. He glanced at the bottle of TUMS, the packet of beef jerky, the bowl of fruit, the bowls of walnuts and cashews, a whole lobster and a red sauce, a loaf of crusty dark bread, several chilled bottles of water and...there was another knock. He padded across the thick carpet and opened the door.

"Mr. Smith. It's good to see you again." The man he knew as Mr. Jones strode into the room and walked straight to the table.

"Apparently, it likes to breathe," he said, picking up a corkscrew and the bottle of Clos de Vougeot. "Mr. Jones likes it better that way. As for me, I can't tell the difference." He pulled the cork and placed it, red end up, on the table next to the wine bottle.

Another knock on the door and Smith admitted two men he had probably never seen before. They both introduced themselves as Mr. Jones. Smith was not surprised – over the years he had met several Mr. Jones, and the only one he had seen each time was the man he had first admitted to his room – at least that's what he thought, but he could never be sure. In the past, at meetings like these, that man had done all the talking and the other two, or sometimes three, just sat and listened. This evening's meeting was probably going to follow the same pattern, but there was already one difference. Room service, and the items on his table, were not part of the usual plan. He had little opportunity to examine the Mr. Jones's in the room with him before Mr. Jones A (he decided to give them letter suffixes based on when they entered the room) indicated they should sit at the table. He noticed they all wore white shirts, dark suits and ties.

He sat across from Mr. Jones A at the narrow part of the rectangular table. Mr. Jones B and C sat at the ends. He noted both B and C were probably in their seventies, had remains of white hair on their almost-bald scalps, but were otherwise not alike. One was thin, and still over six feet tall despite his aging stoop, and the other was shorter and fatter – his dark suit bulged as he sat revealing a flash of white shirt. Both wore glasses, but had no reading material in front of them. In keeping with the previous meetings there were no writing materials either.

Mr. Jones A divided the items on the table. Mr. Smith noted he slid the lobster to his right and the wine to his left. The table, instead of being randomly set, as he had assumed, was clearly set to facilitate Mr. Jones A distributing the items. Remaining in front of Mr. Jones A and Mr. Smith were the bottles of ice water, the nuts, a small bowl of grapes and a bowl of pretzels. Mr. Jones A opened a bottle of ice water and poured it into a glass.

"Forty dollars was too much," he commented looking up and directly into Mr. Smith's eyes.

"I...I agree," Mr. Smith replied, broke the gaze and poured himself a glass of ice water. He couldn't be sure, but based on his past experience it was likely both Mr. Jones B and Mr. Jones C could have added six or seven zeroes after the forty and still had change for a Mercedes or two. The money wasn't important; it was letting Mr. Smith know who was in charge. He looked up from his glass at Mr. Jones A.

"Still, I've always liked the work you've done for us in the past," Mr. Jones A continued, relaxed his gaze and reached for a grape. Mr. Smith glanced down and noted both the absence of a Rolex, and the skin on Mr. Jones A's hand seemed tight and red. When he looked up he noticed there was a similar tightness to the skin around his mouth. He wondered if he had been the victim of a plastic surgeon. He hadn't noticed this at previous meetings, so maybe he hadn't met Mr. Jones A before?

"What have you got for us?" Mr. Jones A asked.

"Four congressional seats and one governor's," Mr. Smith replied.

"And which states?"

"Five different states. New York, California, Florida, South Dakota, and Washington State. Two Democrats and three Republicans."

"And each of these is an incumbent who would benefit from extra... attention?" Mr. Jones A asked.

"All except one, and I'll come to that in a minute. We've been in contact with each of these candidates and they have a need for some extra funds to help them stay where they are. Some have not had stellar careers and the races are close, but with a little help at critical times they should remain in their jobs. They are already grateful for the help which I have indicated may come their way."

"Should remain in their jobs?" Mr. Jones A echoed Mr. Smith.

"There are no guarantees, of course, but since we have been doing this we have had over a 90% success rate." Mr. Smith spoke quietly and confidently. He knew that the questions and answers were for the benefit of the other Mr. Jones's in the room.

"Define the 90% number?" Mr. Jones A suggested.

"We have had a 90% success rate in getting our people elected, and you reported to me a 95% success rate in ensuring their compliance to our principles afterwards. It has been mutually rewarding for the candidates and for us," Mr. Smith replied. He glanced to his sides and noticed Mr. Jones B was methodically dismembering the lobster and Mr. Jones C was looking at him over a glass of the Clos de Vougeot. He returned his gaze to Mr. Jones A.

"What happened to the ten percent and the five percent who didn't comply?" asked Mr. Jones A, knowing the answer.

"They are no longer in politics," replied Mr. Smith. "If you discount them, we have been one hundred percent successful."

"I agree you have been successful. Democracy doesn't always proceed in the correct direction, so giving it a little push, seems entirely appropriate," said Mr. Jones A. This was received with a grunt from Mr. Jones B who did not look up from his lobster.

Mr. Jones A continued, "We don't want to know all the details, and certainly don't want to enquire into your methods, but give us an outline of what you intend to do, and how much it will cost."

For the next thirty minutes Mr. Smith explained the reasons for the choice of candidates and his expectations of how he could influence the outcome of the forthcoming mid-term elections. He paused and took a sip from his glass of water before continuing.

"Over the years we have been able to make our work more efficient. We know what works and what does not. Sometimes we improve our candidate's reputation, and sometimes we...we don't improve his rivals." He thought that was a reasonable euphemism. "So, we have been able to be more specific with costs and more focused in our endeavors. The four seats I have been talking about, the governorship and three of the house seats come to one million nine hundred and fifty thousand. Looking at these seats I can almost guarantee we will have compliant candidates and dependent allies when they get re-elected. Basically, any legislation you choose to promote will be sponsored by them. Any committee they are on will be almost like you have a vote in the room. It is also probable, after this election, you'll have a majority in two or more of the more important committees. It'll have taken you about ten years. It'll be interesting to see how you get on over the next ten. However, I should add that you will expect to spend at least another five hundred thousand over the next two years on two of these candidates. For the other two you only have to remind them of certain documents and videos in your possession to ensure their compliance, but even then you will sometimes have to provide a carrot with the stick, so assume two hundred thousand for both of them, maybe a little more."

"So, about three to four million total?" Mr. Jones A asked, "And does that include your reimbursement?"

"No, as usual I'll cover my expenses from here out, and I want twenty percent of the total for each of the next two years."

"So, you would expect to receive about one to one-and-a-half million over the next two years?"

"That assumes all are elected. If not, I only get that sum prorated. That's what we've done in the past. That's my guarantee to you, but it will be a little more. We have not yet discussed the last candidate."

"Tell us about him, or is it a her?" asked Mr. Jones A.

"It's a him. His name is William Shanty and he is standing for election in District 12 in Washington State as a Republican. This is a new district. With population growth Washington has qualified for another seat in Congress. So, the state carved out an interesting area in western Washington. They took a big part of Norm Dicks's district, gave him some nearer Seattle instead, and extended the new district north and south. It includes a mix of rural, suburban, and some urban voters. Historically, this area has voted Democrat, but the redistricting has probably had the effect of making Norm Dicks's Democrat seat more secure for him, but the new district has concentrated Republicans' voting power. The local Republican Party in the new district is all fired-up, and they should be. Current polls put their candidate, Shanty, with 38% of the vote, his rival with 41%. There are no other candidates. The state is obliged to hold a meaningless primary in a couple of months, when the two candidates with the most votes proceed to the general election, but since there are only two of them the result is a foregone conclusion. However, coming in first in the primary always helps, so the local Republican Party will be promoting their candidate for the primary, and we are not going to get involved in that. We have been looking at the democratic candidate and we find he has certain faults we feel we could exploit."

"If he has faults couldn't we promote his chances instead? If he's already a few points ahead, wouldn't it be easier to make him the proverbial offer he can't refuse?" asked Mr. Jones A.

"We thought about that, and he would probably comply, but he's unreliable. He's a typical political narcissist and an alcoholic. It's not a good combination. He thinks he can't do anything wrong, but the public will disagree. Believe me. This is Washington State we're talking about, not Washington DC, and you might get away with all sorts of capers in the capital city, but in this state it should be basically easy to bury him politically so he'll never raise his head again. So, we'll be indirectly promoting the Republican candidate, Shanty. It remains to be seen how we can convince him of the benefits of aligning his political career with us, but we will be able to...one way or another." Mr. Smith finished, leaned back in his chair and felt himself relax. He was surprised how tense he had been. He hadn't proposed anything he hadn't done before, so he couldn't figure out the cause of his tension. Maybe he was getting older. Maybe he should retire and become a...

Mr. Jones A interrupted his train of thought, "And how much extra will this cost?" he asked.

"Another $750, 000," Mr. Smith replied.

"About four and a half million then, and with your reimbursement?"

"I figured about six million tops."

There was a short pause. Without looking at the Mr. Jones's at the ends of the table for agreement Mr. Jones A said, "OK, it's a deal."

From this Mr. Smith deduced they had already decided on an appropriate sum before they came into his room. He wondered if he had undersold his talents.

The three Mr. Jones's stood to leave. Mr. Smith stood and accompanied them to the door. Mr. Jones B and C shook his hand first and wandered towards the elevator, but Mr. Jones A called them back so they could hear what he had to say to Mr. Smith.

"I feel I need to thank you for all you have done for us, and hopefully we will continue to use your services," he said quietly. "Mr. Jones is not feeling well and may not be around to meet with you much longer, but he will be watching these elections closely. If you need any more assistance get in contact in the usual way. Nothing must go wrong." He looked Smith in the eyes, shook his hand, turned, and with the others made for the elevator.

Smith closed the door and puzzled over Mr. Jones A's parting remarks. He wasn't sure if he had been threatened or not. He wasn't sure which Mr. Jones might be sick, maybe Mr. Jones A, or maybe it was a Mr. Jones not in the room with them, but he found Mr. Jones A's comments unnerving. He'd done well over the last decade since he'd first put forward his ideas in the bar at that conference in Maui. Maybe it would be just as well to get out of it now. He was still young and he had enough contacts to expand the use of his talents into other ventures, or maybe he should head back to Maui, buy that house on the beach, and forget about performing these little subservient charades every year.

    He wandered back to the table. The bottle of wine was still two-thirds full and the lobster hardly touched. He took both into the warm evening on the balcony, sat down and relaxed. He placed his feet up on another chair and poured himself a glass of Clos de Vougeot.

2

The Kitsap Airporter leaves SeaTac Airport at twenty minutes past the hour. While it can be delayed by off-airport traffic it is not affected by the vagaries of departure and arrival times, gate availability, seating position, or baggage-handling whims. I have arrived on the hour knowing I have twenty minutes to succumb to, or survive, these quirks. Sometimes I make it with seconds to spare, and at others I search in vain for my bags as the impartial carousel rotates, hope fades, and the bus leaves without me.

This time the plane was in a few minutes early at 5:45, and despite being in row 34, seat F, I thought I had enough time. I only had a carry-on backpack and had flown from Oakland. I was in the same time zone and I was focused. I didn't have to catch the subway from an outer terminal, so it should have been simple. There was some delay with the lady in 32 C getting her walker to fit the aisle, but by five minutes past six I was striding along the corridor from Concourse C, passing all but the youngest, determined fellow passengers.

That's when I bumped into the brick wall of the press conference.

I understand the press has to do its job, and in a free society they are allowed to photograph, video, interview, and harass anyone they wish to, but at 6:08 I didn't need any of that. In fact at that moment I was secretly hoping for a military coup which would install a totalitarian, puppet-dictatorship curfew in Seattle to let me get around the cameras, boxes, lights, wires, hangers-on, coffee cups, and noise. The wave of passengers hitting this immoveable object was being directed by the police to a single exit. My pace slowed in the pressure of people squeezing towards the door.

By 6:16 I made it through. My fellow travelers and I were released, like water from a hose, and sprayed ourselves in different directions over SeaTac. I still had three hundred yards to cover. I could have run it in under a minute, but that might have attracted the attention of the authorities, and things would have probably flown out of my pockets forcing me to stop, so I just increased my speed to an uncomfortable walk. Now I was passing even the youngest, determined passengers.

At 6:20 I made it to the bus area of the airport. It was still there! I had fifty yards to go, the door was still open, so I broke into a jog, ran for the open door, up the steps and onto the vehicle. I'd made it.

I looked around the bus. There were ten passengers. and most were ignoring anything else but their own cell phones. They were calling relatives and friends, with various degrees of incivility, to let them know they were on their way home. I found an empty seat halfway down the bus, put my backpack beside me, and pulled out my own cell phone. I had just turned it on when the passenger in the aisle across from me leaned over and said,

"Doc, you shouldn't run like that. It'll give you a heart attack."

I looked over and smiled. "I always run like that. It's to stop me getting a heart attack. How are you, doc?" I asked.

"Pretty good," was the reply. I had known Al Dorfman for years. He was a former colleague and a firm friend, whom I did not see nearly enough now I was retired. Al was still working, and two ex-wives and three children in college meant he wouldn't be easing up any time soon. "What were you running like that for anyway?" he added.

"I got in nearly forty minutes ago," I said, confirming the time on my watch, "so I thought I'd plenty of time to make it, but there was a press conference, or something, and it took me ages to get through that. I don't know what it was about. Do you?"

"Yeah, it was for that candidate for District 12...oh, what's his name... oh, yeah, Bill Shanty. You know the new congressional seat we're getting here. He was coming in from DC apparently, and the press found out or were told to be there. Who knows? Anyway, he's been attracting a lot of media attention. It seems the seat could be critical in November. He's a Republican. The Democrat is getting just as much attention. It should be interesting."

The driver hurried on to the bus, briefly apologized for the late departure, said he would collect the tickets later and backed out of the parking space. He accelerated away a little faster than is usual for airport bus drivers. I looked up in time to see a couple with heavy roller bags leave the terminal, notice the bus departing, briefly speed up, stop and wave, then realize the driver hadn't seen them. I saw him glance in the side mirror, hesitate briefly before continuing to accelerate, and then I realized it was more likely he didn't want to see them. With dejected shoulders they turned to each other and resigned themselves to waiting for the 7:20. I knew how they felt. I turned back to Al.

"With all the fuss in there I thought it would have been someone important, like Madonna, or a baseball star."

"Normally, you'd have been right. After all, that's the American way, but the eyes of the nation are on

Kitsap County. Well, Pierce, Mason, and Thurston Counties too. Bits of them are in this new district, but he lives in Kitsap... by the way, name a baseball star."

"Oh, uh... Joe DiMaggio. "

"Anyone living?"

"You mean he isn't?

"Now, you're playing with me, "Al smiled again."How long have you lived here now? Over thirty years?" he asked.

I nodded.

"And you still don't know diddly-squat about American sports."

"I know Joe DiMaggio was married to Marilyn Monroe, and I thought marriage was an all-American sport."

Al snorted.

"Well, I wasn't brought up with American sports. I played hockey, field hockey, the real hockey, and rugby in college. You know...the sports of gentlemen."

"Huh!" Al replied with a flick of his head, "And you are now a gentleman?"

"Of course, but I suppose it depends on your definition."

"Let's not go there. What were you doing flying in today anyway?"

"I was at a conference in San Francisco, and then I had a couple of days to hang out with Laura at Berkeley."

"What year is she now?"

"She's beginning her doctorate."

"I seem to remember her in first grade," Al said. "You sure she didn't skip any?"

"No, she did the standard thing. She got older and we got old."

"You can say that again...what were you doing at a conference anyway? You're not still filling in are you? I thought you were retired?"

"Well, so did I. They call me occasionally. I still work a bit, and I have to keep my license active, so I have to stay educated. It was a diabetes conference."

"Any good?" Al asked.

"Well, there's always something interesting, but there were too many presenters, who probably only see one patient per hour, trotting out their latest research on the newest expensive drug, and claiming to have the definitive way to manage diabetes. And, of course, no one says it would be less expensive if the drug company promoting the newest expensive drug didn't fund, maybe indirectly, the monthly payments on the speaker's yacht."

"I'd say you were being cynical, but I think there's probably a lot of truth there. And I sometimes wonder if it isn't directly going to the speaker's yacht."

"I hope, even in America, that would be too obvious, but it's still interesting to go to these events. You get a different perspective on the medical industrial complex than sitting at home, or in your office, or combing through the records in a local nursing home," I said. "I enjoyed San Francisco. I walked around. Laura took an afternoon off and we did Alcatraz. We went out to dinner. It was fun."

"Where'd you stay?"

"The King George. It was a better deal than the conference hotel and I got to walk along Market every morning – that's always fun, but it convinced me, once again, living in the big city is not for me."

"I agree. I prefer living within reach of Seattle, not in it."

We chatted. Al was returning from visiting family in

Denver. The bus made its way south through the end-of-evening rush hour on Interstate 5 to Highway 16 in Tacoma, over the Narrows Bridge and north again to Kitsap County.

I said my good-byes to Al, who was staying on until Silverdale, both of us promising to meet up again very soon, got off the bus in Port Orchard and into the waiting arms and lips of Ann. It was good to be home. I pulled her closer to me and wondered why I didn't spend every minute of my life holding her tight.

We came up for air. She looked at me with her blue eyes, and said, "It's good to have you back here, doctor. I missed you."

"You did, nurse?" I replied. I linked her arm in mine and we walked to her car.

"Of course."

"But I've only been gone five days."

"You sure? It feels like a lot longer to me." She gave me a peck on the cheek and added, "How is Laura?"

"She's doing fine. I met her new boyfriend and he seems likeable enough. She likes her work. She's working on insects now. Who knows? Maybe she'll get a Nobel prize for biology."

I threw my bag on the backseat of the Camry and we set off.

"How was SeaTac?" Ann asked.

"That's interesting. It didn't bother me. It was busy. I thought I wouldn't make the Airporter, and I was rushed, but otherwise it was fine."

I had never found any airport relaxing, but since I had been involved in a bomb blast in the parking garage in 2001 I had been apprehensive about flying through SeaTac. I had no physical injury, and although it happened before I met Ann, we'd both lived through the consequences of that day. Overall, we survived with only a few scars to our psyches. We'd bought a house and had been living together in unmarried bliss for over two years.

We were making plans to change that.

"So, it's all going as planned?" I asked.

"You mean the big event?'

I nodded.

"Yes. Ten days to go to my thirty-ninth birthday party."

"I should be so lucky," I said.

"Maybe one day you will be," she said.

I laughed.

3

Christopher Miller was not a happy man.

He knew the reason. He hated Washington DC. Everything about it seemed so wrong – the money, the misplaced confidence, the sense of superiority, the lobbyists, and more than anything else, the politicians. If DC were an island, and somehow floated away into the Atlantic, the rest of the country would be much better off. He hadn't always felt like this, but the reality of his life was slowly becoming more apparent. It wasn't going anywhere. He felt stuck.

At 3:35 pm on a drizzly, windy Friday in late March he was not the only one in the building at 935 Pennsylvania Avenue who was wondering what the hell they were doing there. He thought about slipping out early and heading to his home in Newington, but Interstates 95 and 395 would already be creeping with fleeing, irresponsible federal workers.

And then there was that appointment at 4:00 pm. He glanced at his schedule on the computer screen. It had the single word, "Preston". The computer let him know who had scheduled the appointment. It looked like it had been his personal assistant, Eloise. However, she was currently sick at home with the flu, which had been coughing and aching its way through the building, so he had no idea if he was to meet a girl scout or an orangutan. There was probably a memo somewhere, but he couldn't remember seeing one.

He stood, walked to the window and looked down through the distorted wet glass on to the red brake lights of 9th Avenue. He plugged in the kettle on the window table and waited for it to boil before selecting a decaffeinated green tea-bag and dunking it in the steaming mug of water. His 'phone rang. He carried his mug and his Friday afternoon chocolate-chip cookie back to his desk, reached over and pushed the intercom button.

"Your four o'clock is here, sir."

Miller glanced at his watch. It was 3:50.

"Send him in."

"There are two, sir."

"Send them in. Thank you."

Miller turned and two men entered his office. He recognized one immediately. Now he knew there had been no memo.

Preston, or more specifically, the impeccably dressed Senator Robert Preston, removed his hat, strode into the room, and shook his hand.

"It's been a long time," said Preston.

"Over thirty years," replied the surprised Miller, "...and... you haven't changed a bit."

They both smiled at the sociable lie. Preston introduced his companion.

"Chris, I would like you to meet Father Andrew Riley. He is my spiritual guide."

Miller felt the firm handshake of the priest. He was small, red-haired, thin, freckled, and at about age forty-five, was ten years younger than Miller and Preston. Miller gestured for them all to sit and moved to the other side of the desk and his own chair.

It had been nearly thirty-five years since he and Preston had been midshipmen at Annapolis. Miller had gone on to do his twenty, had thought about another five, but had balked at the idea when he was told he would be posted to the Pentagon. The stories of the internal politics and back-stabbing he'd heard about in those corridors of power had made the medieval activities of the Borgias sound like the kindergarten tea-party cliché. He'd fled from involvement in politics and for five years the only time he had left his home in the Virginia backwoods, and gone to DC, was to use one of its airports to escape. Maybe he'd have been back there now if his wife hadn't died and a friend had not suggested his grief could be lessened by using his talents in the FBI. He'd waited and resisted, at least he thought he'd resisted, but eventually he had been drawn into the life of DC.

Preston, however, was different. He was taller, at six feet two inches; his groomed black hair had lasted longer than Miller's now bald head, and he'd only just started sporting a hint of grey at the temples. He had stayed in the Navy for three years after Annapolis. It was supposed to be a minimum of five. Somehow he'd got around that rule with no apparent consequences to his reputation. He had family money and his sights set on bigger game. Although he was not related to the actor, Robert Preston, having the same name and Hollywood looks did him no harm with his political ambitions. His New Jersey twang had morphed into the ubiquitous west-coast accent with a hint of southern drawl, so at age thirty-four he'd become a junior senator in a southern state and his star had been rising ever since. There had even been talk of a run for the presidency, which he had vehemently denied in front of the cameras on many occasions. Everyone knew, of course, this made it more likely he would humbly accept the nomination at his party's next convention. Miller was not impressed. He had sat in class with the narcissistic Preston, and heard of the relief his fellow officers felt when Preston left the service. He'd thought of Preston as an arrogant ass-hole back then, and nothing he had seen in the press had made him change his mind. If Preston was in his office now it was for one reason. He wanted something from him.

"How can I help you, Senator?" Miller asked with his best customer-service voice and smile.

"Oh, please, Chris, call me Bob," Preston drawled.

"OK. Bob, how can I help you?" Miller asked again, retaining his equanimity.

Preston glanced at Father Riley, before replying, "I have a confession to make, and I wanted to make it to you."

"Why me? I'm not in the confessions business. Well, not like the Father here," replied Miller, a little taken aback.

"I thought it would be the right thing to do."

Father Riley adjusted his position in his chair and looked directly at Preston.

Preston was aware of this and hesitated. "I apologize, Father Riley thinks it's the right thing to do."

"Does that mean you don't think it's the right thing to do?"

"Not exactly."

Miller looked into the famous blue eyes and for a moment could see they were troubled.

"If you have a confession, Senator, sorry, Bob, to make to a law-man, I will need to record this and ask a duty marshal to sit in on this too."

"I prefer it if we have this conversation between ourselves only," said Preston. "I think you'll see why."

Father Riley added, "I would prefer any conversation stays in this room, at least until you know what you're dealing with. Is that reasonable?"

"Yes, Father, that can be done. It's against protocol, but I don't think anyone is going to fire me over it. Let's carry on. Bob, you were saying, you have a confession?"

"It's...it's not easy to admit, but I made a mistake...I don't know if you remember, but I've always had a proclivity for younger members of the opposite sex. I know I am not alone in this – most men seem to favor younger women." He paused. "Well, it's one thing for a twenty-year old at Annapolis to be interested in younger women, but it's not considered acceptable when I was, oh...about forty-five, a US senator, married, and with three children in their teens. My work takes me away from home. My position sometimes makes me think I can do whatever I want."

'Or maybe it's because he feels he can do whatever he wants to he got the position, ' thought Miller.

"Of course, at that age, and a US senator I couldn't get access to young women easily and discreetly without paying for it, and that's what I did. I think I'm not the only one in congress who does so. Anyway, I thought I was discreet, and for many years, when I was in DC and away from my family, I satisfied my sexual needs and fantasies this way. I had an arrangement with...I'll call it an agency. I'd drive to a house in the suburbs for an evening's...entertainment, and be back in the Senate the next day. I'd use their services once or twice a week to once or twice a month. It seemed a comfortable enough arrangement to be able to...you know, see young women." He paused.

Something about the way Preston had repeated "young women" caught Miller's attention. "Young women?" he asked, "How young?"

Preston hesitated, "Well, the nearer to sixteen. Well you know..."

Preston smiled, hoping to get the same reaction from Miller.

Miller stared back at him, took a deep breath and carried on. "And you used your own name?" he asked, hiding his astonishment and disgust at a politician admitting to these foibles, even with what seemed a mixture of rehearsal, reluctance, and excuse.

"No, I paid in cash and I used the name Myron Rockefeller."

"The former speaker of the house?"

"Yes."

"That's an interesting twist on using a false name," said Miller.

"He and I have different political views, so it seemed appropriate," said Preston," and no one I was having sex...relationships with was...well, the matter didn't come up."

"Carry on," Miller said, and noticed from the lack of expression on Father Riley's face that none of this was news to him. Either that or he would make a great poker player.

"Each time I went there was a new girl...I don't know how they did that. Then, about six years ago when I went back it was the same girl. I remember she said she had such a good time with me the last time, she wanted to repeat it. Well, we did, and she was there again the next time. She suggested we try some different positions and well...she was quite...adventurous. She also liked to smoke a joint before we had sex."

Miller could see where this was going.

"Then one day she wasn't there, and I've never seen her again. Nothing happened for a month or two. I went back to the suburbs and one evening, it was a little like this, cold and raining. I got in my car to leave, and as I was putting on my seatbelt a man opened the passenger door and sat next to me. To begin with I was angry, then afraid. He reached into his coat and I remember thinking for a second he was going to pull a gun on me, but he just pulled out an envelope and gave it to me. He told me to open it. I did, and...maybe you can guess what the photos showed. They showed in painful detail my escapades with that girl. He also said the videos were even more interesting, and he knew who I was and where I lived. He called me Senator Preston and repeated my home address to me to emphasize this. He said he would be in touch, took back the photographs, and said if anyone called Myron Rockefeller contacted me to make arrangements to meet them in private. He also told me not to make any more trips to the suburbs. That was probably good advice."

"Did you heed his advice?" asked Miller.

"Of course," replied Preston defensively. Miller thought he was lying — a lot of what he was saying seemed practiced. He was probably following Clinton and a whole host of politicians who lied about their sexual activities.

"So, did you hear from Myron Rockefeller?"

"Not for another couple of months. I'd mentioned to my staff that if a Myron Rockefeller made contact in any way to let me know. Most of them thought I was talking about the former speaker, so that was easy. I was wondering how much it was going to cost me, and I'd even thought the whole thing may have been a mistake, and I'd be let off the hook. But one evening, in late March, I had a call from someone calling himself Myron Rockefeller, telling me to meet someone by the Vietnam Memorial, just before dark. I was to walk normally and slow down near the M's, look at the names and wait to be contacted, but to not stop moving. I did this. It was a cool evening, so it seemed sensible to wear a hat and coat. I didn't think I'd be recognized, and there were only a few people at the Memorial. I slowed down, as ordered, and as I reached the M's a man in his sixties, long grey hair, bearded, wearing worn army fatigues, and looking like a Vietnam veteran is supposed to, walked by me and put a piece of paper in my hand. I walked back to my car and read the paper. It said, 'Vote no on SB 410'".

"Senate Bill 410?"

"Yes."

"And how did you vote?'

"I voted 'no'."

"Well, were you intending to vote 'no' before you received the note?" Miller asked.

"I hadn't made up my mind. I forget the details now, but it was a bill for relief aid somewhere in Africa. It had passed the House and it eventually died in the Senate."

"Did it go down with a small or large margin?"

"I seem to remember it was just two or three votes, and mainly along party lines. It didn't make much of a headline in the newspapers – there was unrest in the Middle East, or something else that week, to distract readers."

There was silence for a moment as Miller took in the implications of this revelation. "Then, what happened?" he said.

"Nothing for another couple of months, then another call to another meeting, and another note asking me to vote in a certain way."

"So, this was about six to eight years ago?"

"About that."

"How many times have you been asked to vote 'a certain way'?"

"Twenty-three, but that includes notes to vote, or influence, committees I was on too."

"And did you vote as they asked?"

"Yes, most of the time."

"Most?"

"Well, most of the times I was voting the way I would have done anyway. That's what's so strange about it. And at no time was it only one vote which stopped or carried a bill."

"But did you ever vote against the way you had been told to?"

"Once. It was a bill to close a loophole in an inner-city, kindergarten support program. I couldn't see it would make any difference. It seemed inconsequential, and the little mail coming in from the constituents in my state was in favor of it. I also thought a vote in favor would be politically appropriate for me. You know, supporting kids and education."

Miller knew exactly what Preston meant and wished he didn't.

Preston continued, "Well, I voted in favor, and the bill passed by a slim margin. I think it was one vote only. A couple of days later my office staff opened an envelope with a large photo. The faces were blurred, and details were hard to make out, but I recognized it as one of me and that girl. I got the message."

"And you've toed their line ever since?" Miller asked.

"Yes."

"Any idea who is blackmailing you or what they are after?"

"I've thought about this a lot. As I said most of the time when they ask me to vote a certain way it was going to be how I voted anyway. At other times the votes have been...maybe a little more, shall I say "right wing" than I would have normally voted, but there was no other pattern. I think some of the time their voting orders were just to let me know I was not off the hook. As to who is behind this, I haven't a clue, but I have realized a couple of things." Preston paused, stood, and moved from the desk to stand at the table by the window. He poured himself a glass of water. Miller waited.

Preston turned to face the desk and continued, "I have recently been approached by a few influential members of my party. They want me to be their next presidential candidate nominee. I know I'll have to go through the primaries, make speeches in Iowa and New Hampshire, and press-the-flesh from Maine to California, but they assure me they will grease the skids to make it happen. And that's my concern."

"You mean you don't think it would be appropriate for a president, or a presidential candidate to be blackmailed and be told how to vote?" Miller asked, trying to keep the sarcasm he thought in his head out of his mouth. He needn't have bothered. Preston seemed oblivious and carried on.

"My concern is when this all started I was not being considered a presidential candidate, and when I voted over these years it was not as if mine was the only vote that made a bill survive or die. That's my other point. If you think about it, as I have, you would come to the same conclusion. Others were also being told how to vote."

Preston paused to let this sink in. Miller thought about the implications of this for thirty seconds and said, "If that is correct there would also be others who could be being groomed for the presidency. Or, to put it another way, there may have been a number, unknown, of potential candidates recruited over the years, but you may be the one closest to becoming president. Do you agree?

"Yes."

"That's interesting, or maybe it's terrifying...of course there is one other possibility. Any of these potential candidates, including you, could become the fall guy, not the president."

"What do you mean?"

"The blackmailer can keep the photos and the world will never know, or he can give them to the press at an opportune moment and destroy your chances of becoming president in order to promote someone else's."

"I hadn't thought of that."

Miller thought those might be some of the first spontaneous words Preston had said in his office. He was also not surprised he hadn't thought of it – what arrogant ass-hole would? He continued.

"You remember Gary Hart, potential presidential candidate in '88, I believe. He was found to be having an affair. He claimed he was being unfairly treated by the press, but I don't think he made it to the primary after he was found out. I don't know if it was the FBI, the CIA, NSA, the maid, or who knows, but someone leaked the story to the press."

"Monkey Business," Father Riley spoke.

"What?" Miller and Preston looked at Father Riley.

"Monkey Business," Father Riley repeated. "The boat."

"Oh, yes... the name of the boat where the liaison occurred." Miller smiled and nodded at Father Riley. "You have a good memory, Father."

"Especially for stuff we would all prefer to forget."

"Father, I have conducted all sorts of interviews in this room. Some people come alone, some with an attorney, some with a relative, but you are the first priest to be here as a witness, or for support?"

"I think I am here for both," Father Riley answered, "but I think Bob has a little more to say."

Miller again thought Father Riley would have made a good poker player, or maybe all priests were good at deflecting questions. They both turned to look at Preston.

"I am aware that not everyone has a favorable opinion of me, " Preston began," and my behavior has not been exemplary, but the thought of someone in the White House who could be blackmailed is abhorrent to me, so I'm resigning and not seeking re-election. I don't want this to carry on any more." He paused. "There is one other factor which made the decision easier...I went to the doctor eight weeks ago and had some routine tests run. I felt fine. I still do...maybe I shouldn't have had the tests, but they showed I have prostate cancer and it's going to kill me. I don't know when. The doctors say I may have four or five years. I hope I have, and if I have, I realized I don't want to spend it in DC. I want to be with my family. Maybe it's the diagnosis, maybe it's those damn shots they're giving me, but it's changed me. I am going to announce this on Monday. I have a press conference scheduled."

Miller could see Preston was telling the truth. His eyes watered and his voice broke when he talked about the cancer and being with his family. For a moment Miller felt sorry for him. Father Riley placed a hand on Preston's shoulder. Miller spoke.

"I am sorry to hear about the prostate cancer. I wish you well. However, what would you like me to do about the information you've given me?"

"I think that's up to you. What do you suggest?"

"Well, you have committed a crime, not a federal one, by employing the services of a prostitute, but I can't prove that. You voted according to someone else's instructions, but you could argue ninety percent of congress does that every time they accept funding from lobbyists and other organizations to fund their re-election campaigns. Or maybe that's just my prejudices coming out. I'm sure the Senate Ethics Committee would haul you over the coals. Your family might disown you if the photos became public, and it's unlikely you would survive this politically, but it's possible. I suppose my real concern is you have been part of what seems to be a conspiracy to undermine what is left of the democratic process in this country. If I put you on a witness stand somewhere, and assuming you choose to not deny anything, there are no others you can name. We might be able to guess a few names, based on voting patterns, but it would be very difficult to prove. So, I don't like what you've done, and there is nothing I can do about it, but if there is a conspiracy, I need to root it out, or rather the FBI needs to root it out."

"How do you propose to do that?"

"I have a couple of ideas, but maybe you can help me here. Bob, and you too, Father. If you were trying to recruit or blackmail people to vote according to your wishes, when and how would you go about it?"

After a few seconds Father Riley replied, "Interesting question...I assume not all members of congress get themselves photographed in compromising situations, so the only time when more of them would be vulnerable to persuasion would be around re-election time. What do you think, Bob?"

"I agree, but if I were trying to recruit members of congress I would work on them even before they are elected the first time."

"How would that work?" asked Miller.

"Let me see...you could give them under-the-counter financing for their own campaign, but that isn't a guarantee, and it's already being done a lot of the time. You'd be better off doing a...doing a Gary Hart on their opponent. That would give you the most bang for your buck and would probably be more controllable. Of course, if you could do both it would help. You do a Gary Hart on someone you don't want, and get the photos on your guy. That way you show how you can help and how you can destroy someone. If you want someone in your political pocket forever that should work."

"So, it's the carrot and stick. You can't use one or the other indefinitely, but you can use both?"

"Exactly."

Miller knew what the stick was for Preston. He guessed the carrot had been further trips to the suburbs where his anonymity was guaranteed. He needed time to think. It was time to wrap up this interview.

"Well, Bob, Father, you've given me a lot to think about over the weekend. I can't guarantee anonymity, or where any investigation we start will go, but I can't see letting your name out to the press hounds will help us or you. In fact, it would be much better if nothing of this conversation leaves this office. I'll get back to you next week?"

Preston replied, "Not next week. After the press conference on Monday there will be all sorts of interviews on all sorts of TV channels. You won't want to be seen with me next week."

"That's OK. Most politicians don't ever want to be seen with an FBI man. If anyone asks why don't we say you and I met to discuss a dinner at Annapolis." Miller smiled and the tension which they had all been feeling in the room relaxed.

"Why don't you keep in touch with me?" Father Riley asked.

"It would be unusual, but I suppose it's no different than going through someone's attorney," said Miller.

"It's a lot different," Father Riley smiled, put on his hat and handed Miller his card.

Miller rose and pocketed the card. "You're right. I apologize. It is a lot different, Father."

"Chris, thanks for your help in this matter. I know I can trust you," Preston said. He put on his hat and pulled it low over his forehead. They shook hands. Miller walked them to the elevator and returned to his office.

His mug of green tea was almost untouched and cold. He micro-waved it back to life and stood looking out of his window again.

Miller was not sure how much influence Father Riley had over Preston, and he wondered if Preston would have admitted his wrongdoings without prodding from him. Coming in with a priest instead of an attorney was a good idea. Attorneys aren't supposed to talk but do; priests never talk. On the other hand, if it hadn't been for the prostate cancer maybe the country would have elected someone whose strings were being pulled by...well, he didn't know who. He also doubted Preston had chosen him to confess to because of their time at Annapolis together. It was more likely because he was high enough in the echelons of the FBI to be given enough independence to start his own investigation, but not high enough to be weighed down by political considerations. However, Miller realized this made no difference. He had been given a problem to solve.

There was one other thought which concerned him. If some organization was blackmailing politicians it would be in their interest to know what the FBI was up to also. There was nothing he could do about today's visit. He'd noted Preston and Father Riley had been wearing hats, maybe to reduce the possibilities of being identified, but this was the FBI; Preston would have been recognized.

He couldn't do this alone. He would need a team, and a team working away from DC. He smiled. He could get out of town for a while. It would be good for him. He realized, as he was interviewing Preston, he was becoming too cynical, even by DC standards. It was time for a change. He finished the last of his tea, picked up his briefcase, and headed for the parking garage.

He had a lot to think about.

4

"Everything ready?" I asked.

"Everything ready," Ann replied.

We looked at each other, smiled, high-fived, and I started the car.

We'd loaded my aging Subaru Forester with the cakes (two), the changes of outfit, the orders of service, and the food.

It was going to be a celebration for Ann's thirty-ninth birthday party, except it wasn't. It wasn't her thirty-ninth birthday, and it wasn't a birthday party. Most of our friends knew it wasn't the former, but we hoped none knew it wasn't a birthday party. Lying to friends can be fun, but tonight it was going to end. Tomorrow we would be back to telling the truth.

We had rented a local church for the celebration. It had a kitchen, parking, heat, and it didn't matter what bottles we brought in as long as they all left with us. We'd dropped off the wine and the beer that morning. Most of the food was being catered for by Le Chat Gourmand. We'd tasted their cooking at previous gatherings, liked it, and we wanted something different from the usual offerings out of The Lutheran Church Recipe Book (how to make macaroni and cheese for fifty). We had talked to the owner Elizabeth Francois, a transposed French cook from Lille, and decided on the menu. I wondered why she named the business after a food-loving cat, but she declined to tell me. I told her I assumed it must have been named after a special cat, rather than cat for food-lovers, or cat food for lovers, but she had just smiled and snorted at my suggestions.

She was probably right to do so. In retrospect I'd been more nervous than I needed to be.

We arrived at the church two hours before any guests. Laura, my daughter, Clare, Ann's daughter, and their respective boy-friends were already there. Laura had flown in from her PhD work in Berkeley, where she was hoping to save the world from cockroaches (at least that's what I told her I thought she was doing) and Clare had arrived from Purdue where she was in her final year of a psychology major. We told them the previous night about the party and they had taken it in good spirit. They'd even stayed up late working on a speech and enrolled their boyfriends' help. The church had been transformed. It's amazing what you can do with young lungs and fifty or sixty balloons. It was bright, colorful, and the "Happy 39th" banner was installed with a quick-release mechanism courtesy of Ishmael, Laura's boyfriend. We tested the sound system, for which Brian, Clare's boyfriend took responsibility. We worked on the entrances and exits, and the timing, and by 5:30 pm we were ready. The first guest was due at 6:00.

A few guests had bought cards and presents, despite our express requests on the invitation. I suppose some people just have to bring something to a birthday party or it wouldn't feel right — I'm probably one of them. But we didn't ask these transgressors to leave, despite the dire warnings on the invitation. The conversation flowed, Ann accepted congratulations on her birthday, and the Costco carrot cake emblazoned with "Happy 39th, Ann" was displayed prominently. For an hour we wandered among friends in our casual birthday-party clothes while they enjoyed the selection of Le Chat Gourmand's delights, and the wine and beer we had provided. No one seemed to notice neither Ann nor I were touching any alcohol.

At 7:00 pm I turned on the microphone and announced, "Thank you all for coming this evening. I hope you are all having a good time (A few cheers around the room.) Ann and I have arranged a short entertainment skit for you this evening. So, please refill your glasses and your plates, and we'll be back in about ten minutes." I switched off the mike and we both left the room.

It's surprising how long it takes to change your clothes and get the new ones on. It would have helped if I had knotted a tie more often, but ever since I had been told, years before, doctors' ties were the source of all the evil and infection in the world, I had taken to not wearing one, and no one seemed to care. I kept getting the wide part too short and the narrow part too long, so it was not until eight and a half minutes after leaving the room that I was ready. I needn't have worried, Ann was taking longer, but she had the help of Laura and Clare. In retrospect she only took fifteen minutes, and considering what was involved she probably created a new Guinness world record.

However, we had a critical audience. We'd said ten minutes, not fifteen, and by the time we stood again outside the doors to the party room the slow handclap had started. The room had two sets of double doors, separated by about twenty feet. I stood at one, Ann at the other with Laura and Clare. We gave Ishmael the signal, counted to thirty, nodded at each other and opened the doors.

Brian increased the volume of the orchestral introduction to The Moody Blues' "Days of Future Passed" to overcome the applause as we entered the room. Ann was wearing a white dress with a train followed by our daughters. I was wearing a grey suit, white dress shirt, and a passably knotted tie. As we hit the dais the orchestral strings came alive, Ishmael dropped the "Happy 39th, Ann" banner. The applause died away. They still didn't get it. They told me later they thought it was some sort of skit we were putting on — in a way it was.

Only when Colin Dougan, our Unitarian minister friend, stood, stepped between us, turned to face the party and opened an official-looking book did they get it. It wasn't a party; it was a wedding. Then the applause, the smiles, the laughter and the cheers overwhelmed The Moody Blues. Colin called for calm, the room settled down and we started the ceremony. I put the ring on her finger, I kissed the bride, we waltzed around the room to Moon River, and it was done.

We were husband and wife.

Well, not quite. It's not a real wedding without the speeches and wedding cake. We left out the Costco birthday cake for those who wanted it, and served our own, deliciously rich, two-tiered, traditional British wedding fruit-cake for the aficionados. With cake on the plate, and champagne glasses in hand, our guests settled down for the speeches. Laura and Clare went first.

Clare began: "Thank you for all coming today to my mother's thirty-ninth birthday party. It was news to me that she had been a teenage mother, or maybe I hadn't done the math right? Still, I suppose it was one of those things that parents don't tell their children about, just as children don't always tell their parents what they are up to. Laura and I however, are exceptional. We always tell our parents what we are up to, unless of course, we're sure they don't want to know."

Laura's turn: "So, imagine our surprise yesterday when we arrived here and found out the speeches we had written on our way here were redundant. It wasn't a birthday party after all. It was a wedding and we had to participate in the deception. This, of course, was against our highest principles."

Clare: "But sometimes, as children, you have to make sacrifices to help your parents. They may not see it that way, but you hope, one day, they will appreciate all you have done for them."

Laura: "So, we had to re-write our speeches. It wasn't easy, but by 3:30 this morning we felt we had hammered out a reasonable compromise, and we made a list of the reasons we think this marriage is a perfect match. Do you have it Clare?"

Clare: "Oh yes, here it is." She held up a 2" x 3" Post-it note. "Oh, no, that's not it. Here it is." She held up five feet of taped-together copy paper. "Shall we read some of them to you?" She asked her audience?"

"Yes," was the reply.

"All of them?"

"No," they roared back.

Laura: "Well, of the fifty or so reasons we wrote down, here are our favorite five."

Clare: "Number five. The Skype medical and nursing advice has doubled. When we ask for advice we get double the conflicting opinions now."

Laura: "Number four. There has been a substantial increase in the number and quality of chocolate chip cookies at home. Thanks, Ann."

Clare: "Number three. I now have a new sister."

Laura: "So do I. And, number two. My dad seems to be able to sing in tune now, well, at least more often than not. Ann's musicality has worn off on him."

Clare and Laura together: "Number one. It is great to see them so happy together."

Applause.

Clare: "One last thing. This is an Apache blessing."

Clare and Laura read alternate lines.

"May the sun bring you new energy by day
May the moon softly restore you by night
May the rain wash away your worries

And the breeze blow new strength into your being.

And all of the days of your life may you walk gently through the world and know its beauty."

Hugs, kisses, and a few damp eyes (including mine) and it was Ann's turn.

"Thank you all for being here to share in our special occasion! For any of you who really thought it was my 39th birthday – I want to invite you to my 38th next year.

Some of you may know we originally met at a medical conference about ten years ago. I think it was a particularly boring gastroenterology conference and so we found each other more interesting than the conference. Back then I wondered to myself, 'maybe'... or 'I wonder if...,' but it was not until a few years later we met again, dated, and the 'maybe' and 'wonder if' became...'oh, yes'. Of course, I've always wondered if the conference had been more interesting, would we have met and been here today? On the other hand, it's hard to make a gastroenterology conference, and a thesis on bowel movements, interesting, so I think it was fate, and here we are.

And it's been a lot of fun. Life these last six years of being together has not always been smooth. There have been tests of our relationship, but John has not hesitated or faltered once. If he had I would still love him.

Today I married my best friend, my greatest love. John is my Renaissance man – a special person who is genuine and kind, a mastermind who is humorous and romantic; I cannot imagine anything better than spending the rest of my life with this man."

More hugs and tears and it was my turn. I faced Ann, held her right hand in my left, and started.

"Shall I compare thee to a summer's day?
Thou art more lovely and temperate
Rough winds do shake the darling buds of May
And summer's lease hath all too short a date.
Sometime too hot the eye of heaven shines,
And often is his gold complexion dimmed,
And every fair from fair sometimes declines,
By chance, or nature's changing course untrimmed,
But thy eternal summer shall not fade,
Nor lose possession of that tho ow'st,
Nor shall death brag thou wand'rest in his shade,
When in eternal lines to Time thou grow'st,
So long as men can breathe, or eyes can see,
So long lives this, and this gives life to thee."

I gave a short bow to Ann, who leapt up and hugged me, much to the audience's appreciation. We disentangled and I continued.

"That was a short poem I wrote over breakfast this morning.'

Boos and jeers.

"Oh, I'm sorry. That was a short poem William Shakespeare wrote over breakfast."

Boos, jeers and laughter. I continued.

"Thank you once again for coming this evening. I am sure some of you are disappointed this is not Ann's thirty-ninth birthday party, but I would like to reassure you...no one is more disappointed than Ann.

It's true we met years ago at some medical conference or other, but even then the main attraction at the conference was Ann. But we were cautious. When we got together a few years later we started slowly. We even went to a couple's retreat on Gabriola Island to help us make sure it was the right thing and the real thing. Actually, we didn't need much reassurance – we knew we were on the right track. Of course, all the retreats in the world won't tell you everything about your partner. I remember a psychiatrist with whom I worked once said you never really know anyone until you-

1- Know how they spend money.

2- Know how they play games.

3- Know how they have sex.

Consequently, we never really get to know many people in our lives.

So, let's go through these.

1- Money. I know there is a rumor Ann and I had our first date in The Dollar Store, but that is incorrect. It was the Goodwill store, but it was the Gig Harbor Goodwill store.

2- Games. Ann and I have played many games of Scrabble and Boggle together. Of course, we also tried playing Doctor and Nurse, but we both agreed I just don't look right in a nurse's uniform.

3- Sex. I want to reassure all of you, and our children that Ann and I are good in bed. Of course, at our age, all that really means is we don't snore too much or get up to pee too often (laughter).

What does this mean? We have a winning combination.

The last few years have been some of the best years of my life.

Being with Ann is a joy.

For her the glass is always half full, never half empty.

She will sit down with a book at the end of the day and contentedly sigh what a wonderful day she has had.

She has brought music into my life again.

She is caring, considerate, practical, loving, and I feel privileged to be with her.

She is the light of my life and I want to spend the rest of my life with her.

And...she lets me make speeches like this.

Please raise your glasses to Ann and the next forty years. She'll only be 79 then."

We raised our glasses, toasted Ann, and the party re-started. A few of the younger, and a few of the older, members of the audience danced while Ann and I made the rounds talking to individuals and groups of friends.

It was all something of a blur. There was hand-shaking, joking, and back-slapping and I can't remember most of what was said. I would have probably forgotten what Dick and Harry said too if later events hadn't reminded me. Dick was a longtime attorney friend who had gone into the personal investigation business with one of his former colleagues, Harry. Together they had formed a successful small company which employed them and one part-time receptionist – Harry's wife. We'd worked together successfully before, although not in a way they or I had anticipated, so I wasn't entirely surprised when Dick asked me if I would be available in about a week to help them with a project they were working on.

"Sure," I said, "And..."

I was about to ask a little more about the project when Colin, the minister, tapped me on the shoulder and asked us if we could fill out the paperwork. I made my apologies to Dick and Harry, and Ann and I followed Colin to a quiet room so we could add our signatures to the official documents. This took longer than I thought, and when we got back to the party room, the music was still playing, but all the guests were putting away the tables, vacuuming the carpet and taking down the balloons.

Al Dorfman, my medical colleague, came up to us and explained he had asked everyone to pitch in. He'd told everyone we were not as young as we used to be, and we still had the wedding night responsibilities ahead of us. It would help if the wedding guests could clear everything away so we could get home and consummate the marriage.

"You didn't really say that did you?" Ann asked.

"Well, no. I said we should help out, so you could get out of here. The rest is what they inferred," Al replied.

"How do you know that's what they inferred?" Ann said.

"I'm a doctor. I'm always right," he said with a smile, turned around and picked up a chair to stack.

The building was almost cleared, guests were taking their leave, and we would soon be alone with only our family again.

Ann murmured in my ear, "Do you think we should have told Al about 2:30 this morning?"

I muttered, "You mean how we anticipated the wedding night problem and dealt with it preemptively?"

"Yes, something like that."

"No, if we mention anything like that, they'll feel obliged to put up the tables and chairs again and spill cake on the floor. Let's not mention it."

"Good idea."

"Besides, the night is still young. We may still be able to take him up on his suggestion when we get home." I gave her a peck on her cheek.

We arrived home and got into bed. The night may have been young, but we weren't, and sixty seconds later we were both asleep.

5

"He what?"

"He asked for you."

"But I don't even know him."

"Apparently, he knows you. Any idea how?"

"No, and how would he know I had anything to do with you two anyway?" I asked.

It was one week after the wedding and I was meeting with Dick and Harry.

We had met monthly for years. Dick and I had started the tradition when The Ale House was still in business, and Harry had joined us occasionally over the last two years. When The Ale House had closed its doors we looked around for another meeting place and discovered Dick's sailboat, moored in the Port Orchard Marina, was ideal. It was quiet, private, warm, and the smell of diesel was slowly fading. It would never go away completely. I had helped Dick find the small diesel leak which had left an oily scum on the water in the bilge of his forty -year old, Luders sloop. Dick had bought it from a local contractor who had lovingly, but intermittently, cared for the mechanics, if not the appearance, of the thirty-three foot sailboat. Dick and I had sailed it around most of Puget Sound and the Gulf Islands in British Columbia. It was built for function not luxury, and broadly fitted the definition of a boat being a hole in the water, surrounded by wood (or fiberglass in this case) into which you throw money. Fortunately, it was not too much money, or at least not too much money too often. Dick had been an attorney for the prosecutor's office in the county, which never paid well by lawyer standards, but he had been careful, and his shared business with Harry was bringing in a steady income which he was supplementing with occasional legal work.

I repeated my question, "So, how did he know I was in the picture?"

Harry avoided my gaze for a few seconds, sighed, and said, "Well, he asked about medical help and first aid and having someone around, and I thought of you."

"Couldn't you have found a boy scout?"

"Not one I could trust," Harry replied.

For a moment I wondered if Harry knew something about the Boy Scouts of America that I didn't. I still didn't get it and told them so. Dick stepped in.

"Apparently, Harry mentioned your name, almost in passing, and he said he knew of you, thought you were a good guy, realized it was not your usual field of excellence, but asked us if you might be available. Harry got the impression if you said yes the deal would be ours, so he mentioned we'd worked together on a couple of things in the past and you were a good team member. Anyway, it looks like we have the contract, but we would really like you on board. It won't be too much work. It will get busier later in the year. I thought you might like it. It would be a change for you."

Change was the operative word. My degree says I am an MD; my later certificates modify that to a family doctor, general practitioner, jack-of-all-medical-trades, primary care physician, or whatever the current political terminology was for my skills. In theory I could take out your appendix, suck fluid out of your chest, fix your broken wrist, control your diabetes and heart failure while eating my breakfast. In reality, if I had to do that, I would throw up my breakfast. At one time I had done all of those, but I was almost completely retired and was enjoying it that way. Dick and Harry were proposing a major career change.

"You mean I'd have to wear dark glasses, surreptitiously talk into microphones, and carry a gun?"

"No, no," Dick replied. "I don't ever carry a gun," he added. He put the emphasis on the 'I', which made me wonder if Harry did. "It'll be nothing like that. We are coordinating security and keeping an eye on things."

"That sounds incredibly vague," I replied.

"It is, and speaking as a lawyer, I think it will work out best for both parties if it stays that way."

Harry added, "I asked him more specifically what he wanted, and he doesn't want big security involved. He does not want a bunch of testosterone-muscled bouncers around him. He wants it low-key."

"Well, he'd get low-key with us," I said. Dick was a few inches taller than me and probably weighed about two-hundred pounds. His graying beard and shoulder length hair, which he had recently tied in a pony-tail, may have had some intimidating effect. Harry, at about five foot, ten inches, was the same height as me, but had a slight stoop. He usually wore a Seahawks baseball cap to cover his balding head. Since I was catching him up with the hair loss I was wondering if I should start wearing a cap too. We probably both weighed about the same, just under a hundred-and-seventy pounds. We had no intimidating potential.

"I think that's the point," Dick said. "He wants it to look like there is no security. He wants to look like a man of the people."

I snorted, "Man of the people!" And then I asked, "How come he asked you?" I was looking at Harry.

"I know him... well, I knew him. We were in high school together. We weren't in the same grade, but we were at the same school."

"Yes, but when did he ask you?"

"I went to one of his meetings. Meg likes his ideas and has been helping his campaign. She introduced us. So, she told him what we do and he started talking about what he thinks he is going to need until November. Apparently, he has the money to pay us. His campaign may attract big donors."

Meg was Harry's wife, our part-time office person, and the campaign we were discussing was of William Shanty, the Republican candidate for the new District 12. His press conference at SeaTac Airport had nearly cost me an extra hour of waiting, so I was not immediately drawn to like him, or his principles, but I had begun to follow the campaign. I didn't live in the twelfth district, but it was close, and the campaign was visible enough that it was impossible to avoid the flyers, roadside signs, and hullabaloo of the forthcoming election. The press kept reminding us that whoever was elected from this district could be critical to the political direction the nation, even the world, would be taking over the next two years. From my perspective this meant I had even less reason to turn on my television than normal.

The dilemma I found myself in was for some odd reason it appealed to me to work with Dick and Harry on this vague job they were offering me, but it was totally outside my realm of comfort. Coming from the British parliamentary system, and not being able to vote in the USA for the twenty years I remained a 'resident alien' I had not taken much interest in the American political system. I had been able to vote for the last ten years I had been a citizen, but the system still puzzled me. Maybe I'd learn a little more about it. On the other hand, from what I had heard of William Shanty's campaign so far, it did not fit with my political ideals. I said so.

Dick said, "Super. That way you can be perfectly objective. So, you'll do it then?"

"I'll think about it, but I need to pass it by Ann first," I replied.

Dick and Harry visibly relaxed, so maybe they knew me better than I did, or maybe they knew what Ann would say. Clearly, they thought I had agreed to working with them, and I probably had.

We opened another beer, finished off the pizza Harry had brought, and avoided talking politics.

6

The Wednesday after his meeting with Preston, Christopher Miller flew to Portland, Oregon. Portland was one of his all-time favorite US cities, but he knew he wouldn't have much chance of browsing Powell's book store, or wandering the street markets on this trip. The airline had given him a copy of USA Today which he had tucked into his overnight bag. The only article of interest to him was an editorial reaction to Preston's news conference when he had announced his resignation the day before. The piece wondered if Preston couldn't have stayed to the end of his term – after all there was an election at the end of the year. Now there was speculation about whom the governor of Preston's home state would appoint to fill the position until the next election. There would be plenty of pressure on the governor to influence his choice of replacement, but Miller didn't think whoever had been blackmailing Preston would be able to work themselves into manipulating that decision. On the other hand, if Preston had not told him the entire truth and had suggested the governor pick his choice of replacement... he decided he'd better not follow that line of investigation. Time was short anyway. There would be an election and he was still not quite sure what he was going to do.

One thing he did know; he would have to tread carefully. He had no evidence to back up his story of the conversation with Miller. He hadn't had time to review the video records of the lobby to see if Preston had been easily recognizable. He wasn't sure if he should do that. A request would have to go through the usual channels and others would review the records too, so it might end up drawing more attention than he needed.

If he was going to start investigating members of Congress, he had to make sure as few people as possible knew about it. If the press were to find out he was involved in checking into voting patterns, for a reason he could not disclose or support, he would have no support from his seniors. He would be virtually hung, drawn and quartered. The trouble was anyone working with him might suffer a similar fate, so he hoped he'd chosen his confederates wisely. He'd find out in the morning.

He checked into the Red Lion on Hayden Island, ate a light supper, and with his brain on DC time was asleep by 9:00 pm. He awoke at 4:00 am, dressed and went for a walk in a light drizzle along the Columbia River waterfront. It was magnificent to be out at this quiet hour with only a few hardened, Gore-texed joggers for company. By 7:00 am he had showered and was eating his breakfast. He returned to his room and at 8:15 the knock on the door announced his first visitor, Jack Straw, who had driven down from Seattle. A few minutes later, Pedro Sanchez arrived. He had caught an early morning flight from San Francisco.

Miller introduced them to each other and welcomed both to Portland. They took off their coats, rearranged the chairs around the small table, opened their briefcases and made small talk.

Room service arrived and while Straw and Sanchez helped themselves to coffee and muffins, Miller related the substance of his meeting with Preston. Straw was over six feet tall, dressed in jeans, jacket, and open-neck shirt. He sported a full beard, shoulder length black hair, and managed to make himself look like anything but the public expectation of an FBI agent. Sanchez, as his name suggested, was Hispanic, clean shaven, with closely cropped hair, only about five-and-a-half feet tall, and dressed impeccably with suit and tie. He did not look so much an FBI agent as a successful California business man, and he spoke with an impeccable Californian accent.

Miller continued, "The problem I have is there's no direct evidence of any blackmail or voting irregularity. Before I take this any further you both have to realize there are dangers on starting an investigation into Congress, especially since it involves influencing voting. Our job today is to see if we can take this any further. Maybe we'll decide there's nothing we can do, but if we start we will have to keep any investigation as quiet as we can. The fewer involved the better. I would like you to share this with staff you really trust, and who don't mind living with ambiguity."

"Ambiguity?" asked Straw.

"Maybe ambiguity is not the right word. The problem is we've been told of a threat to the system, but we may not be able to do anything about it."

Sanchez commented, "In some ways the system is the threat."

"What do you mean?" Miller asked.

"Well, we are meeting to help put a stop to something which threatens our democracy, but if we are found to be investigating, basically doing our job, we'll be the ones who suffer," Sanchez replied.

Miller said, "Exactly. It could be the proverbial hot potato."

Sanchez shrugged and said, "We can at least look at our options. Let's look at what we could do from what you've told us. Let's look at the extremes. We make it a major investigation. We look at voting patterns for all of Congress over the last ten years. We use a lot of manpower and it may lead to identifying some Members of Congress as potential victims, if that's the right word, for vote-buying or blackmail. Who knows what we might find? If we find anything the politicians will deny they voted as they were told, the press has a field-day, and we limp away with our tails between our legs."

Straw said, "I agree that won't work. It might have the opposite effect of making any blackmail impossible to identify. We could narrow it down. Since Preston is a senator, we could just look at Senate voting patterns and see if any are in concordance with him, especially on close votes. The trouble is I believe he's very much a toe-the-line-for-the-party senator, which is probably one of the reasons he was asked to consider running for president, and he is not alone in voting as the party directs."

"Then there are the times he voted, or didn't vote, in committee, so there might be a different pattern there. Do either of you know if it's easy to find out about politicians' votes?" asked Miller.

Sanchez replied, "Oh, it's relatively easy. There are government web sites which have those details, and then there are sites run by special interests who want you to know who voted for, or against, their philosophies. There are some allegedly independent sites that monitor votes too. I suppose it would be possible to correlate votes, but I'm not sure it would get us anywhere. If we identify a pattern, then what? It would be too easy for a member of Congress to display moral indignation of any statistical evidence the FBI produces. What we really need is hard evidence. We need written statements. We need something like the photos and video of Preston, and we have nothing like that."

"Do you think we should just forget about it?" asked Miller.

"No," Sanchez replied, "we just can't do that. In a way we would be just as morally responsible then."

Straw nodded and said, "I agree, we just can't leave it. We have to try something, but voting patterns aren't going to work. So, if we don't try to find out about the results of blackmail, maybe we should look at those who are being blackmailed."

"How?" asked Miller.

"You said Preston thought the best way to ensure a politician would vote the way you want them to is to use a carrot-and-stick approach. Maybe we should look at that aspect?" said Straw.

Miller said, "Well, we know what the stick was for Preston, and I assume the carrot was anonymous trips to a brothel in the suburbs. I don't know that. It was something I assumed from the conversation. I don't like Preston, so I'm sure I'm biased, but how are we going to find out what the carrots or sticks are for any other politician?"

Sanchez answered first, "We don't know. Each year there are a few scandals involving members of Congress, which the press discovers, or is told about, but there is no way in which we can identify who's being blackmailed or what carrots and sticks are being used out there."

Straw said, "And we still only have Preston's story. He is implying there are others in the Senate who are being told how to vote, but we don't know, and we have no idea if this is going to apply to the House."

"I agree," said Miller. "I think am going to have a longer talk with Preston when we I get back to DC. He must have some idea of who else might be involved."

"Do you think you'll get any more out of him?" asked Sanchez.

"Maybe. I was left with the feeling of not being told everything, but I get that when I speak to most politicians."

"It's time for you to leave DC, Chris. You've given enough already," Sanchez said.

"I agree. I am thinking about it. This investigation might be my swan song. I went for a walk this morning along the Columbia — I'd forgotten how much I like being near a river. Well, a river other than the Potomac. I'm working on getting out.

"Don't wait too long, Chris," added Straw.

"I have waited too long already. I'm working on it," he emphasized. " Now, let's get a refill and get back to business." Miller obviously did not want his personal life discussed, even though the two colleagues in the room with him were also two of his firm friends. He'd always maintained a strict separation between his work and his social life. At least he thought he had, but as he reached for his cup he realized most of his few friends were FBI. That was not a good sign.

They stood, refilled their coffee cups, stretched and sat back at the small hotel-room table.

Straw spoke, "I think the only way we're going to be able to identify any potential past or future blackmail targets is to look at the Gary Hart effect."

"How?"

"Let's look at scandals around election time which have caused a candidate to lose."

Miller replied, "The only problem with that is I called it the Gary Hart effect. Preston hadn't even considered it a possibility before I mentioned it."

"I agree, but let's look at it from the blackmailer's perspective. Say you want to make sure your candidate wins. It's a close race. You can pour extra money into your candidate's election, and that might work, or it could back-fire on you if you over do it. So, it's much easier to disgrace your opponent close to the election."

Sanchez said, "OK, so it works. Your opponent is disgraced and you win, but just because your opponent has lost doesn't mean you are now going to vote according to a blackmailer's wishes."

"In some cases that may be all a blackmailer has to do. If a candidate is elected who votes as you want anyway, all you have to do is make sure he is elected."

"Well, let's take it a little further," Sanchez said. "If you were going to disgrace a political candidate how would you go about it? For men I'm thinking the usual women, alcohol, gambling, drug, sexuality, religion, motel-room scandal. For women members of Congress it might be harder, or it could be similar – perhaps throw in abortion history. It doesn't have to always be the truth."

Miller added, "What you want is to some extent the opposite of what worked with Preston. There you wanted to have compromising evidence and plan to never make it public or you lose your ability to use it as a threat. For a disgrace to work you want to have maximum publicity, and you have to time it right. For that you need the press."

Straw said, "I agree, but what coverage do you need? Say you have, well for example, a motel set-up. You have to have the police, the press, TV cameras, all there at the same time. That's not easy. You can get the police there in minutes, but not the press. The interviews outside motels on the evening news are the neighbor, the brother, the best friend all being asked their opinion at the scene of the crime, but not at the same time as the crime. You need the press there at the time of the crime if you want to really make sure it'll grab the headlines."

"The only way you can guarantee that is to notify the press in advance," said Sanchez.

"Exactly," Straw continued, "so you call the local newspaper, but that wouldn't work. They may not have a reporter available, and the editor may be friends with the candidate. Hey, he may have even booked the motel room, so you have to tell maybe a regional newspaper, maybe even a national one. You should probably also notify a TV channel, maybe two."

"You'd want a minimum turnout of the media. How are you going to guarantee that, but not make it too obvious?" asked Miller.

Straw replied, "Let's think this through. You may not need the full TV cameras and newspaper exposure. It depends on how you are going to discredit the candidate. Take Preston for example. It would not have been too difficult to follow him and get photographs, at least of him going into a cat house, and build up enough evidence over time to disgrace him. You could then give this to a newspaper, and then twelve hours later give it to the rest of the press. For extra drama you might have a reporter try to interview him as he leaves the brothel. On the other hand, if you are trying to disgrace someone who is lily-white, you have to have the maximum press coverage in a short time, just at the critical time before an election. You have to have a set-up, maximum media exposure, and a week's follow-up. The candidate will deny everything, but by the time he or she is being shown to be telling the truth, the damage will have been done."

Sanchez said, "That could be the potentially weak link in this. You have to make sure the press is going to go along with your plans. You could let different newspapers and TV stations know when to turn up, but they might not comply, or they may get suspicious. Perhaps you should feed your reports to a news agency."

"You mean like Associated Press or Reuters, or one like that?" asked Miller.

"Yes, but the news agency has to know it is coming from a reliable source, or one they have worked with before, or why would they have anything to do with it?" replied Sanchez. "So anonymous tips won't work. What you need for anyone in the press to pay attention to you is a history of providing reliable information, or at least tips."

Miller said, "You two are a little young to remember the Watergate scandal which undid President Nixon, but the informant, who was called Deep Throat, gave reliable tips and managed to remain anonymous, so you could have an anonymous source."

Straw smiled and said, "We're not that young, Chris. It was only just before my time, or maybe the time I was old enough for politics to register on my mind, but we went over it, sometimes in excruciating detail, at the Academy. And, as we all now know, all these years later, Deep Throat turned out to be an FBI man. He worked with a couple of reporters from the Washington Post I believe?" The others nodded. "It wouldn't have worked if he'd contacted multiple reporters or other media outlets for a couple of reasons. One is it would have been more difficult to maintain anonymity, and two, he would have had less control over when to release the information he was providing."

Miller said, "So, what we need to look for is a pattern of reports from a news agency, newspaper or maybe TV? It would probably have to be a nation-wide pattern and so a nation-wide news organization. "

Sanchez said, "That's probably a good place to start, but don't forget Facebook, Twitter and the other social media sites. They can disseminate information more quickly than any news service. How about we try to identify scandals which have led to a candidate losing an election and see how they got reported. Maybe we'll find a pattern."

Straw added, "That seems like a good place to start. I was thinking of maybe concentrating on close elections, but if you had a scandal which basically stopped a candidate from ever participating in political life again, it wouldn't necessarily have to be that close. It would depend on your time perspective."

Miller said, "I agree. There are a couple of points to consider though. We shouldn't just concentrate on times when there was a scandal. We have to look at times when a candidate, and here I think we will just have to concentrate on close elections, was disabled from participating in the election and it may have let their opponent win. You don't have to be 'Gary Harted' to lose. You could have a heart attack, maybe cancer, or even the rumor of cancer. You could break a leg, get seriously injured in a car wreck. In fact anything that might make the electorate hesitate before electing you."

Sanchez said, "You could even be assassinated."

Miller and Straw looked at Sanchez. Miller spoke first, "You're right, Pedro. I don't know what stakes these people are playing for, and I hope it doesn't go that far, but it's something we can't exclude. I wonder what we are getting ourselves into."

The meeting continued for the rest of the morning. They broke for lunch and decided to leave Miller's hotel room for a restaurant overlooking the Columbia River. They also promised to talk about topics other than Gary Hart, Richard Nixon, and FBI politics. By 1:30 they were back in Miller's room. They agreed on their assignments and bringing in one or two others in their respective offices to help with the investigation. The Seattle and San Francisco offices would coordinate their research. For the time being Miller wanted DC kept out of the investigation until he could see what the other offices had turned up. He planned to talk to Preston as soon as possible to see if he could get information to help focus the investigation.

At 2:30 Miller checked out of his room and both he and Sanchez accepted Straw's offer of a ride to Portland International Airport. There was one other assignment which Miller suggested on the journey. He asked both agents to start to look around the country for political races which looked like being close, or critical, in the November elections.

Straw headed north for Interstate 5 and Seattle while Miller and Sanchez said their goodbyes and headed for their departure gates. Miller found a seat, noted his plane was on time and closed his eyes. He was tired. It was just after 4:00 pm in Portland. In DC it was dark and on a normal day he might have been home by now, but it looked like he wouldn't get there much before 3:00 am. He sighed and wondered if he should let himself fall asleep. His head fell forward and he tried to ignore the sounds around him, but through the airport noise and announcements something caught his attention. He stood and moved closer to an airport television. It was showing CNN and a female reporter on the scene in Washington DC. It was dark and raining. She was wearing a yellow reflective safety vest, and holding an umbrella against the weather. There were flashing lights in the background.

She continued, "...and that is the story from Arlington. I repeat it looks like Senator Robert Preston, who announced this week he was resigning and would not seek re-election, Senator Preston, who was considered a potential presidential candidate next year, was seriously injured and died on the way to hospital in an apparent hit-and-run accident this evening. This is Amanda Holte on the scene of the hit-and-run returning you to Bill in the studio." The picture changed and Bill, the immaculately groomed and immaculate anchorman wore his serious face and continued with the rest of the news.

Miller was about to call Sanchez, but then checked his watch. Sanchez's plane had already left and he was in the air and unreachable for another two hours. He called Straw, who was approaching Centralia on Interstate 5, and told him the news.

Miller added, "I'll check when I get back to DC. I'll get some of our people to find out what the Arlington police know."

Straw replied, "Maybe it doesn't really matter if it was a hit-and-run which killed him, or he was murdered. I think we have to assume he was murdered, even if we can't prove it. This changes the complexion of what we're doing...I have one major concern though – do you think you are in any danger?"

The question caught Miller by surprise, "I don't know. I don't think so. I really hadn't thought about it."

Straw said, "Well, think about it on the plane back to DC, and let me know what you come up with. What time does your plane get in?"

"About one."

"Well, I'll still be up. It'll only be ten here. I'll call Sanchez too. I like the way he thinks."

"OK, I'll call when I get to DC and...yes, I thought you'd like him. Call you later. Bye."

Miller hung up and put his phone away. Was he in any danger? He didn't really think so, but there was no sense in ignoring risks. Evaluating risk was part of his job. He'd think about it on the flight.

At another airport, in the same time zone as Miller, the man known as Mr. Smith, was also evaluating the risk. As he watched the same CNN report he felt the realization creeping over him. He could no longer ignore the facts. He should have given up the game long ago. He had to accept he was in danger, and he had to plan accordingly.

Preston had been one of his early targets. He'd arranged the photo and video sessions, handed over the information, and then watched Preston's career proceed, seemingly unaffected, for the last ten years. He also had a 'photo session' with the governor of Preston's home state, and Preston himself, when the two visited a 'ranch' outside Las Vegas. Again he'd handed over the evidence, and said he no other copies. Well, at least he swore he had none. That part was sort of true. He no longer had the copies in his possession — he'd stashed them elsewhere. The Las Vegas Chamber of Commerce may attract visitors to Sin City with their "what happens in Vegas, stays in Vegas" slogan, but it didn't really apply to anybody. There was no anonymity. It especially didn't apply to politicians and their antics.

He'd assumed that since he knew little about those who had hired him, they knew little about him too. Now he could take nothing for granted. He would have to resurrect the plans he'd made for disappearing, but the timing would have to be right. He was still valuable to them and had work to do.

He had a four-hour flight to Chicago to think it over.

7

"I agree. Something has to be done about immigration. It's completely wrong that we should allow people into this country to take jobs from Americans. What would you suggest?"

It was one month after our meeting on Dick's sailboat and the three of us, Dick, Harry and I, were providing "security" for William Shanty's primary election campaign meeting at the Lutheran church in Belfair. There were a few unoccupied seats, but for a hot Monday night in mid-July it was a good turnout. There were no television cameras, but a couple of reporters from local and state newspapers had turned up.

Shanty was answering questions about his policies and ideas after his short introductory, why-you-need-to-vote-for-me speech. He was impressive. This was the fourth meeting I had attended and he clearly knew how to woo the audience to his side. More than that he managed to do one thing politicians usually failed at.

He knew when to shut up.

This time he was bouncing back the question to a bald, grey-bearded, two-hundred-and-fifty pounder in the second row.

The red-neck question had been, "When are you politishuns gonna get real and stop these damn Mexicans sneakin' across the border in Texas and stealin' our jobs up here?" The reply could have agreed with the questioner's premise and cited figures showing medical services and welfare costs incurred caring for illegal immigrants. On the other hand it could have included studies showing the benefits of immigration for current residents, or the finding that immigrants mostly take jobs shunned by Americans. Shanty could have questioned what jobs in Mason County, Washington State, were being stolen because of a leaky border two thousand miles away in Texas – none of this would have had any impact. Asking what the questioner would do was smarter. There had been no reply so Shanty repeated the question in a level, unemotional tone, "What would you suggest, sir?"

The man hesitated for a few seconds, regained his bluster and said, "Well, secure the borders, arrest any illegals...shoot...you politishuns should do it. It's your responsibility." He was clearly doing his best to not swear, but for a second when he said "shoot", when he really meant "shit", I had a fleeting vision of guard towers, machine guns, a Berlin wall and bodies lining the bottom of Texas.

Before it could seem like he was belittling the questioner Shanty commented, "It is a difficult issue, sir, and thanks for your question."

Shanty nodded towards the man, who seemed suitably mollified, and continued, "I wish there was a simple answer. I know some of my colleagues. Oh, I'm getting ahead of myself (smile)... some of my prospective colleagues. I haven't been elected yet. Well, some of my prospective colleagues would like to put a ditch, fence, and guard dogs along the border. I don't know about you, but do I want billions of my tax dollars going to 'secure the border'? Hell, no. And if I'm a farmer in Yakima with crops wasting in my fields do I want to spend more money keeping away good help? Hell, no. Well, I suppose I could always get it for twenty-five bucks an hour, and do you know what that would do to the cost of an apple in your supermarket? No, sir, like I'm sure you agree it's a complicated matter. It needs to be fixed, and when I'm elected you can bet I'll be working on it."

There were some nods in the audience and Shanty, without saying anything of substance, moved on to the next question. I was not sure if the audience thought the question had been answered. They seemed happy, but that may have been the result of the extra beer or two from the Black Bear Bar before the meeting.

Shanty stood about six feet tall, was in his late forties, and used his hands and arms like an Italian to help convey his message. He was moderately good-looking, with well-groomed, straight black hair and brown eyes. He was a few pounds overweight, which made him emaciated in comparison to his audience's standards. He was wearing blue jeans and a white T shirt emblazoned in red with the words, "It Shall be Shanty". Corny though it had seemed to me, and most of the members of the press, the slogan seemed to be helping him. He was currently the only Republican candidate for the new 12th District seat and was campaigning for the primary. I wasn't quite sure why a primary was necessary, since the Democrats had only fielded a single candidate too, but apparently, despite the cost to taxpayers, the State's constitution demanded it. The first two past the post would be on the ballot in the November election, so the result of who would be on the ballot was a foregone conclusion. The only reason the candidates were campaigning now, when everyone was supposed to be enjoying summer, was the first in the primary was said to have a better chance of winning in November.

The meeting continued. Did he believe in the Bible? "Hell, yes, of course I do." But he moved on quickly from that question, and from the inevitable abortion question to which he answered, "I believe in the sanctity of human life, at all stages of that life, whenever that life begins."

This established his pro-life and pro-Christian principles for those who were only interested in single-issue elections.

He, and the audience, seemed a little surprised when he was asked about America's position on Cuba by a woman with a Hispanic accent. But this wasn't Florida, so most agreed with him that if the US had wanted to devise a way of keeping Castro in power for over fifty years...well, they couldn't have done better than recommend the embargo that was still in place.

Overall, it was a benign meeting. There was very little rancor, and most of the audience were chatting and smiling when the meeting wrapped up at 9:15. My job was more like a movie-theater usher than a Secret Service agent. I'd even wondered if I could have made a little more money selling popcorn and ice-cream from a tray hanging around my neck. The job paid well too. I could have earned more money playing at doctor, but it was refreshing to sit in these meetings and see another side of life. Occasionally, I'd recognize someone who had been a patient of mine and we'd share a word or two. One asked if I'd thought about a second career as a Wal-mart greeter when I told him I was there in an official capacity.

I was having fun and there was only one problem.

I didn't believe in William Shanty.

But much more of a concern was I didn't think he believed in himself. It was hard to pinpoint why I felt uncomfortable about this. Dick, Harry, and I were only three of about fifteen people who hovered around him at all times. No one else in the entourage seemed to have the least doubt that he was District 12's answer to the rampant liberalism, laziness, foreigners, government intervention, abortionists, and godless gun-control nuts who were tearing the country apart. It's not as if those issues were close to my heart, and if they had been maybe I'd have been sitting in the audience enraptured by the candidate. It's just something didn't seem to fit. On paper he had the right credentials. He hadn't lived in the area for long, but his family had spent weekends at their cabin on the north shore of the Hood Canal for decades, so he could be called a resident. His website detailed his conservative credentials.

His father had amassed a reasonable fortune from a career in the pharmaceutical industry. The website displayed a photograph from the eighties of his father shaking hands with Ronald Reagan, which I realized was second only to receiving a personal blessing from the Pope. William Shanty had gone to high school in Seattle and on to The University of Michigan in Ann Arbor. He then acquired an MBA and a wife from Duke. They had three good-looking photogenic children, who were now at college themselves, and also featured on the website. His life had not been without tragedy. His wife had died in a skiing accident when the children were in middle school. He had carried on, cared for the children and worked hard in his import/export business. He had experienced running a small business and building it into a medium-sized business, which he had sold three years previously with the intention of retiring, but he found (according to his website) that he just couldn't sit and watch the country continue as it was doing and so had ventured into politics. He was just what any political party would want. He was young, well young enough, and wealthy, which paradoxically, attracted more campaign money from out-of-state donors.

So, why didn't I believe any of it? He wasn't a chameleon, changing colors to suit his surroundings, and he wasn't a psychopath, changing who he was depending on what he could get out of people, but he did have the ability to make those around him think he was wholeheartedly behind the issues they were interested in, whether it was the moderates in his party or the vociferous right-wing. Everything looked good on paper, but somehow it wasn't. It reminded me of a patient I once saw who came to see me after a minor earthquake. His house had shaken and for a few seconds he thought he was back in Vietnam and under fire. The flashback caused him extreme anxiety which settled after a week or two. It was then that he brought in his medals, commendations, and letters from his tours in the Vietnam War. I looked them over and said they looked impressive. He told me they were all lies. He wasn't where they said he was, and he didn't do what they said he did.

There was also the fact Shanty was single. He had not remarried and the companionship of a member of the opposite sex was not mentioned on his political web page. The companionship of a member of the same sex would never have been mentioned, after all this was an election campaign, but I had no reason to suspect he had any inclinations to either end of the sexual spectrum. That was part of my problem. He seemed too perfect. Of course, if he'd had a doting wife by his side that may have made him even more politically perfect, so I was undermining my own argument. Basically, something was unsettling me and I couldn't put my finger on it.

Two weeks later I again found myself in his driveway, listening to the welcome rain on the car roof and the squeak of the intermittent wipers smudging the windshield. It was an hour after the last speech of the primary campaign. Postal votes had been coming in for a week and it was only three days to the primary election. The polls had us coming in just behind his Democratic opponent. He'd worked hard, narrowed the gap, and in a few days we would have the results. In some ways it was going to be something of an anti-climax, and of course, it didn't matter – the general election, when he squared off against his primary opponent, didn't take place until November.

That evening he'd given a rousing speech at another Lutheran church in Shelton, answered the questions appropriately, and I'd driven him home again, but this time, when he sat in the car, he looked as he should have. He looked drained. He reclined the seat part-way, closed his eyes, and it was not until we arrived at his house that he spoke.

"John, I apologize. I have not been good company this evening. For some reason that last meeting exhausted me, and then I realized this is only the primary. In another month we'll be back at it again until November. And then, assuming I win, I'll be commuting to DC to work. I wonder why anyone would want a job like this."

"You're talking to someone who wouldn't cross the Tacoma Narrows Bridge to commute, so I just couldn't imagine what going back and forth to DC would be like. Actually, I'm wrong, I could imagine what it would be like, and I prefer not to. And, you don't have to apologize – you're entitled to be exhausted."

He made no offer to get out of the car. He moved his seat upright, looked at me and said, "We were sitting here a couple of weeks ago and you said you wondered if I believed in myself. I think you wondered if I was trying to be white bread. What did you really mean by that?"

"I don't think I communicated exactly what I meant. We ended the conversation with you being a croissant, and I drove away unhappy; that's where it ended." We both smiled at this.

I continued, "I was wondering if you believe in yourself...you know...what you are doing, and I wasn't convinced you are. Are you?"

"Do you think I'm dumbing things down?"

"No, that's not it. You don't dumb things down. People see through that act quickly. I've seen that in my own profession, and soon it sounds patronizing. You don't do that."

"So, I am not the great patrician come down from on high to somehow get the masses in order?"

"No, not at all," I replied, "but maybe that's it though. I wonder if you are playing at being a politician. You don't need the money; you don't seem to need the fame. Your website says you want to get elected to try to change the way the country is going."

"Have you checked out other politicians' websites?"

"No."

"They all say that. It's like loving apple pie, small dogs, babes-in-arms, and the American flag. If you don't say that there must be something wrong with you," he said, allowing a little cynicism to creep in where I had seen none before. He noticed the slight pulling back of my head as I reacted to this and continued, "Yes, they all say that, and you've touched a nerve there. I suspect one in a hundred believes all what they say. They daren't say they want to get into congress because of the status and power it will give them, but that's what most of them are in it for." He sighed deeply. "I just hope I can see this through. It's harder than I thought it would be. And besides, there are a few other reasons people go into politics – at least I hope there are. There are for me anyway."

"Your website doesn't mention any," I replied.

He looked at me for a full twenty seconds before replying, "John, are you my doctor?"

"No."

"So, any conversations taking place in this car are not covered by doctor-patient confidentiality?"

"I suppose not, but I don't plan on making our conversations public."

"But they would be 'discoverable' by an attorney?"

"I suppose so." I was curious.

He reached into his jacket, pulled a five-dollar bill out of his wallet and handed it to me.

"This is your retainer," he said, "and if I want to ask you about my heartburn, the aching in my knee, or a persistent rash, then I am now your patient. Is that correct?

"Maybe, if I choose to accept you as a patient. Accepting the money isn't necessary – you know that." I handed the five dollars back to him and he accepted it. I couldn't see where this conversation was leading.

He hesitated before saying, "So last time you wondered if you could believe in me and if I believe in myself, or maybe believe in myself as Will Shanty, Member of Congress."

I nodded.

He eased his head onto the head-rest, closed his eyes, then continued, "So, I am going to assume this is confidential and not one word will get out of this car?"

"Of course," I answered.

"How can I put it?...I... well, I do want to become a member of the US Congress, but it may not happen for reasons other than electoral. Because of, what I at least consider the highest motives, it may not work, and I feel guilty about that. I have a lot of people who believe in me and want me as their representative, and I think I can do a good job, but it's just not that simple."

I waited a couple of seconds, just in case there was more, and said, "I haven't a clue what you're talking about. Maybe you have morphed into a politician after all."

He chuckled, opened his eyes, looked at me and said, "You're right. I didn't say anything did I? Maybe now is not the right time to confess all." He sat up, put his hand on the door handle and continued, "I need to share something. It can wait. Enjoy your vacation. See you after Labor Day when we get down to business again."

He opened the door and was about to get out, but I couldn't let him go with that statement. Before he could get out of the car I said, "Come on, you can't leave me hanging like that."

For a moment he hesitated then replied, "Look at the website." He got out of the car and jogged through the rain to the shelter of his front porch. He turned, gave a brief wave and let himself into his house. I drove home.

8

We lost the election, but did better than expected. The turnout was low – only 21% of the electorate had bothered to vote and who could blame them? It had been a hot summer and there were more interesting distractions than voting in a primary of minimal significance. For once I agreed with Fox news whose pundits thought our 52% to 48% loss showed we were still very much in the running for the November election. William Shanty's opponent, the democrat Chris Hall, tried to appear conciliatory but came off as condescending when he was interviewed on the local CBS channel. As predicted, the result made very little difference, and the electorate went back to sleep for the rest of August.

The Shanty election machine wound down for the rest of the summer too. The candidate himself managed the press enquiries, letters to the editors, and radio and television interviews. This was enough to maintain his name recognition, and we had agreed there would be no more meetings and debates until after the first week in September. It helped that his opponent took off for a three-week European vacation the Saturday after the election. Everyone was being very civilized.

Ann and I had other plans. Dick was hoping to spend time on his boat exploring the Hood Canal. We had a mutual friend whose house overlooked the Canal and had agreed to let Dick moor the sailboat there for the rest of the summer.

Hood Canal was apparently named by George Vancouver on one of his explorations to the area in the eighteenth century. He called it Hood Channel in his notes, but named it Hood Canal on his charts. Both terms were wrong. It is best described as a fjord – an inlet caused by glacial erosion, but the name Hood Canal stuck. It has a surface area of about 150 square miles and is about sixty-five miles long. William Shanty's family cabin was ten miles from the lower end, but Ann and I only planned to go as far as Bangor on its eastern shore; less than thirty miles from its opening into Puget Sound at Foul Weather Bluff.

Ann had taken a week off work and we were going to sail Dick's boat there. It was also going to be a delayed honeymoon. The trip plans reminded me of the song, "I'm going to get you on a slow boat to China". We weren't anticipating getting to China, but it was certainly going to be slow. With no trade winds, just the fickle breezes of Puget Sound in August, we made sure the fuel tank was filled before we caught an early outgoing tide on a Monday morning and headed north. We found a little wind, but by noon the tide had changed and we were in danger of sailing backwards, so we cut our losses, fired up the "underwater sail" and made it to Liberty Bay by 4 pm.

By 6 pm we had moored at the public dock in Poulsbo and were sitting down for a meal at Campana's. It had been a sunny day, with a weak south-easterly breeze, but the weather was changing. The wind had picked up a little and backed to the south-west, clouds were moving in and the temperature was dropping. After a post-dinner walk we were back at the boat just as the first few rain-drops began to fall.

Well, I suppose we needed the rain – rain is always welcome in August. Unless, of course, you are trying to sleep in a boat in a marina. It wasn't the noise of the rain on the top of the boat; it was the drumming from the wind beating the rigging against the mast that kept us awake. I minimized it as best I could by attaching lines to the shrouds to pull the halyards off the mast, but it wasn't ideal, and we spent a restless night listening to the thumping.

We awoke the next morning and stayed in bed until we could hold off emptying our bladders no longer. The wind had died, but it was still raining and misty. We scurried to the marina's bathrooms and back to the promise of warm oatmeal and scrambled eggs.

Six hours later we motored in to a slip in the marina at Kingston near the ferry dock. It was still raining.

It's hard to keep dry, or to dry yourself, when you are sitting in a boat surrounded by 100% humidity which takes every opportunity to invade your footwear, clothes, and living space. As we sat in a mediocre restaurant, picking over a mediocre dinner, looking out through fogged-up windows on the grayness of Puget Sound, Ann commented,

"For the same investment in time, and maybe even money, we could have had a few days in Vancouver."

I nodded and said, "It gives you new respect for what the Pilgrim Fathers must have endured."

"Ah, but they weren't on their honeymoon, so their expectations must have been less."

"I don't think they had honeymoons back then, and at least by reputation they weren't supposed to enjoy things like honeymoons, even if they didn't have them."

Ann asked, "What do you think the essential parts of a honeymoon are? I mean, apart from the sex."

"Well, if suffering hours of rain, diesel fumes, sea-sickness, and engine drone aren't on the list, that would exclude us...and any cruise ships. So, they must be on the list, or why would cruising honeymoons be so popular? If not, then I suppose the only thing on the list is sex."

"How is it I feel anything but interested in sex then?"

"I know what you mean. It's hard to feel enthusiasm when you can't get dry to get wet in the first place."

"That sounds like you just said something naughty."

"I apologize," I said. "It was unintentional. It was not meant as a pick-up line or seduction attempt. It just came out."

Ann raised an eyebrow.

"It came from that movie," I continued. "You know the one...the comedy with Billy Crystal as the therapist; 'Ride me hard and put me away wet'. That's what one of his patients said."

"To his therapist?"

"No, to his wife and Billy Crystal said it was OK. At least I think he did."

"What does it mean?"

"I'm not really sure. Maybe I don't have enough imagination."

"Oh, you have plenty of imagination. Sounds more like a line from a John Wayne movie. If it's such a good line, why haven't you used it on me?"

"Probably because it sounds like a line from a John Wayne movie... Anyway, we don't seem to need lines like that."

Ann smiled. "We don't need lines like that tonight. We just need to sleep."

"I agree. Let's toast to that. I just hope we have a better night's sleep tonight."

We raised our glasses and downed what was left of our drinks, squirmed into our wet "water-proofs" and scuttled back to the boat.

We might have had a good night's sleep if condensation hadn't dripped from the roof onto my face, and if the early ferry to Edmonds hadn't stuck to the shipping rules and announced its departure with its foghorn at 4:55 am. We even went back to sleep after that, but the foghorn of the 5:30 ferry blew away the last chances of sleep.

The oatmeal was welcome, but it seemed not as tasty as the previous day's. We couldn't face making scrambled eggs.

I started the motor. Ann untied Roho and we eased out of the slip and into the windless rain and fog of Puget Sound. We headed north at a weary five knots If we tried to go any faster the engine vibrations set up annoying harmonies with other parts of the boat. About four hundred yards from the shore the cliffs disappeared in the mist and we were alone, tired, bedraggled and wondering why anyone would ever buy a boat. Another definition of sailboat ownership came to mind; sailing is like standing in a cold shower tearing up $100 bills. I am not sure who first thought that up, but for us it was more like standing in a cold shower tearing up honeymoons.

Then, a miracle happened.

It stopped raining, a light breeze picked up. An hour later the fog melted away and the sun came out. The light breeze became a gentle breeze, and another hour later the gentle breeze became a moderate breeze. By then, with the main hoisted and the Genoa filling, we were heading north on a broad reach in an east wind at six knots. We turned off the engine and opened every port hole and hatch to banish the moisture and memories of the rain.

Finally, we were having fun.

We rounded Foulweather Bluff at around 1:00 pm and turned to head south along the western shore of Hood Canal. The wind held as we headed towards the floating Hood Canal Bridge. I was pretty sure we could make it under the fixed structure of the bridge at the eastern end, but wished I'd checked earlier. We were coming in with the tide and I would have to make a decision soon. I'd wanted to avoid the eastern side of Hood Canal because the wind would not be as reliable there.

It turned out I did not have to make a decision – a much taller sailboat than Roho had requested the bridge be opened to allow passage. I contacted the bridge operator and we were told we could follow the other sailboat if we could be there less than five minutes after it was through. We were less than a quarter of a mile away. I could see the warning lights on the bridge roadway start to flash, the barriers came down, and the traffic in both directions stopped and began to back up. The middle of the bridge deck began to open. The other sailboat was a little downwind of the bridge, threw in a tack to port, sixty seconds later tacked again to starboard and headed for the opening. We were still on a broad reach and my concern was not that I would not make it in five minutes, but at the same time the other boat reached the gap. Fortunately, her skipper headed a few degrees to starboard and caught a little more speed as he went through the opening. Fifteen seconds later we followed him through the gap, tightened the sheets and headed away from the bridge and the other sailboat. I heard a voice crackle on the VHF radio. Ann answered and turned to me.

"That was the bridge. They want to thank you for your timing."

I looked around, the barriers were already lifting and traffic would soon be moving again. I raised a hand and waved to the control tower.

"Do you think they were being sarcastic or did they mean it?"

"I think they meant it."

"So, it looked like I knew what I was doing then?"

"I had complete faith in you, doctor."

"Thanks, nurse. Now who's being sarcastic? I must admit I had a few moments of life-flashing-before-my-eyes back there."

"No one will ever know," she smiled. "I won't tell a soul, as long as you...well, I'll think of something later." She kissed me on the cheek and headed below to tidy up the cabin.

We were now within an hour of our destination and I continued mid-channel. I didn't approach the eastern shore until we were well past the Navy base at Bangor. I started the engine and pointed her into the wind. Ann lowered the Genoa and stowed it in its bag, then together we lowered, and covered, the mainsail on the boom. We eased closer to the shore, tied up to the buoy, and turned off the engine.

It was so peaceful. The boat rocked gently, the late afternoon sun warmed us and we fell asleep lying on the foredeck propped up by pillows, life jackets, and cushions.

I would like to say we stayed one more night on the boat, but civilization was calling and we answered. It was only fifty yards away and when we woke from our nap we pumped up the inflatable. With two quick trips we took our belongings from the boat and found ourselves back on terra firma. Dick had arranged for my car to be at our friend's house and we drove home to a warm shower, a horizontal, dry, immobile bed, peace, and sleep.

There was one problem we discussed over breakfast the next morning. It had been a life-affirming, bonding, moist, sleep-deprived honeymoon, but it had been totally sexless. We could of course tell no one, and if we encountered any innuendo about our experience we would have to remain silent and smile knowingly. We tried smiling knowingly over breakfast – it doesn't work well with shredded wheat in your mouth. However, we both agreed ours must be an advanced relationship to be able to go on honeymoon, have no sex, and laugh about it.

9

There were only a couple of weeks left in August and the weather remained warm and dry. Ann and I made the most of it, relaxed when we could, took hikes into the mountains, and one Sunday afternoon lazed on the lawns of the Olympic Music Festival.

September arrived and with it Labor Day weekend and Seattle's Bumbershoot festival. On cue the drizzle started. It wasn't that hard, or cold, but it persisted and by the third day any remaining blackberries on the vines we passed on our morning walk had turned to moldy mush. The warm summer was leading to an early fall and the first leaves were yellowing and drifting to the ground.

Politics were changing too. The Wednesday after Labor Day we met at William Shanty's campaign headquarters in Belfair. Our numbers had expanded and twenty of us listened as his new campaign manager outlined the strategy for the next two months. Apparently, the closeness of the primary results had encouraged even more big donors to chip in and support the campaign. This was American politics at its best, or maybe worst.

For Dick, Harry, and me (the security team) the new plan meant we would be driving the candidate around more. Dick and Harry would be driving the most and I would only be called on for back-up and the bigger meetings. This suited me. I wasn't interested in being a chauffeur, but I still found the whole show fascinating and it was hard not to be carried along with the enthusiasm of the campaign team.

There was one thing I had postponed investigating during the summer, and which candidate Shanty had mentioned the last time we met, and that was to look again at his website.

One rainy evening in early September I sat down in front of my desktop screen, found his website and started to look around. It was basically very simple. It gave a history of his life and political activities. There seemed nothing particularly interesting, or new. He hadn't been in the military, so there was no opportunity to create any acts of valor. There was a short photo gallery of Shanty with his family, but none with his deceased wife. Mixed in with these was the one of his father with Ronald Reagan.

There was a large, green "contribute now" button. I wondered if I donated to his campaign if I would gain access to more information, but a twenty-dollar contribution brought me back to the same page. I wasn't about to give him any more in the hope it might lead me to a high-donor-realm webpage.

I sat back and thought about the website a little more. The only slightly incongruous post was finding the photo of his father with Ronald Reagan included with the other family snapshots. Probably thousands of people in the 80's had their photos taken with The Great Communicator, so nothing seemed unusual there, but the website furnished a link to another site where I could find out more about his father. I clicked on it and a Wikipedia page opened.

It seemed William "Bark" Shanty senior had been an exemplary capitalist. He had started to amass a sizeable nest-egg by the end of the sixties, and at the end of the seventies this had become a small fortune. By the beginning of the eighties he had moved his money, "using his experience in the pharmaceutical industry," into a couple of small companies in the Seattle area. One had failed, but the other was still a successful biotech business. He had been the major financier, shareholder and board member, and had sold his investment for half a billion dollars in the late nineties. He had died in 2002 and his fortune had been left to his one son, born in 1963. There was no mention of any political activity and, even for a Wikipedia entry, the biography left out many details. Before the sixties there was no information at all, and it wasn't until 1975 that more details of his life were listed. Even these seemed bland and uninformative. There were gaps in the entry, and although I searched the webpage I couldn't find who had written it. I hesitated and decided I had better things to do – I played a video game for ten minutes, then turned off the computer.

The campaign went on into October with each week becoming more frenetic than the last. The pace was telling on the team. There was an occasional raising of voices, and once a stand-up argument; one resigned, three left to return to college, and a couple more lost a week to coughs and colds. Through all of this William Shanty maintained his equanimity, but even he lost a few pounds, despite the efforts of the pizza shop close to his headquarters to convert the campaign staff into pepperoni and pineapple. Dick and Harry supplied most of the chauffeur services during the day (including fetching the pizza) and I helped out when there was a meeting.

On one occasion I ended up being the only one willing and available to take Shanty to interviews in Seattle. He was to be at the NPR station, KUOW, in the early afternoon, and at the Fox network TV station, KCPQ, an hour later. He could have probably taken both interviews from Kitsap County, but had the conviction that travelling to Seattle, and being questioned live and in person, was better than the remote interviews preferred by his opponent. He was probably right, and the last opinion poll suggested the race was close enough that he should be concerned about details like this. Normally, I would hesitate before driving to Seattle. It's fun, occasionally, to spend time in the city, and I have had a lot of good times there, but why would I want to take three to five (or more) hours out of my day driving to and from a city which was only sixty miles away by road, and twelve as the crow flies? And then, when I got there...well, most times it's easier not to go, but this time we were taking the ferry. It didn't save any time, but it did make the journey more pleasant.

By 11:15 we were second in line for the ferry from Southworth to West Seattle. It's usually a quiet time of day, and we were twenty minutes early. I thought about going for a stroll and leaving Shanty to his paperwork, but there was a fine gray drizzle dampening the outside world, so I read a couple of articles in the magazines I'd brought with me. I glanced at the rear-view mirror occasionally and could see the line filling up behind me with other vehicles. I turned on the fan to minimize the condensation on the windows. The ferry from Vashon arrived and disgorged its passengers and cars. I noticed a lone bicyclist approaching from the right rear of the car. The vehicle in front of me started to move onto the ferry. I started the engine, put it into gear, and was about to release the handbrake when there was a knock on the passenger window. It was the bicyclist. His lower face was hidden by a muffler and a hood over his bicycle helmet covered his forehead.

Shanty lowered the window before I could stop him.

The bicyclist pushed a thin package in through the gap in the window, turned and pushed his bicycle away from the ferry. The driver behind honked for me to move. I made a decision and moved forward. As I drove onto the ferry I looked in the rearview mirror and caught a glimpse of the bicyclist slowly pedaling in the opposite direction. I followed the directions of the ferry crew and pulled to a stop near the front of the car lane, turned off the engine, took a deep breath, and looked at Shanty.

"I suppose I shouldn't have done that?" he asked, looking a little penitent.

"No, you shouldn't." I took another deep breath. "I think I'd have done the same, but I'm your security detail, so I am supposed to act differently."

"You're right of course. I shouldn't have done it." He glanced down for a few seconds, then added, "Look...I'm just getting on a ferry in Washington State. I've done it hundreds of times before. I'm not thinking security...I suppose it might have helped if you were wearing a uniform, or I seemed to be doing anything other than being with a family doctor I know driving a small car."

"Right. You are going to have to pretend I'm not a family doctor driving a small car. Think...think we're in Kabul and I'm driving you between military bases in a militarized Humvee."

"That's going to be hard. It wouldn't work," he replied.

"Yeah. We couldn't keep that up, and I don't think we'd want to anyway.'

"I agree."

I paused, shook my head and asked, "So, to back to plan A. What have you got there anyway?" I asked, looking at the envelope on his lap.

He picked it up, turned it over and said, "It's a standard letter, size 8x11, beige envelope. It seems to have some papers inside it. It's flexible. No writing on the outside. Should I open it?"

I didn't think it could be a bomb and it probably didn't contain anthrax spores, so I told him to go ahead.

Using care, and a small screwdriver from the glove box as a letter opener, he removed four sheets of paper from the envelope and placed them on his knees.

The pages were clipped together and the top page bore the words, "We will be in touch", printed in large font size across the middle. He turned over this sheet and looked at the underlying three pages. They were photocopies of documents, but I couldn't quite make out what they were. I leaned over to get a better look. He noticed my movement and put his hand over the documents and replaced the top sheet.

"I'm not sure you want to see these," he said.

I was a little surprised by this, but just said, "OK."

He seemed to reconsider his reluctance to let me see what was in the envelope and said, "On the other hand, we've been over this before, you are my doctor, sort of, and I think this qualifies as confidential information I would share with my doctor." He hesitated a few more seconds then gave me the envelope. I took out the papers and looked at them.

The first sheet was a photocopy of an entry in the Seattle Times of November 5th, 1962. The article mentioned the conviction of a Jeffrey Williamson for possession and dealing of marijuana. The jury found him not guilty of charges of dealing cocaine and LSD. The judge had given him six years. With time already served and good behavior, he would be released in less than four years. Even for those days this seemed a harsh penalty.

The next sheet was a copy of two birth certificates. One was for a boy, John Elvis Williamson in January of 1963, and the other for a girl, Emma Peel Shanty in 1969.

The final sheet was a copy of a change of name authorized by a King County judge in 1968. Jeffrey Williamson had been allowed to change his name to William Shanty.

I thought for a few seconds, "So Jeffrey Williamson is ...?" I asked

"My father."

"And Emma Peel Shanty is your sister?"

"Correct."

"And you are, or were, John Elvis Williamson?"

"I was, and now I'm William Shanty junior."

"This isn't what your website says," I pointed out.

"That's correct too."

"I don't get it," I said.

"In some ways it's pretty simple. I wanted to keep my sister out of any political shenanigans that might go on, and I wanted to keep my family history out of sight too."

"Well, it doesn't seem to have worked," I said.

"Maybe, maybe not. This information is not general knowledge yet."

"If it becomes general knowledge it wouldn't do your campaign any good. It's probably just about OK to have a family history like this, but if you try to hide it then it becomes a problem."

"Exactly," he said without any apparent emotion.

He'd been handed a blackmail note, but didn't seem too concerned. I still didn't get, it and told him.

"Let me tell you about my father," he replied. "He was a total ass-hole all his life. Why my mother put up with him I will never know, but she did. He was also a ruthless, mean, abusive businessman. At the end of the fifties, and beginning of the sixties, he was pulling in good money controlling a large chunk of the drug scene in Seattle. It was just beginning to take off, and the Vietnam War, and all the other changes in the sixties, would eventually make him a multi-millionaire. However, he'd made a few mistakes and in 1962 he and my mother got out of Seattle one step ahead of the law. They came over to the Olympic Peninsula and hung out here for a month. They stayed with friends in Quilcene. There's not much in that town now, but you can imagine what it was like forty years ago. Apparently one day they went for a hike. I think it was on the Lower Big Quilcene River trail, and they stopped at a place called Bark Shanty for lunch, a joint, sex, and I was conceived. At least that's what my father told me on many occasions, and usually in graphic detail. I don't suppose most of us care or know about when they were conceived, but when he later changed his name he gave me and the world a perpetual reminder of that day. He also remembered it because when he got back to his friend's house that evening the cops were waiting and carted him back to Seattle. The month he'd spent away from Seattle was not idle, and he had made arrangements for concealing his cash and making sure his business carried on if he was not around. He got a long sentence because it was apparently common knowledge that his marijuana conviction was just the tip of the iceberg. At least as far as his drug-dealing activities were concerned.

"I was born the following year and didn't really know him until his release nearly four years later. Prison hadn't made him any more likeable, but he'd resolved to never go back inside again. He continued with his drug activities. By now he had several intermediaries between him and the street customers, and he was good at knowing when trouble was brewing and stepping back, but he knew there was always the possibility of betrayal. He'd probably been betrayed when he was arrested in Quilcene. He once hinted he'd dealt with that before he was imprisoned, and I can only guess what he meant by that. So, one day he changed his name and mine too. I think he paid off a judge to get it done. He shaved his long blond hair and abandoned his sunglasses, dyed his hair brown, and bought a respectable suit so he looked like any anonymous businessman. He made my mother disguise herself too. We moved to a house on Lake Washington and became completely legitimate, or so the story goes. I suspect he never completely gave up his illegal activities, but he certainly used the ways and means he had lived by for so long to get ahead in the so-called legal drug trade. The rest of his bio on the website is mainly accurate."

Something about this story didn't quite ring true. I asked, "So no one knew William Shanty, the businessman, was Jeffrey Williamson the drug king-pin? You'd have thought someone would have recognized him from one or other of his alternative lives. I mean... well, he was in the same city."

"If you'd known him you could see it would be possible. He was a psychopath and a performer. He could change his walk, his appearance, his accent, his voice. He could be what he thought you wanted him to be. He was not a nice man. My sister hated him."

"What happened to your sister?"

"She's alive, well, clean now, and living in Indianapolis with her husband and two kids. It took her a long time, and a hard struggle, to get where she is. She does not need it undone by my political ambitions, so that's why she's not mentioned on my website. She knows about it and she agrees."

"But it seems the intention of giving you these photocopies is to blackmail you. Aren't you worried your sister could be involved?"

"She's pretty well covered her tracks. She and I have mainly communicated by mail for several years, so there should be no email or phone contacts which could be discoverable. If I want to talk to her I use a pay phone. She wants it this way. My father cut her out of his will and I have offered her money, but she wants to have no contact with the Shanty fortune, and I think it's just as well. She has a good life in Indianapolis and doesn't want it damaged."

"Good... well she seems safe. So, what is the point of sending you this stuff apart from trying to embarrass you politically?"

"I think that is the point. It could be politically embarrassing."

"And what are you going to do about it?" I asked.

"I'm not sure. I don't think this was sent to me to get money out of me, but that's a possibility. I'm going to have to think about it."

With that he gave an affirmative nod of his head, leaned back and closed his eyes. This conversation was apparently over for the time being.

I hadn't been paying attention to what was going on around me during our conversation. I looked out and noticed the ferry had docked on Vashon Island, taken on more vehicles and passengers and was on its way to our destination, the dock at Fauntleroy. We'd be there in less than fifteen minutes. I spent a couple of them thinking about the idea of blackmail and Shanty's reaction, but then biological necessity checked in.

"I need to pee before we get there," I said.

"Good idea."

I locked the car and we both climbed the stairs to the restrooms. Before attempting any driving to, from, around, or anywhere in Seattle it's a good idea to have an empty bladder, because you never know when you'll be stuck, or for how long. Normally, I would have taken this opportunity to stretch my legs and walk around the ferry's passenger deck, but today was different. The episode with the bicyclist had alarmed me and I suggested we return to my car for the last few minutes before we docked. It felt safer in the vehicle.

As we drove off the ferry and into the normality of West Seattle traffic he said, "I am going to try to not think about this for the next hour or two. I need to focus on these interviews."

I nodded. I couldn't disagree – all my attention would be directed to getting back into the lanes I should have been in, but had forgotten about because I didn't drive to Seattle frequently enough. I drove and, once again, he reclined his seat and closed his eyes.

Almost thirty minutes later I dropped him off outside the KUOW offices in the University District, miraculously found a parking spot, retrieved my umbrella and walked back to the building. I sat in the waiting room for a half-hour reading an article in a medical journal about autosomal dominant polycystic kidney disease. At least I had the journal open at the article, but found I wasn't concentrating on the topic. This was because it's hard to write a dynamic, erudite article on autosomal dominant polycystic kidney disease, and I couldn't turn off the part of my brain which was wondering at the implications of the materials delivered by the anonymous bicyclist. I hoped Shanty was doing better at focusing on his interview.

I asked him how it had gone as we left the building. He gave a non-committal shrug and said it had gone much as expected. In the shelter of my umbrella we made it back to the car, and following the instructions on my GPS I drove the short distance to KCPQ on Westlake Avenue North . Fortunately, this time, parking was provided. I stayed in the car and since it was warm and dry in there, I took a leaf from the Shanty travel manual, reclined the seat and closed my eyes.

I was awakened by Shanty knocking on the windshield. It took me a few seconds to realize where I was. I unlocked his door, moved my seat upright and shook the cobwebs out of my brain. He sat in the car and looked at me. He was smiling.

"So, the interview went well?" I asked.

"Not too bad. It's a Fox Network station, so they weren't too hard on a Republican candidate. They had what they thought were a few minor ambushes, but nothing I hadn't had to deal with in Mason County already. No, I was smiling because I realized I hadn't seen a doctor asleep before."

"Me asleep? We don't normally sleep. In fact I wasn't asleep. I was just receiving Wi-Fi immunization updates from the CDC. They are beamed straight into our nervous systems – closing our eyes and reclining helps the transmission."

"Pretty good for someone who's just woken up."

"Thank you. At least I will be fully alert for the drive back now. Let's get going."

I started the car, worked my way back to Mercer and the relatively painless access onto Interstate 5.

"I've been thinking this over," Shanty started, "and I have to react in some way to the notes the blackmailer, or maybe potential blackmailer, left me."

I managed a nod and affirmative grunt. I was paying attention to my mirrors as I attempted to cross four lanes of traffic to get into the carpool lane.

"If nothing else I should take out the link to my father from my website."

I accelerated past a Honda Civic and made it to the carpool lane unscathed, relaxed a little and answered.

"I am not sure why you had the link in the first place, but I agree it should go."

"There was a very good reason for it to be there, and I think you should know about it, but not now. I have to talk to a few people first."

"That sounds mysterious. Didn't we have a conversation like this before? Do I really want to know?"

"I think you will, but I suppose I can't be sure. I'll think about it."

"OK," I answered, not sure what else to say.

"In the meantime, it's about an hour to home, so I think I will recline my seat again, close my eyes and see if the CDC communicates with me too."

I drove while he napped.

10

Chris Hall liked his Ford Taurus. It was five years old, painted red, so it was noticeable, and American-made, which made for good politics. Until the election was over his wife would be driving the silver Audi.

The democratic candidate for the twelfth district congressional seat was pleased with his lunch-time presentation. He was sure he would receive their endorsement. The International Brotherhood of Boilermakers meeting had gone on longer than expected, and he probably shouldn't have had that fourth beer, maybe not even the third, or the wine before that, but everyone had been very encouraging.

He was being extra careful, as only a drunk knows how, driving along Callow. He was going to turn left on 6th and take Kitsap Way to Highway 3, then home for an afternoon nap. He slowed, indicated he was going to take a left turn and started to move into the turn lane. The lights were changing and he slowed to make the stop.

The bang and the jolt happened simultaneously and his Taurus sprung forward.

He managed to stop the car with only the front wheels over the line. For a second he wondered what had happened, then he heard the roar of a leaky muffler and an aged Lincoln passed him on the right. It ran the red light in a cloud of smoke and disappeared down Callow.

He'd been rear-ended!

He looked in his rear-view mirror. There was a white van behind him. A man dressed in dirty white overalls, wearing a Seahawk's baseball cap and dark glasses got out of the vehicle, walked up to his door and tapped on the window. Hall lowered it.

"Are you OK?" the man asked.

"Did you just hit me?" Hall replied.

"Me? No, not me. It was that guy who drove off." The man pointed down Callow.

"Oh...did you get his number?" Hall asked.

"No," the man answered. Hall undid his seatbelt, got out of his car and walked back to see the damage. As he did he felt a little woozy. The man noticed this and clasped both hands on Hall's shoulders and looked him in the eyes.

"Steady," he said. "Are you sure you're all right? These things can be scary."

"I'm OK."

Hall didn't feel the needle prick in his left shoulder.

The man released him and Hall looked at the crumpled rear bumper and trunk, the smashed light, shook his head and said, "Shit."

"Are you OK?"

"Yes, I think so."

"Well, if you're OK I'd better move my van," the man said.

Hall nodded. Somewhere close a police siren started to wail. The man got back in his van, moved it to the right lane, turned right, and disappeared on 6th Street.

It was less than three minutes since the accident.

Officer Randy Black, a fifteen-year veteran of the Bremerton Police Department had been sitting in his cruiser at a light on 11th Street when he heard the dispatch. He'd turned on his lights and siren, made a U-turn, and headed for Callow. When he came to the intersection on 6th he saw an obese, white, middle-aged male leaning against a red Ford sedan. Officer Black drove his cruiser through the intersection, pulled ahead, turned off the siren, kept the lights flashing, then backed up behind the Taurus, effectively blocking the north direction lanes. He got out of the car and quickly surveyed the scene. The Taurus had obviously sustained some damage, but it did not seem major; the nearside light and the edge of the bumper must have received a glancing blow. Traffic was backing up, but that could wait. The middle-aged male was slowly making his way to the driver's door. Officer Black picked up his pace, passed Hall and stood in front of him.

"Are you OK, sir?" Black asked.

Hall did not reply but held on to the car to steady his swaying and looked around him, apparently dazed and confused. Another police car arrived. Black looked over his left shoulder at his emerging colleague and shouted, "Call an ambulance and work the..." He hadn't finished his sentence when Hall pushed him in the chest. It wasn't very hard, but it knocked Black off balance and he fell across the hood of the car encumbered by the fifteen pounds of his duty belt. Hall opened the car door, and tried to get in but seemed to have difficulty coordinating his limbs. Black had no problem with his. He recovered, and in three paces reached Hall. He held him from behind against the Taurus. Hall struggled weakly, and Black handcuffed him. His colleague joined him.

"What happened, Randy?"

"I get here and this guy's out of his car. I stop him getting back in, turn my head and he pushes me away," Black replied.

"You OK?"

"Yeah, he didn't hurt me. I wasn't expecting it. He's not behaving right. I don't know what's up with him. Maybe he's just a drunk. Let's put him in my cruiser until the ambulance gets here. You can work the traffic. OK?"

"Sure."

"I'll call for a tow truck and sit with him."

"OK."

The ambulance arrived. Hall was transferred, easily restrained by the paramedics, the cuffs were removed, and the ambulance left.

Another cop arrived. Officer Black moved his cruiser and ten minutes later followed the ambulance to Harrison Hospital emergency room. There, he introduced himself and was shown to Hall's room. He knocked on the door and saw Hall was being moved off the ambulance gurney and on to the ER's heavier bed. One of the paramedics was just finishing her report to the charge nurse. Both looked up when Black opened the door. They all recognized each other. They'd been through this before and moved into the corridor out of earshot of Hall. Black gave his brief summary of the accident and Hall's confusion and aggression at the scene. He requested to interview Hall and ask him to take a breath test. The charge nurse asked him to wait and a couple of minutes later returned to the corridor.

"You can see him. He knows where he is now, but he claims he doesn't know why or what happened. I think I can smell alcohol on his breath, but I can't be sure. I've told him you want to see him."

"Does he have a name?" Black asked.

"Christopher Raymond Hall," the nurse replied, looking at the chart.

Black made a note of the name.

Officer Black talked to Hall for five minutes while IV's were started and blood was taken. He confirmed Hall seemed to have no memory of the event or pushing Black. He seemed to have a vague memory of being hit by a white van. Black tried to persuade Hall to take a breath test, but he refused. Hall couldn't understand why, if he'd been rear-ended, he was now the subject of a police investigation.

He demanded to know why the police didn't try to find out who had hit him. Hall was no longer confused and for once that day may have made a good judgment; he realized it was going to be easier to fight a refusal to take a breath test than a damning breath or blood test result. He couldn't remember what had happened, but he did recall his lunchtime alcohol intake. He also didn't believe Black's version of the events. He'd never hit a policeman.

Officer Black recorded the refusal to take a breath test and advised Hall of his rights. He left the emergency room and asked to be called if Hall was going to be discharged.

Dr Bruce Alawi reviewed the nursing records before interviewing and examining Hall. He found an angry, but lucid patient. He calmly explained that because of Hall's confusion at the scene, despite any evidence of trauma, a CAT scan of his brain would be ordered. The lab tests were not yet back, but if everything was normal he would be released in an hour or two.

The lab tests were mainly unremarkable. His blood alcohol was 0.14%, over the limit for Washington State's 0.08% threshold, which was not unexpected. No one thought to check for any other intoxicating substance. Why would they? If they had checked for narcotics there would have been none detected, but a check for ketamine, a short-acting sedative, would have produced a positive test and explained Hall's earlier behavior.

In the end it made no difference. The ER became busy dealing with a mixture of cardiac arrests, abdominal pain, domestic violence, bladder infections, and psychoses.

Back from the CAT scan, which he had been told was normal, Hall found himself waiting in his room and called his wife.

His wife, a dentist, was just finishing with her last patient of the day. She drove to the hospital still wearing her white lab coat and scrub suit. She wisely avoided the gauntlet of the ER main entrance and approached from the hospital side. Without asking permission she found the door to her husband's room open and walked in.

"What happened?" she asked.

"I don't know. I was driving home, I think I was rear-ended, then I can't remember much about what happened until I got here."

"You been drinking?" she demanded.

"Well, I had a few over lunch," he replied.

"You ass hole. Were you drunk? Did they check you?"

"No, I refused it."

"Hell you did. Oh, shit! Did they arrest you?"

"No, not yet. Well, I don't think so. Like I said, I don't remember it all."

"Oh, God! Let's get you out of here."

"Do you think that's right?" Hall asked.

"I think. You don't. That's obvious. Shut up and let's get out of here. How could you do this you screw-up?"

She pulled out his IV and told him to keep his arm bent to stop any bleeding. She took off his hospital gown, and helped him put his jacket and shoes back on, led him through the hospital and out to the waiting Audi.

When his absence was discovered thirty minutes later no one thought to call Officer Black.

The news editor, Simon Undergrove, at KOMO TV in Seattle reviewed the email and the video. There was one hour to go before the evening news. The email, from "Concerned Citizen" contained one sixty-second video. The email said, "You will have exclusive rights to this video for three hours, then the other Seattle TV stations will also receive it and it will be posted on the internet." It went on to detail the time, the people, and the place the video was taken. Undergrove played the video a couple of times before calling in his editorial team and playing it again. They recognized Chris Hall looking at the back of his car at the intersection, his staggering gait, the arrival of Officer Black, the push to the chest, the off-balance Black, and the cuffing. The events leading up to Hall's arrival at the intersection and the arrival of the ambulance were not covered.

They concluded they had to go with it. They'd play it down for the 6 pm newscast and only show ten seconds of the video until they got more information. They'd get a reporter over to Bremerton to find out more before the 11 pm broadcast. In the meantime they decided to upload the complete video to the KOMO news website with minimal accompanying content and a bland by-line. They settled on "Politician in trouble in Bremerton?"

By 8 pm the video had been posted on Facebook and YouTube.

At 8:30 a reporter for the Kitsap Sun in Bremerton picked up on these posts, captured a couple of shots as photos for his newspaper, and called a contact in the Bremerton Police Department. The contact checked the log and confirmed a Christopher Hall had been involved in a traffic accident in the early afternoon and had been take to Harrison Hospital.

The reporter had no contacts in the ER at Harrison, but had once been a paramedic. He called a friend on the off-chance he may have been involved with taking Hall to Harrison. He was lucky. His friend hadn't been involved, but he knew about it. Another colleague had taken Hall to the hospital, and returned to the ER about three hours later. Apparently, Hall had left AMA (Against Medical Advice) and no one had missed him for an hour or two. Someone had thought to call his home. His wife answered and said he'd left when he'd seen how busy they were so someone could have his bed. Both the paramedic and the reporter thought this strange, but neither would get any more information that evening about the event. The reporter thought he had enough for a back-page story for the next morning edition and at 9:45 sent the article to his editor. It was published the next morning with no changes.

By 6 pm the next day the national press aired the story.

The man known as Mr. Smith watched the developing story on the television in his room at the Seattle Hilton. He almost felt sorry for Hall, but he'd made it so easy. Hall hadn't just lowered the window, he'd got out of the car and staggered, giving Smith the opportunity for a friendly arm support and the chance to inject nearly fifty milligrams of ketamine in Hall's left shoulder. The icing on the cake had been the pushing of the cop and his subsequent hand-cuffing – it made great television. The ancient Lincoln had sustained minimal damage and was now back with its owner in rural Mason County. The van was back with the rental company with its legal license plates in place. It had cost him less than ten thousand and it had been worth every penny. He hoped those who were paying him appreciated his work. He doubted it, and it wouldn't make any difference anyway; his arrangements for dealing with his exit from this business were going as planned. He slept well that night.

Two days later the first mail-in ballots were mailed to Kitsap, Pierce, and Mason County voters.

11

Ann and I watched the video clip of Chris Hall's accident online. The TV stations didn't show the full sixty seconds, so it was left to Facebook, and a dozen other news sites, to air all the dirty laundry; if that is what it was. After the initial surprise of viewing the scene it was hard to not wonder why the cell-phone filming had been so steady, and what was going on with Hall at the time. Certainly, he could have been a drunk, but he looked so uncoordinated and confused that it was difficult to see how he could have driven a car to that intersection. On the other hand drunks have successfully commanded armies and nations, so we put it out of our minds and, after a few days, so did the media. They resurrected the story briefly for a "moral indignation" segment about all politicians when they published the tastefully censored photos of a Georgia senatorial hopeful with his mistresses, but their main goal seemed to be to make all election coverage entertainment. To do this they filled it with as much hyperbole and hysteria as possible while presenting it as "news".

Ann and I would have switched off the television and ignored all the hype, insults, blame and fame, but our television was already gathering dust in the garage. We voted by mail as soon as the ballots hit our mailbox, and we could have missed the election completely, but for my job, and it was now a real job; I was getting busier.

There was just over one week to go before the election. William Shanty (or Will as everyone called him) was on television being interviewed and appearing in advertisements between shows. Since neither he, nor Chris Hall, had any record of voting or supporting fringe political viewpoints, the ads were remarkably positive, or at least non-negative. Shanty had been asked for his opinion on the Hall video and had wisely declined comment. This probably earned him a few extra votes and it seemed, from the few polls that had been taken, he might need them. Both candidates were running neck-and-neck – every vote was going to count.

The media loved it. We had reporters in the campaign headquarters, reporters following our vehicles whenever we were transporting Shanty, and reporters in the toilets. We soon put a stop to that practice; there are some places you don't want to be interviewed. They weren't around us all the time, which was a relief, but we were never quite sure when they would appear next. In private Shanty likened them to acne (just when you think you've got over it another zit appears) but in public he was always willing to stop and give them time. This gave Dick, Harry, and me one extra task; we had to make sure we kept him moving and away from the press. There was one place he had not been bothered and this was his home on Hood Canal. By the time we had taken him home on most nights he, and any reporters within fifty miles, were ready for peace and quiet. I'd taken him home on several occasions, and we had sometimes talked in my car for ten minutes or so, but I had never been invited into his house, so I was surprised when one night he asked me in. He said he wanted to show me something.

We walked through the light drizzle to the shelter of his porch. He opened the door, entered the hallway, switched on the lights and I followed him in. He busied himself adjusting the thermostat and laying out the mail he'd picked up from his mailbox. He asked me to feel free to look around while he heated up water for the hot chocolate he'd offered me.

The house was about fifty years old. I'd made this supposition from the outside on my previous visits, and the interior confirmed this, but it had been extensively modernized. In keeping with most waterfront houses it had large picture windows on the side facing the water. From what I could see most of the space was taken up by a huge open room which contained at one end an extensive kitchen, and at the other a grand piano. In between was a circular oak dining room table, surrounded by a dozen chairs, and numerous white leather sofas and easy-chairs. I tried to look out, but all I saw was my reflection in the window until I hit a switch which illuminated a wrap-around cedar deck and a path to the water. It was all quite magnificent.

I sank into one of the leather sofas and Shanty brought me my drink and said.

"Don't get too comfortable there. I want to show you something, or more correctly I want to introduce you to someone."

"You mean there's someone else living here?" I sat up.

"No, not exactly, but there's someone I'd like you to meet. I think he's playing pool in the basement."

This seemed really strange. There was minimal heating and lighting on when we entered the house, and it had seemed empty. I followed him back to the entrance hall, hot chocolate in hand, and we took a door which led to the basement stairs. As I followed him down I could hear the murmur of voices and the clack of pool balls. I found myself in a large pool room illuminated only by the table light, so although I could see there were two others in the room, I couldn't make out their faces. Shanty found the switch and turned up the rest of the lights. With the room fully lit I half-recognized the man walking towards me with his hand outstretched and a broad smile lighting up. As I reached for his hand I finally realized who he was.

"Jack, Jack Straw!" I said and grasped his hand.

"Yeah, Doc. It's me. How are you doing?" he asked.

"It's the beard and the hair. Last time I saw you they weren't there. They are real aren't they? You're not in disguise are you?"

"No, they're real, and it's still me, and I'm still with the Bureau."

"Well, now I'm jealous...of the hair I mean, not the Bureau."

Straw laughed and said, "Let me introduce you to a colleague of mine. Dr. John Beaton, this is Christopher Miller. He's come all the way from DC."

"Pleased to meet you, Doc." Miller shook my hand. He had a distinct east coast accent.

I replied, "Good to meet you too. But I bet you haven't come all this way just to play pool with Jack or talk to me." I was feeling a little tense. It was good to see Jack again, but here I was in a basement with the FBI. Who wouldn't feel tense?

"You're right there," Miller replied.

He looked at Shanty who said, "Let's sit down. We have a lot to go through and I'm pretty tired already."

That I could believe. He'd spent the day on the phone calling individual voters, and answering questions from media as far away as Europe. He preferred getting out of the campaign headquarters and door-belling (we all did) but the late October weather had kept him inside.

We sat in sofas and I noticed there were no windows in the room. It turned out this was important. Jack spoke first.

"We need to give you some background about what's going on here. It's probably best to explain why you are here. "

I had met Jack a couple of years before when he helped me deal with the aftermath of a bombing incident I had been involved in. He'd been friendly, open, and supportive during a difficult time in both Ann's life and mine.

He continued, "I sort of asked for you."

This was a shock to me. The FBI wanting me? What for? The surprise must have shown on my face.

Shanty said, "Well, you remember how you got into this in the first place? Dick and Harry wanted you to help them with my security and they said I'd asked for you. When you asked me about that I said I'd heard good things about your work as a doctor. I remember you said I might be better off with a boy scout, but you joined the team anyway."

I nodded but kept quiet.

"I wanted you around because I needed someone I could trust, but I haven't been completely open with you. I may have implied there was more going on than I talked about, but for various reasons I couldn't tell you."

"That's because I didn't want anyone involved who didn't need to be." It was Miller who spoke. "I was overseeing this operation, and a few others, from DC and the fewer people in the know the better."

I opened my mouth, but decided to say nothing.

Miller continued, "I don't know if you remember Robert Preston, the US Senator, but he came to see me earlier this year. It seemed he was being blackmailed into voting certain ways. This had been going on for a while, and I'm not sure what made him come to me. It may have been his diagnosis of cancer, but we discussed what was happening and concluded his blackmail could be part of a larger conspiracy to control voting in Congress. I'd planned to have more discussions with him, but he was killed in a hit-and-run accident shortly afterwards. You may remember that?"

"Yes," I said.

"Preston had come to me confidentially and I had no evidence to start an enquiry, and to be honest, I was not sure the FBI in DC was completely safe. If I had to start something I wanted it to be out of range of the DC political radar, at least for a while. Jack and I met, and I also had a few meetings around the country with people I trust. We discussed what to do, and we decided that doing something was better than nothing. However, as you can imagine, we had to be very discreet. We couldn't be seen to be interfering in voting in any way or we would be strung up by our balls on the White House fence, probably literally."

That didn't seem like a pleasant fate.

Miller continued, "In Preston's case it seems he was being blackmailed because of evidence of his liking teenagers for sex. The trouble was we didn't know if any others in the House or Senate were being blackmailed too, but after talking to Preston I became convinced there were. What their indiscretion or foibles were, which made them vulnerable to blackmail, we might never know. So this left us with a problem. What could we do about proving if there is a larger conspiracy, or at least try to prevent further blackmail? Well, we looked at voting patterns, and again this had to be done away from DC. Even looking at voting patterns might invite scrutiny from higher up. Preston had said he had been asked to vote certain ways when the voting was going to be close on certain bills. This made sense; if a bill was going to lose or win anyway, why risk being seen to vote strangely. We used Preston's voting record as a comparison and found a couple of senators who had nearly always voted like him. In the House it was more difficult, but we found a group of five who seemed to have concordance with voting patterns on close bills, and didn't always vote according to party principles. Our concern is we may have included representatives who are completely innocent, and I am sure we left out many who are involved. And then, what could we do with this information? We concluded the answer was nothing. We were stuck, but then Jack had an idea."

Jack said, "Will and I go way back. We were in high school together and at college. We both attended each others' weddings and I was at Joy's funeral. Joy was Will's wife. We still meet a couple of times each year for a game of golf and go out for dinner afterwards. I knew he was interested in running for office, but I wasn't quite sure when or where, or for that matter, which party. He's always been more of a middle-of-the-road independent in the past. I asked him to run."

"Just in case you think the FBI is now fronting candidates for political office," Shanty said, "I was seriously thinking about running anyway. The only thing is I was thinking of running as a Democrat, but it turned out their political machine already had a candidate in mind. So, I'm running as a Republican. If I get elected I'm going to be a moderate Republican. I know at one time you questioned my belief in me. You were correct to do so. I believe I am doing the right thing now. "

This was beginning to answer some of the initial doubts I'd had about him.

He continued, "We weren't certain what would happen, but Jack convinced me that anyone wanting a politician in their pocket, either through bribe or blackmail, would be better off getting in at the beginning of their career – in other words around an election, and even better, around a close election. The trouble was I didn't really have anything in my past, or my current life, that would be embarrassing or fatal to a political career. There was the problem of my father, but that could have been easily dealt with, so I wasn't sure how I could help."

"You mean the idea was to set you up as a potential blackmail target?" I asked.

Jack replied, "Basically, yes. And it may have worked. We aren't quite sure yet. "

"The man on the bicycle at the ferry?" I said.

"Yes."

"I wondered why you weren't too surprised to get that envelope from him."

"I know," Shanty replied. "I was going to tell you on the way back from Seattle, but I thought I would talk to my handlers first, and that's why we are sitting here now."

Miller said, "It's one of the reasons we set up Will's website so anyone curious might want to learn more about his father. Jack went through old FBI records and discovered some information about his dad, but most of what he found was available through Seattle newspapers' records. The idea was to provide something which the candidate would prefer not to reveal. Revealing the fact his father was a gangster might lose him some votes, but trying to hide that fact would lose him more. In an election this close it might make a difference. However, we didn't know if Will, or anyone in the country, would be contacted, so we had to leave it to Will to let us know if anything happened."

"Well, you were there. Will was contacted," Jack said, "and we were figuring out what to do about it when the Christopher Hall video hit the news. That got our attention. We've looked at the video, and purely by chance we got some information from the medical records. It seems he was drunk that day, but not at a level which would normally leave him that impaired. He is probably an alcoholic, so he should have been able to tolerate a level of...I think it was 0.14. Do you agree, John?"

"Yes. He's probably quite tolerant. I watched that video too. It seemed almost too good to be true," I said. I wondered how they'd got hold of the medical records, but decided I preferred not to know.

Jack continued, "It was. He was definitely out of it at the scene, but the hospital records indicate by the time he was seen in the ER he'd become fully alert. We checked it out with some of our experts and they think a short-acting narcotic, or maybe ketamine, could have been used. How it got into him we don't know. We don't think it could have been given to him before he left his meeting, which leaves the probability that the whole thing was a set-up. The filming of the incident must have taken place from just across the street. It was a little unsteady, but not too much. It was well done. We checked CCTV in the area and there were none concentrated on that intersection."

Miller said, "It seems the video was done with one purpose and that was to disgrace Hall and hand the election to Will. We'll know in a few days if it worked. We won't know if Will wins if he would have won anyway. Will doesn't like that." He looked at Will, who said.

"If I win I want to win fair and square, and not because of interference from outsiders, so I'm having some problems with this. It's got nothing to do with the FBI. They didn't have any part in the video."

He stood and was clearly troubled by this.

"That's why we need to catch whoever is doing this and put a stop to it," said Miller. "There is one other point we need to consider, which Jack and I were discussing over pool, and that is what if whoever took the video intends to place the responsibility, or blame, for it on you?"

"How could they?" Shanty was surprised.

"They could plant incriminating documents in your office. They could bribe witnesses. They could produce another video. They could do half a dozen sneaky things. Don't forget, it doesn't have to stick. It just has to be good television." Miller replied.

"I mean, wow... that's ...that's quite unscrupulous," Shanty said and sat down again.

Jack said, "We don't really think that's going to happen. The election is less than a week away and postal votes are coming in now. There would be little point in disgracing both you and Hall. If anyone was going to use this strategy it would have to be used sooner in the campaign. One of the hopefuls would look petty, manipulative, and deceitful by trying to embarrass his opponent, and the opponent, after appearing magnanimous and statesman-like on the evening news, would be exonerated from his very human minor slip...or something like that. The trouble is if the intention was to malign you, then there would be no guarantee that Hall would be magnanimous and statesman-like. However, using it to blackmail you could be part of the package. The first part would be the relatively minor threat of revealing your father's past, the second would be the threat to blame you for the Hall video."

Miller said, "The trouble is when I look at both of those I can't see how individually, or combined, it would be enough to blackmail you into voting a certain way. It might tip the balance in a future election, but you could ride out whatever storm revealing them might cause in the meantime. Can you think of any other leverage they might have with you?"

Shanty gave Miller a how-many-times-must-I answer-this-question look and said, "No, like I've told you. I'm not gay. I have a girl-friend. She's Guatemalan. We met at a University of Washington conference last year and she's back in Guatemala at the moment. She's an anthropologist and is currently on a field trip near Lake Atitlan. She has a contract to teach for two or more semesters in Seattle, beginning next year. When this election is over I'm going to check on my kids then fly to Guatemala to see her for a couple of weeks. She is not an illegal. I didn't want her to be involved in this election fracas. I am sure you've checked her out?"

The Guatemalan girlfriend was news to me.

Miller replied, "Yes, we have, and we checked you out, and your children are normal college students. You have nothing on your record, and your girlfriend works for the University in Guatemala City. I just hope we haven't overlooked something. Some way someone could get to you."

It was about time I said something.

"Does it matter?" I asked. "If they are going to use some other leverage to blackmail Will it will be apparent when they contact him. Maybe there is no other leverage. Maybe they just hope his being elected will make him vote the way they want, and since he doesn't have a voting record, they may wait to see how he votes. "

Miller said, "I hope you're right and maybe there will be no more contact. Just getting the election to go their way may be enough, but I also hope you're wrong. If there's no more contact we may be left high and dry, and have to wait until the next election. We may never get so close to who is behind this again."

Jack said, "We have to assume contact will be made and it will be person-to-person. It will also most likely be unannounced. I doubt it will be a note asking Will to be at a certain place at a certain time, but it could be. We have to assume, from now on, Will is being watched, probably not all the time, so Chris and I will be nearby, but not visible. We have some help, but we're trying to keep this quiet inside and outside the Bureau. We think the most likely place he will be contacted is here, at his house. This is the only place he isn't surrounded by people. We thought about wiring the house, but were concerned our wiring might be noticed if 'they' try to wire it too, or if the house is being observed. Will has agreed to wear a wire and let us know if person-to-person contact is being made. John, I believe you are driving Will home every evening now. It is possible your car could be bugged too. If you notice anything strange let us know, but don't remove anything or behave differently. There is one other point I need to emphasize. We don't think there is any danger to you, Will, or you, John, but don't take any risks. If contact is made we can be here in less than two minutes."

And that was it. We had to go over a few details, add a few emergency numbers to our cell-phones, and Will learnt how to use the device he was going to wear. I wondered why I'd been allowed into this conspiracy to catch a blackmailer, but the new pattern, when I dropped him off in the evening, was going to be for me to accept the invitation to have a hot chocolate before I left for my own home. This way there would be some check of the house and grounds. We had been reassured the FBI would be close all the time. I wasn't completely convinced. I'd had this reassurance once before and the contact between the FBI and me had failed. Jack was aware of this and sought to calm my fears. I thought I ought to wear a signaling device like Will, or some other form of communication. Jack thought about this and said he would arrange for me to be fitted with a microphone and transmitter. I'd turn it on when we left the last public event of the day and before I started the car to head to Will's home. This reassured me a little, but the big unknown was if, or when, there would be any more contact between Will Shanty and his potential blackmailer. Collectively, we all thought it wouldn't happen until after the election.

    We were all wrong.

12

I was home later than usual that evening. Ann woke briefly, put her arms around me for a hug, and was asleep again within thirty seconds. I couldn't sleep so easily and found myself staring at the ceiling trying to unwind from the events of the evening.

I'd left Shanty at 11:15. At the time he said he was planning to be asleep by 11:15 and thirty seconds, but I wondered if he was still awake. Jack and Miller were planning to leave by a side door after Shanty turned out the lights. I hadn't noticed any other vehicle in the driveway, so I assumed they had access to a nearby house or summer vacation cottage. I was certain they were asleep, and if not, they were supposed to be. I think I was feeling a little sorry for myself. I hadn't seen much of Ann – she was working days and I was sort of working a swing-shift – so we weren't eating together or sharing our day-to-day stories. It made me think about all those families I had seen over the years where spouses were working opposite shifts. For some it was how their marriage survived, but for many it was the cause of their marriage's failure. Ours was not failing, but it did seem to have been put on hold. In between thoughts of marriage stagnation came fantasies of capturing blackmailing criminals, but more frequent was imagining a painful death, or being tortured, by blackmailing criminals. I think I eventually fell asleep after resorting to sheep-counting; they were the fat, extra-woolly variety with black faces, and I counted them jumping over a low stone wall somewhere in Yorkshire. Of course, even then, I had to have one get itself caught on a loose strand of barbed-wire only to be rescued by the grey- bearded, one-legged shepherd and his panting border collie. Sometimes it would be nice to turn off the imagination machine.

I was woken by Ann. She gave me a peck on the cheek and got out of bed to get dressed. I was half asleep or half awake, enjoying my horizontal time, when I heard and felt what I thought was Ann come close to me. I opened my eyes a little and an enormous teddy-bear-like creature stared down at me. That got my attention and I grunted myself fully awake.

The teddy-bear had Ann's face, said, "Happy Halloween", handed me a card, a small bag of Hershey's Kisses (the dark chocolate ones) jumped in the bed, wriggled on top of me for ten seconds and then left. A minute later I heard her car back out of the garage. I smiled, my feet hit the sheepskin rug (one of those extra-woolly ones) and I walked down the hallway to enjoy breakfast and NPR. The future didn't seem so bleak after all, except I'd forgotten it was October 31st, Halloween, and one of those days I am supposed to remember. I hadn't made any plans for the morning. I was not due to appear at the campaign headquarters until 3:00 pm, but I had an idea of how to make amends for my lack of Halloween spirit. The previous Sunday Ann and I had staked out a seat at a table at the nearest Albertson's supermarket. We were there to encourage donations for the local food bank. I wasn't sure if a human presence was necessary; the Turkey Bucks scheme really needed shoppers to stop, pick up a voucher and donate at the check-out line, but most people ambled past us without stopping as they went in and out. The only donations were left as groceries, or loose change, when they were leaving. Still, we passed three hours there, sitting, shopping, talking, reading, and donating. The table was set up in front of the flower display, and I wondered if we were effectively blocking flower-sales all the time we were there. Now I had an opportunity to remedy Albertson's floral accounts. I wrapped up well against the windy, just-above-freezing drizzle, and drove the couple of miles to Albertson's.

I picked pink and white roses, not red (red are for Valentine's Day and anniversaries) and I hadn't had time to forget an anniversary yet, although given time I'm sure I would. To avoid going back out in the rain too soon my roses and I wandered over towards the fruit and vegetable section, passing an in-store Starbucks on the way.

In contrast to the rest of the population of the Pacific Northwest I am not a coffee nut. I have been in plenty of coffee shops for meetings and to use their Wi-Fi access, but as I leave one Starbucks in Seattle I can always see another a block or two away. I'm not sure there is any Starbucks coffee shop in Seattle where you cannot see another close by as you leave. Maybe, like musk ox, they huddle for protection, because they all seem to thrive. However, the one inside Albertson's was almost deserted. There was a single barista busying herself with cleaning chores, and I noticed one of the two small tables nearby was unoccupied except for an unopened New York Times edition of October 31st. It called to me. I ordered my skinny, decaf, tall, latté (apparently called a "why bother?") took it to the table and opened the newspaper.

A man sat down opposite me. I looked up. He was wearing blue jeans, a Seahawks' sweatshirt, Seahawks' baseball cap, open rain jacket, and apart from his dark glasses was a generic South-Kitsapper. I gave an acknowledging nod and returned to my newspaper.

"I believe in dressing like the natives. What do you think, Doc?" He asked. His accent was generic Pacific Northwest too.

"Uh?" I looked up again and this time paid more attention. From what I could see of his face and his salt and pepper curly hair he seemed to be in his early forties. He was a little taller and heavier than me, but not overweight. He was white, but with no other distinguishing features. I noticed he was wearing black leather gloves and didn't have a coffee.

He repeated, "I said I like to dress like the natives."

"I got that, but should I know you?" I asked politely. I thought he may have been a patient of mine at some time.

"I hope not, Doc. I suppose I don't really know you, but we seem to have a common interest. Tell me, Doc; Shanty's old man, and the stuff on the website you took down. Was it for real, or was it a trap?"

Somewhere in the dark recesses of my brain a couple of connections came together. I think I intended just to think it, but my mouth moved.

"Oh, shit!" I said.

"Well said, Doc."

I didn't say anything else. I wasn't sure where to start.

"Let me introduce myself." He leaned forward, his accent changed to east coast, and he said quietly, "My name is Mr. Smith. That's my real name. I don't need to tell you where I live, or what I do. Maybe you already know what I do? Well, it doesn't matter. What matters is here we are today because I'm curious and suspicious. I'm curious about the website. I checked, and Shanty's old man was a gangster, and he made his money selling chemicals to teenagers before he went legit, but the website just didn't seem right. Shanty could've stopped at the photo of his old man and Ronald Reagan. He didn't need to have all that other BS about his dad, but I went along with it. I gave Shanty the photocopies at the ferry-line and the next day the BS was taken off the website. Great, but not so great. It just didn't seem right. Your man, Shanty, has precious little leverage I can get on him. No one's going to really care if his dad was a gangster since it's obvious he isn't. If that was just one part of his being a scum-bag, it might have some benefit. You know; the last nail in the coffin so-to-speak. I checked his girlfriend out, but she's in Guatemala for another month or two. Her dad was something in the government down there in the eighties and nineties, so he may have blood on his hands, but it's all a little vague. No, in all the time I have been doing this job I haven't had as much trouble working an angle. What do you think?"

While he'd been talking I had the presence of mind to take a few sips from my coffee. My mouth was no longer dry and my pulse rate was settling. I said the first thing that came to mind.

"Couldn't you hang the video of Hall, his opponent, at that intersection on him?"

"Whoa!" He leaned back and thought for a few seconds. "Doc, where did you get that idea?"

"That video seemed to be too good to be true too," I answered.

He thought for a few more seconds then said.

"I don't know who you been talking to, or maybe I do, but that wasn't the point of the video. The point was to show Hall for what he is. He likes his booze too much. He also has other weak points which I didn't want to expose to the public. If you had a ball-busting wife, and the IQ of a brain-damaged jock, like he has, you might have other weak points too. True, the video could be attributed to Shanty, but it would only stick for a short time. I'd have to think that one through, but it is an idea."

"Do you think it was right to set him up like that?"

"Oh, yeah. It's very rare that I do anything other than demonstrate weaknesses. As far as Hall is concerned I'm sure they hoped he wouldn't auto-destruct during the campaign, but I doubt he would have made it through his first term before screwing-up in some major way."

"So, what did you use to make him look so wasted?" I asked. I was feeling a little more curious.

"You noticed?"

"I thought he looked like he was more than just a drunk, but I assumed that was all he was since I couldn't figure out what else it could be. That, and the video quality was a little better than your usual bystander video, so I was a little suspicious it was a set-up. What did you use?"

He waited before replying, "Ketamine. In the left shoulder. I don't think he even felt it. It had the desired effect."

"And what was that?"

Again he paused. "The effect of making Shanty win the election."

"You don't think he'll win anyway?" I asked.

"I think it's probable he would win anyway, but this way it's likely to be a big enough margin to avoid a recount."

"You seem pretty sure of yourself."

"Not of myself, but of American voters. I think I know them well enough by now."

Something from a recent news report jogged my memory.

"That senator in Georgia. I can't remember if it was for state or federal office. He was in the news recently. Did you have anything to do with that?"

"The one with the two hookers and the motel?"

"I thought it was two mistresses, but I think that's the one."

"It was state office, and I had nothing to do with it. Politicians screw up all by themselves most of the time. And I don't bother with state elections. It doesn't make good use of my time."

"Also, if I think this through, I suppose you would prefer to keep dirt like that on politicians secret. It gives you more leverage."

He laughed. "That's it, Doc. You're getting to understand how it works, and it's not me who exerts the leverage. I leave that bit alone."

"Who does then?" I asked.

"Now you're getting ahead of yourself. Let's not go there."

Despite his apparent confidence something in his body language made me wonder about that reply. I couldn't see his eyes so I couldn't be sure. I decided to press on.

"So what do you want from me? Did you follow me here today?"

"I did and I apologize for that."

"You were watching my house?" Now I wasn't just thinking I should be annoyed; I was getting angry.

"Yes, but hear me out."

"Now, I'm getting pissed off," I said.

"I can understand that. In the circumstances I would be too. I don't know what you expected when you started driving him around, but I bet it wasn't this."

"You bet correctly."

"So I can understand you being upset. I would be too, but let me explain. Like I said, something didn't seem quite right about Shanty and this election. I've been able to stay in the game this long because I've a nose for signs of trouble. You can call it a sixth sense, but it's helped me survive. I also operate alone most of the time. For the game we played with Hall I used a team I've worked with before. I pay well, in cash, they don't ask any questions, and all they have ever seen of me is what you are seeing now, but I prefer to work alone when I can. I've been to a few Shanty and some Hall electioneering speeches, and if you already didn't know it, Shanty is a better candidate than Hall. I know your two colleagues Dick and Harry, I believe, carry out most of the security duties, and you tend to help most in the evenings, or when you're asked. You drive an older, dark green Subaru Forester which is becoming easier to spot because it's not a current Subaru color. I couldn't find out anything more in that zoo of a campaign headquarters, so for the past couple of nights I've been sitting outside Shanty's house on Hood Canal when you've driven him home in the evenings. It was a long shot. I'd tried to observe his house from the other shore of the canal, but couldn't find a suitable place. I'd thought about watching from the water, but a boat anchored out there would attract attention and I couldn't come and go as I wanted to. I was left with sitting in my rental car and seeing what happened.

"Of course, nothing much happened. You would drive him home and sometimes the two of you would talk for a while. He would then go to his house and when you'd seen he was inside safely you would drive to your own home. I'd leave myself shortly after, except on one occasion when I followed you home. Yeah, I know, I'm sorry, but I had to do it."

He'd seen my expression of disgust.

"For three nights I waited outside and I was beginning to think I was being paranoid. I was going to give it a couple more nights only, but then last night the pattern changed. This time you went in the house with Shanty and didn't come out. After thirty minutes you still hadn't come out, so I took a risk, got out of my car, and went around to the back and peeked in. All the lights were on, but I couldn't see anybody. I knew there was a daylight basement from my previous observations, so I decided to have a look. I took an outside path to the basement level and couldn't hear or see anything to begin with. There were no drapes on the patio door so I could see in. It was dark and there was nothing to see except light coming from under a door at the back of the room. I was about to head back to my car when I heard your car start up and drive away. About five minutes later the lights upstairs went out. After another five minutes I noticed the light under the door was still on but there were a few shadow movements. The door opened and two men came out. They switched off the light, and for a moment I thought they'd come out of the patio door. I moved back into the bushes, but they left through a smaller door further along the house and walked across the back of the next property. There I lost them. There was some security lighting from some of the houses, but it was raining and I couldn't see them anymore. It was time to get back to my car and get out of there. I got back to my motel and thought for a long time about what to do. I've had a good run with this and I'm getting out of it after this election. I'd made that decision before last night. My concern is not so much being caught by the Feds. And it was the Feds last night?"

I hesitated, but then nodded my head. He continued.

"Not so much the Feds, as it might be my employers who may not let me retire gracefully. As long as I have secrets or can reveal what's been going on I could be in danger. For someone as paranoid and cautious as me I've only lately come to that conclusion; which is strange. So, I want to hand over everything I have to the Feds in exchange for immunity from prosecution. You can be my intermediary. That's why I followed you today and I apologize for going to your house. I won't do that again because I won't need to again."

He sat back put his hands behind the chair and looked at me.

"How do I know if I can believe you?" I asked.

"You don't. I won't need to sit outside your house and watch you again. You can see there's no need for that. As for the rest you can ask the Feds. I'm sure they'll want to talk to me after this. Give me your cell-phone number and I'll call you twice daily to find out what's happening. Tell them not to try to trace the cell-phone. I take out the battery when I'm not using it, and if they succeed in tracing it and getting their hands on me there'll be no deal, and they won't have a case."

I wrote my cell-phone number on a Starbucks' napkin and gave it to him. I said, "I have a whole bunch of questions, and I suppose they can wait. I'm not sure I'm doing the right thing, but I'll go along with you. But, and you know this, if I find you watching, or if you so much as send a Christmas card to my family, I'll do everything I can to make you regret it."

He smiled. "I wouldn't expect anything less. Bye, Doc. Until we meet again."

He stood, extended a gloved hand which, for some odd reason, I shook, stretched unhurriedly, pointed at the ground by my feet and said.

"Don't forget the roses, Doc."

He turned, pulled up the collar of his rain jacket and headed for the exit.

I waited for a few minutes, feeling drained, wondering what I should do next and whether my threat to him was unrealistic. It felt real at the time, but it hadn't seemed to affect him. I finished the remains of my lukewarm coffee, retrieved the roses from under my seat, paid for them, and headed towards my Subaru and home.

13

On the first page of Frederick Forsyth's book, "The Odessa File", his hero, Peter Miller, pulls off the road to listen to the news of President Kennedy's assassination in Dallas. Forsyth also wrote that everyone seems to remember where they were on that November day in 1963.

That may be true if you are writing a book in 1972, but not forty years later. Probably less than a quarter of the US population remembers that day.

On the other hand, most of us can remember where we were on 9/11 when the Twin Towers in New York were destroyed. I was chairing a morning meeting in the clinic at the time. What did we do about it? What did we feel about it? Not much. That's what happens in medicine. You have a full schedule that's not going to go away, or you have to examine a rape victim five minutes after telling a long-time patient the surgery they had for the breast-lump last year didn't cure the cancer after all. You are a professional and you put your own feelings on hold.

Well, that's what you're supposed to do, but most of us don't succeed. And I wasn't succeeding the afternoon after I'd met Smith. It was hard to concentrate on the task in hand, even if I only had to get dressed and drive to Belfair. I'd called Jack and told him briefly what happened and what was planned for the rest of the day. He said he'd get back to me after he'd talked it over with Miller.

The consensus, when he called back, was for me to carry on through the day and in the evening we would meet at Shanty's house. In the circumstances it now seemed redundant for me to wear the microphone which was waiting at campaign headquarters for me.

We had a short day planned. The distractions of Halloween meant that fewer potential swing votes would be influenced that evening, and by 6:00 pm we were on the way to Shanty's waterfront house. We stopped at Safeway to pick up something for dinner that was not pizza. Shanty was ordering at the deli, and I was on my way to the fruit aisle when I received the first call from Smith.

"Doc, it's me. Howya' doing?" he asked.

"OK," I replied.

"You talked to anyone about our conversation yet?"

"Briefly."

"In that case you must be going to talk more about it this evening. Am I correct?"

"Yes," I said.

"I'll keep in touch, Doc. Bye." He hung up.

Not for the first time did I realize one of the reasons I enjoyed hiking in the mountains so much was the absence of cell-phone access. I picked out some fruit for the evening and rejoined Shanty at the deli. I'd already filled him in about the events in Albertson's and told him about the phone call. Shanty paid for the food and a couple of bags of Halloween chocolate candies. We passed the fifteen minutes driving to his home in silence. I think we were both exhausted. I was still missing sleep from the previous night; I think he was too, and we both knew the day was not yet over.

The rain had stopped for the evening and when we arrived at the house I parked in the driveway and he put on the outside lights.

"I know it's pretty remote here, but it's not raining and we sometimes have trick-or-treaters, so I'd better be prepared," he said, opened his candy bags and left them on the entry-way table.

We both entered the house. Jack and Miller were already there. We exchanged small talk and sat at the table in the upper room this time. We helped ourselves to the food and between mouthfuls of Raspberry Turkey Salad and Asian Chicken I related my conversation and observations of the morning. We had only been sitting for five minutes when the doorbell rang and the first trick-or-treaters arrived. Shanty handed out candy and returned to the table. He'd been sitting for a few more minutes when the doorbell rang and he left the table. This pattern went on every five to ten minutes for the next hour. It appeared the home of candidate Shanty was known and he was considered fair game for Halloween hand-outs. The supply of candy near the door diminished and I was worried I would have none for myself, but at about 8 pm the doorbell stopped ringing. By then I'd finished my fractured tale of meeting Smith and had tried to remember any observations and details of the meeting I might have missed at the time.

At 8:15 I had another phone call from him.

"Hey, Doc, it's me again."

"Yes?"

"All OK?"

"Yes."

"Talking about me?"

"Yes."

"Thanks, Doc. I'll be in touch."

At 8:30 the doorbell rang again and a couple of five-year-old supermen almost cleaned out the candy supply.

At 8:35 the doorbell rang and Shanty came back in the room with Smith.

I think I was too tired to react. I'd seen him before that day, so it didn't seem that unusual to see him. We were all winding down a little, and so when he walked in, wearing the same Seahawks' gear, jacket and gloves, he had that morning, for some reason I wasn't surprised. I realized later he was taking a risk, probably a calculated one, but nonetheless he couldn't be sure of the response he'd get. Shanty asked him to introduce himself.

"Hi, I'm Mr. Smith and I know Mr. Shanty here. I've been to his speeches. Doc I know from this morning and you are?" he asked looking from Jack to Miller.

I wondered if they had both been trained to react to every introduction as if they'd been introduced to an annoying neighbor — courteous, but no smiles.

"I'm Special Agent-in-Charge Jack Straw."

"And I'm Assistant Director Miller."

"Assistant Director. Huh! So you must be from DC?" Smith asked.

"Correct. But I think we need to establish who you are first," Miller replied.

"May I sit down?" He asked Shanty, who nodded. He picked a seat at the end of the table.

"I'm Mr. Smith. That's probably all you need to know for the time being. As I told the Doc this morning, it's my real name."

Jack asked, "OK, it's Mr. Smith, but if you took those gloves off and we finger-printed you what would we find?"

"I'll be honest. You'd find someone who is in your files. That's if you keep files for over fifteen years, which I'm sure you do. You'd find I have no history of violence, but I stayed at one of your more relaxing institutions for a year or two, and I don't intend to go back there. I told

Doc this morning I'm planning on retiring, and I'm thinking I should have done it sooner, but we're not all perfect are we?"

No one answered. He carried on.

"I think we could have a partnership."

Jack and Miller raised their eyebrows. Smith continued.

"Well, maybe not a partnership, more an agreement to work to a common goal."

"What goal and what do you want from us?" Jack asked.

"Not much, or a lot, I suppose, depending on your viewpoint, but before we start I have one concern, which I hope you can tell me about."

He turned to Miller. "Tell me about Senator Preston. I know he died, but was it an accident or not, or don't you know?"

"Why do you want to know?" Miller asked.

"It's important to me. I saw he'd announced his resignation, which was interesting, but then he ends up being killed. I wonder why?"

Miller replied, "So, I'm guessing now. Maybe he was on your blackmail list?"

Smith pushed back his chair and put his hands up, palms forward, in a gesture of denial. "Whoa! Oh no, Mr. Miller! I'm no blackmailer. Where did we start talking about blackmail? I've never blackmailed anyone and I don't intend to start."

"Then what is your interest in Preston?" Miller asked.

"He was one of the first I worked on."

"Worked on? What do you mean?"

"I found out about his interests in little girls and arranged to produce evidence of it. Then I handed the information on," Smith replied.

"So, you are saying you got the evidence, but that's all. You didn't use it for blackmail or extortion."

"Yeah."

"I find that hard to believe. I'll tell you why. I talked to Preston and I know he was being blackmailed, but you're telling me it wasn't you who was doing that."

"That's right."

"If not you, who was blackmailing him? Do you know?"

"No, well, not exactly."

"Well, tell us what you do know then," Miller said.

"It works this way. I am contacted, usually about four to six months before an election, sometimes between elections, to see if I have any potential...um... potential individuals who might be keeping secrets from the general public. They are usually politicians, or wannabe politicians, like Mr. Shanty here. Sometimes, they suggest someone for my attentions, sometimes I have someone in mind, and I also do research on their behalf."

Jack said, "That sounds vague. So, what you are saying is you are sort of 'private eye' who finds out things about victims and..."

Smith opened his mouth to speak, but Jack continued, "You may not like the term victim, but that is what these people are. You find out information about victims and pass it on to others. You say you don't know who gets the information, but you must know it's not used for the good of the victim."

"I suppose the first is true. I don't know about the second. I'm not sure the information is used, and if it is, what for," Smith said.

"I think you're splitting hairs. To me it sounds like you are aiding and abetting blackmail," Jack commented.

"I think my role is to document anything from minor weaknesses to plain nastiness. Others exploit my findings."

"I don't know if a jury would agree with you, Mr. Smith," added Miller.

"And then what about the video? We understand it was ketamine you gave to my opponent, Chris Hall?" Shanty asked.

"It's what I was paid to do, and I didn't expose anything that wouldn't have come out in the next year or two if he'd won. By the way, you're the better candidate, so I'm not losing any sleep over Hall."

Shanty stood, clearly annoyed, and paced the room, shaking his hand at Smith. "Do you know how that makes me feel? I want to win, but I want to win fair and square. What should I do now about this? Should I say I know the video was contrived? Should I step down? You've screwed up the whole thing. What about the voters? Shouldn't they decide?"

Mr. Smith replied in a quiet voice, "You don't need me to tell you the average American voter, if he votes at all, hasn't a clue what the issues are or why he should vote for you or your opponent. Advertising sells cornflakes, deodorants, and politicians. The one with the most bucks usually wins. I've spent the last ten to twelve years watching the way the public reacts and individually, or collectively, shoots itself in the foot every time. What I've been doing is just one small cog in the American political election machine. The more I look, the more I've found that good people don't stand a chance, and I admit I've been part of that, but how do we know there's no one else out there doing what I'm doing? None of you may agree with me completely, but you all know there's an element of truth in what I say. I'm not sure we live in a democracy anymore."

Miller, who, for different reasons, had his own doubts about the American democratic process asked, "So, assuming we believe you, why are you here this evening?"

"Because I don't want to do it anymore. It's part of what I've been, and I don't like it anymore, and it may not be safe. Please, I'd like to help, but I come back to my concern. What happened to Preston? Was it just a hit-and-run accident or something else?"

Miller waited a few seconds before replying, "We don't know. The DC police have kept the file open. We may never know. The vehicle involved was not found. Now, if we'd found a stolen, abandoned, wiped-down, or burnt-out vehicle, then it would have been more suspicious for not being just a hit-and-run. On the other hand, it looks like after he was hit, the same, or more likely, another vehicle ran over him. There were no witnesses who came forward. I talked to the detective in charge and overall it's more likely it was homicide. Does that help?"

"And you said you knew he was being blackmailed?" Smith asked.

Again, Miller hesitated. "Yes, he came to see me and we discussed his being blackmailed for some years. What part did you play in this?"

"I arranged for the photos and the video."

"And then?"

"I handed them on."

"You weren't involved with any later contact with him?" Miller asked.

"No, not at all."

Jack asked, "I still don't get it. How does it work?"

"Well, with Preston I just arranged the photos and the video. I've done that a couple of times... well, maybe more, and I hand the evidence on, but I first have to let the candidate know I have the information and someone will be in touch. With ... well, let's look at this election and Hall against Shanty. I am supposed to provide a potential candidate to my employers and get the dirt on him or her. I think they use it to influence the outcome of the election and maybe it can be used later. Sometimes I act as a catalyst and move things along. This time they wanted a Republican win. At times it's been a Democrat, but most of the time it's a Republican. There was a primary this time which let me know you guys were close. Not all states have primaries, so I have to do more research. I also have to look at the mood of the country as a whole. Which direction is the famous American electorate bending in the wind this time? Which way is the western part of Washington State moving? Who has the most money? Of the two who is vulnerable? Who is the ass-hole? You've probably figured out it isn't worth my efforts to work on safe seats where there is a healthy majority?"

He looked around. I was the only one who nodded. He continued, "So, there were two alternatives here. I could make sure Hall wins. I could discredit Shanty, which was not as easy as discrediting Hall. I could keep the video of the accident Hall had to myself, not let it out to the media, and just let him know I have it. Maybe I could have documented other dirt on him too. It wouldn't have been too hard. I hand this on and there my job ends."

"Why didn't you discredit me?" Shanty asked as he sat down.

"Could have done, but it wouldn't be as effective. It may not have worked. The only thing we have on you is the website white-washing your father, and saying you were the only child. By the way, if it's any reassurance to you we didn't find out anything recent about your sister, or your girlfriend for that matter. We found a few little things, but not enough to discredit you. If I'd wanted to do that we would have had to contrive something and that doesn't always work. Now, we could have had Hall in our pocket, or whatever he might be wanted for, but he's a loose cannon. He'd be unreliable. No, as it's going to work out, you will win the election. I'm sorry if you don't like it that way, but for once, the electorate of District 12 will have chosen the better candidate."

"Except, they didn't, you did!" Shanty nearly shouted.

"Not really; they still voted for you. All I did was influence them. It's no different from a PAC throwing a million dollars into your campaign, or producing a video for your campaign. Maybe all I did was level the playing field a bit."

"You don't think you picked up the playing field and all the players slid to one end?" Shanty asked.

That seemed to be taking the metaphor a little far, but Jack stepped in and asked.

"Why have you come to us this evening?"

"Like I said; it's time to stop what I'm doing. I've enough money put aside for a comfortable retirement and I want to retire. I also don't feel safe anymore. The last meeting I had with my employers didn't feel right, and then the Preston thing makes me concerned. Also, you guys are closing in. I don't think you have anything on me yet, or maybe not enough, but if you did I would have to be concerned I might not make it to court."

"Are you talking about the witness protection program?" Jack asked.

"No way! I want to disappear on my own terms, not yours or anyone else's."

"So, what have you got for us?" Jack said.

"Names, video clips, photographs, documents going back for the last ten years."

"Related to what?" Jack asked.

"Probably at least fifty politicians. Mainly house members, a few senators and a few governors," Smith replied.

There was silence in the room.

"You mean to say you have documentation of...of what, on fifty politicians?" Miller couldn't believe it.

"Well, plus or minus five or ten. There were more, but some left politics, some died, so it's been about six to seven each year."

Miller asked, "So what do you have on them?"

"Well, it could be anything from something like we have on Mr. Shanty here, to photos and receipts from motels. It could be activities like Preston's, or it could be same sex, or opposite sex, liaisons. There are a couple of financial shenanigans in there too."

"And you have all this? All originals?"

"No original receipts, and some of the other stuff isn't originals. Most are copies, PDF files, photos. They're all on discs – about four of them."

"So you give them to us and we...?"

"You let me go. You don't try to follow me, look for me, or have anything else to do with me."

"Why should we do that?" Jack asked.

"You've got nothing on me, and that's the deal."

"Well, I'm not sure you're right there, but let's assume you are. We get the discs from you and we believe you're not the one who has been doing the blackmailing. How do we find out who is doing the blackmailing?"

"That's up to you, but I'll give you one other shot at finding out who it could be," Smith replied.

"OK?" Jack said.

"I haven't been paid yet. I don't know how I'll be paid, but how much depends on the election result."

"Well, you've already said Will, Mr. Shanty, is going to win here, so how much are we talking about?"

"It's not just the Shanty/Hall election. There are four other races in other parts of the country I've been working on too."

Again, there was silence in the room as we collectively tried to get our democracy-biased brains around this revelation.

Miller said, "Four others?"

"Yes."

"Could you tell us about them?"

"I could, but I'd rather not. I can give you details after I get paid," Smith replied.

"And how much are you going to be paid?" Miller asked.

"If all works as planned, and I see no reason why at least four out of the five won't come through for me, I expect to get about one million. Of course, I have had expenses, so I should clear about seven hundred thousand."

"Not bad compensation," Miller said.

"I agree, but if you take the election as a whole, what I get is small potatoes. The money spent on these elections across the country is probably in the billions. I make a small difference in a few selected races. My employers are happy because it's efficient use of their money, and I get paid well enough."

"Let's get back to the people you call 'your employers'. What do you know about them?"

"Not much. They contact me when they need my services."

"How do they do that?"

"They've changed it over the years. Now I monitor Craig's List sailboat section for San Francisco area. I send in an enquiry about a boat they advertise. They reply and tell me where to pick up instructions on what to do next. I do that and the instructions usually tell me to go to an airport and pick up a package from a locker. The package includes airplane tickets, cash, and hotel reservations. I get on the plane and fly to where they want me and we discuss what we can do. They seem to like controlling how and what I do. The package also includes a plane ticket to another destination the day after I meet them. That can be very annoying, but it's how they do business."

"And when you meet them, what happens?"

"I think there is always one man, who is the same, and he brings in one or two to hear what I have to say, and we listen to what they have to say. Most of the times they just sit and watch me interact with the main man."

Miller asked, "Do you know who any of these people are?"

"No. I suspect they are wealthy, maybe very wealthy. They seem to have money, since we always discuss payment, and the one man who is there each time calls himself Mr. Jones. He introduces the others as Mr. Jones too, and, no, I don't recognize them."

"That seems like they are taking a risk. You could recognize them again couldn't you?"

"No."

"Why not?" Miller asked.

Smith sighed. "You'd have to go back to when I first got into this. I was talking to a guy at the Honolulu Sheraton bar. I mentioned I had this idea of how to manipulate politicians, but at that time had no idea, or intention, of how to carry this out. I was there for a few days and the same guy comes back to talk to me the next night. The trouble is I didn't recognize him. He was wearing different clothes and not wearing a baseball cap, so I couldn't place him. He noticed this and confirmed it an hour later."

"Confirmed what?" Miller asked.

"Face blindness."

"What?"

"Prosapagnosia, face blindness. It's the inability to recognize faces. It runs in my family and it's a pain. Most of the time I get around it by remembering other aspects of someone's characteristics. I don't think about it, but I probably remember them by shape of head, their clothes, their voice, their accent, their voice, but it doesn't always work. I probably recognize Doc here from his size, his accent when he speaks, shape of body, and his walk. "

"So this guy in the bar realized you had this... pros.."

"Prosapagnosia."

"And he took advantage of it?"

"More or less. When he realized I had this, and I don't know how he got onto it so quickly, he was consistent with what he wore and how he approached me if he wanted to talk to me. Of course, he also tested me to see if I was faking it or not, by appearing at other times with a different accent, walk, clothing, companion, or whatever. I don't know; I didn't recognize him."

Miller looked at me, "This is genuine Doc? He's telling the truth?"

I replied, "It's a genuine medical diagnosis, but I've never seen one."

Smith said, "That's because most people don't realize it if they've had it from birth. There are ways around it. If you get it from other brain damage, like a stroke, the other features of the damage are more of a problem."

"That makes sense," I said.

Miller asked, "So, you couldn't recognize these people you've met who you call your 'employers'?

"No. They tend to wear the same clothing and not say much. I could bump into them an hour later and not recognize them."

Jack leaned forward and said, "That could have caused you problems when you were in federal prison?"

"No kidding. Any form of uniform and it makes it very difficult to identify individuals. That applied to the other inmates and the guards. I also couldn't mention the problem to anyone or it would have been exploited. It was no fun. I don't want to go back there."

Jack said, "You don't seem to have been the sort of upstanding citizen who might avoid ending up back in prison?"

Smith, silent for once, shrugged his shoulders.

Miller asked, "How are you normally paid?"

"Banker's check."

"Check?"

"Yes, usually from some overseas account. I was suspicious the first time, but it worked out."

"The check is mailed to you?"

"Oh, no. I wasn't going to give out any address. It's handed over when I give them the evidence I'm being paid for."

"So, you'd meet someone, somewhere, and the exchange takes place?" Miller asked.

"More or less. I'd be at a meeting place and drop off a CD or two. I'd then be told to go away and come back in one or two hours. Then I would be informed where the payment would be."

"Give us an example," Jack asked.

"I've dropped the CD's off in a park. I've left them under a table at a restaurant. One hour later I'm told to be somewhere else, and there's a note telling me where I can find the payment check. The note usually says it will be available in exactly fifteen minutes, and to go there immediately. And, usually, it takes me at least that long to get there."

"And where is that?"

"It could be a park or a restaurant or anywhere. It's never been the same pattern twice."

"Why do you think they make you do that?"

"I've wondered about that too," Smith replied, "and I think it's just a control issue. They may be watching me to see if I'm followed, but the fifteen minutes is strange. They probably watch me drop the evidence and pick up the money, but it wouldn't really make any sense to watch me the whole time. It's not like I'm meeting someone to make the exchange."

Jack looked at Miller and back to Smith. "We'll have to think that one through too. But, for now, tell us again what do you have in mind?"

Smith leaned forward and looked from Jack to Miller and said. "I want you to keep your hands off me. I want to know you won't arrest me, and I'll give you what I have, then I am going to disappear. I don't want my face on a Post Office bulletin board, so I'd appreciate you not following me, or trying to find me." He looked to Miller for the answer.

After a few seconds hesitation Miller said, "I think we may be able to do that. I'm not sure we can make a case against you anyway." He paused. "However, part of the deal would be trying to catch at least who is paying you."

"After I've been paid, I hope," said Smith.

Miller smiled. "I can't promise that, but we'll try. We need to think this over and get in touch with you. You said you are normally paid after the election?"

"Yes."

"And how much notice do they give you about that?"

"I get a call and they tell me about four hours before where I have to be."

"But how many days after an election?"

"Two or three usually."

"That doesn't give us much time. Oh, and their cell phone number ID is?"

"Unknown. I've never tried to call back. I assume they either use a number once or, more usually, the ID isn't recognized by my phone."

"That's what I would expect," Miller said.

Smith shrugged.

Miller looked at Jack and asked if he had any more questions. Jack shook his head. Miller turned to Smith and said.

"We'll be in touch?"

"I'll be in touch," Smith said. "I'll call the Doc here every day."

That caught my attention.

"Why me? Why not call one of these guys directly?" I asked.

"Because I like you, and that's how I want it to be," Smith replied.

I was not impressed. "But they're the ones who can help you. They have all the resources and people."

"Exactly, which is why I'll call you." He stood and continued, "Well, let the Doc here know if you have any questions, and like I said, I'll be in touch. I'll see myself out. Doc, keep your cell phone charged."

He turned and left. Shanty followed him to the door, closed it after him, returned to the table and sat down.

I had to say something. I was annoyed.

"Why me? Couldn't we have insisted he call one of you instead?"

Jack apologized, "Maybe. We could have offered, but I think he would have insisted on calling you."

Chris Miller added, "I think Jack's right. He comes across as wanting to be in control, but I bet he's checking his driving mirror every ten seconds as he drives away from here now."

"I'm not convinced," and I wasn't. "I think he's in control. I think he got what he wanted when he came in here, and now I feel as if I'm the one dangling on a hook waiting for him to call. Why don't you take my cell phone and answer his calls?"

"It's not that easy, "Jack replied. "There are a couple of reasons for that. The obvious one is we don't sound like you and he would get very suspicious if you didn't answer the phone. The only reason he has to hang around now is the payment he's expecting. I think he's telling the truth about giving this up. He knows we are on to him and he could just disappear. I think he's also worried. He must wonder if what happened to Preston could happen to him. The other reason is the bigger picture. Chris and I are senior members in the Bureau, but we have been doing this mainly on our own dime. You don't see lots of agents buzzing around for a reason. What Smith could give us is politically a hot potato and doing what we have been doing leaves us open to all sorts of charges of interfering with politics. We've stuck our necks out for this, but we didn't want a wider investigation. It could have compromised more agents, and it would have also been more likely our investigations would have been leaked to the media. We haven't quite decided what to do with any information we get. If it is what Smith says it is I'm in favor of passing it up the line to our seniors. Chris is not entirely happy with that, probably because he has to live next to them, but doing nothing with it is not an option. We both agree to that."

Miller added, "Smith doesn't know how big or little our operation is. He doesn't know it's basically just Jack and me here and a few trusted colleagues in other parts of the country. I don't know if they are monitoring an election where Smith is using his talents or not. We're just lucky here. The other reason Smith popped up this evening is he wanted to surprise us. He assumed, correctly, we would not have any surveillance on him, or Will's house yet. We have to go along with what he wants, and I'm sorry that means you taking his phone calls."

I was still not convinced, but I said I would, reluctantly, keep my cell phone charged and handy.

There were four days left before the election.

14

I opened my eyes. I was in bed, it was Saturday morning. Ann was still asleep but stirring. We were together and all was right with the world.

Except it wasn't.

I'd hoped for an early evening so Ann and I could dress up as Peter Pan and Wendy (I was going to be Wendy) and win the most boringly-traditional-Halloween-couple-outfit prize at a friend's party, but I didn't get home until after ten to a resoundingly quiet house. Ann came home by ground transport just before 11:00, and I found myself apologizing, once again, for my social avoidance behavior. Of course, at the same time, I also found myself admiring her arboreal green, leotarded body with its strategically placed green plastic leaves from the Dollar Store. Apparently, she noticed my noticing her, tipped her Swiss-style, arboreal-green, Goodwill-purchased hat over her left eye and advanced. She gave me a lingering moist kiss, put one arm around my upper back and with the other in my lower back, pulled me to her.

"Peter wants his Wendy," she whispered into my right ear and nibbled the ear lobe.

I could feel myself rising to the occasion (I've always wanted to write that).

"You want me to get into the Wendy outfit now?"
"Yes," ear nibble.
"What, everything, including the bra and panties?
"Everything, well, no. You can forget the bra. You know how bra-less turns me on."

"OK, but be gentle with me...I think...I think I'm ovulating," I said coquettishly.

Ann pushed back, looked at my face. I stared at her and batted my eyelids in my best Betty Davis imitation. We both broke out laughing.

The next fifteen minutes was a lot of fun. Five minutes after that we were both asleep.

But now it was morning and the weekend. I smiled as I recalled our encounter the previous night. I turned over and pulled her close to me in a couple spoon. I put my arm around her waist and she held her hand in mine. It was our own private cocoon. It was warm, normal, and felt so right. I didn't want it to go away.

"I think we should stay here all day and not move. We won't touch the phone or turn on the computer, and we can just ask for pizza delivery," I murmured into her right ear.

"Okay, but you have to answer the door and pay the delivery guy."

"Deal."

"Of course too much pizza and Wendy won't like Peter's waist-line will she?"

I was not quite awake and it took me a few seconds to figure out the gender changes and realize I was still Wendy.

I replied, "Wendy will still love Peter whatever the size of his waist-line."

"Liar," Ann said and wriggled closer to me.

We lay there for another minute before she spoke again.

"How are we going to get pizza delivery if we're not going to use the phone?"

"You don't think they'd know to deliver their special with extra anchovies for me, and the seafood Hawaiian for you?"

"At noon?"

"Yes."

"Well, what happens if I want mine earlier?"

"You have to have faith. I believe in Little Caesars," I said.

"Little Caesars doesn't deliver. You've just been teasing me so you can have your way with me."

She turned in mock horror and rolled on top of me pinning my arms to my side.

"And, furthermore, where were you last night? I thought you said you'd be home early." She gave me a kiss on the lips and flopped down to my left side looking at me. I turned to face her.

"Well, it's sort of a long story. I thought I'd be home early too."

I told her the outline of the previous day's events, from the meeting at the supermarket to the time when Smith left Shanty's house.

"So was it a trap? Did Shanty let himself be a target? I hadn't thought about that," she asked.

I had forgotten my promise to Shanty to not disclose his part in getting Smith to reveal himself. I knew the information would go no further than Ann, but I realized why Cold War spy agencies allegedly trained their female operatives to extract information by pillow-talk. It worked.

I confessed, "I wasn't supposed to tell you that. I don't think he's done anything wrong ethically, although he wasn't happy that he might win the election because of Smith's shenanigans, but there's nothing he can do about that now."

"I could see he might be upset by that. And are you still the one who Smith is going to call? What about those FBI guys?"

"After he left I was a little pissed-off I would be the one waiting for his calls, but they said it was probably the only way he would have agreed to stay in contact. I'm not sure. There are probably other reasons too. I was thinking on the way home that someone is probably going to tap my phone to see if they can listen in to any calls or texts I get."

"Really?"

"Oh, yes. I promised to pass on any information from the calls I get from him, but it would be in their interest to make sure I passed everything on."

"It's going to be difficult to call you knowing someone else is listening in."

"I know. We'll have to be careful what we say."

"That will be easy for you," Ann said. "You don't like saying much on the phone anyway."

"Yes, well that's because I look at it as a necessary evil, having to be in touch all the time. And I've never liked speaking on the phone. I think it's my accent. People, even some of my patients, used to think I must be a telemarketer, and it always took me a few minutes to explain I wanted to talk to them about their cholesterol, not sell them a condo in Florida."

"I like your accent," Ann said.

"It's the only one I've got, so we're stuck with it."

"This man, Smith; he had no problem understanding you?"

"No, he didn't, but he called me first."

"And he's going to call every day?"

"Yes."

"Then what?" Ann asked.

"We discussed it last night. Smith expects to be paid by his employers, as he calls them, after the election. He says he'll probably get a message a few days after the election, and he'll be told how he's going to be paid. He'll let me know what the plan is and I'll pass it on. According to Smith he is told to be somewhere to pick up a message, and this tells him where the money will be. Based on this it's unlikely anything will happen before the election."

"Unless someone else changes their mind," Ann said.

"Agreed. Or Smith has been lying to us. I don't think he has, but I don't quite see why he doesn't walk away now. Both Jack and Chris Miller didn't think they had enough on him to make a case that would stick. However, I don't think it's all as straightforward as Smith makes out. He says he's been working on other elections around the country. If we assume this is true then why is he expecting to be paid here? It may be something as simple as being told he will be paid at the furthest west election district, or it could be a number of similar possibilities. Whatever it is he must know that there's a possibility of his being watched too. He also said he had a bad feeling about this election and wants this to be his last. Jack and Miller didn't buy his suddenly acquiring a conscience, but I think it's a possibility. Maybe I'm just less jaded than they are about the human race."

"Good." Wriggle.

"Thanks." Squeeze. "If he walks now he'll miss out on being paid, and he says he expects to be paid about a million dollars."

"That's worth hanging around for!"

"Yes, and it's probably 'tax-free', but it's only worth it if he gets out of this with his skin intact. I think one of the reasons for his apparent cooperation is he hopes to be paid, and for those who are paying him to be caught. Then he plans to disappear. But that isn't straightforward either. If there's no good case against Smith, there wouldn't be one against whoever is paying him. There might be loss of anonymity, but I doubt any of his employers are going to show up around here. Reading between the lines Jack and Chris Miller think his concern is they may send someone else."

"Someone else? I don't get it," Ann asked.

"Maybe it's better not to. Smith asked Chris about what happened to Robert Preston. Do you remember him? He was a US senator who was killed in a hit-and-run accident earlier this year."

"I remember."

"Well, it seems Preston was one of Smith's victims and the circumstances of his death were unusual. Miller had apparently met with him in DC. and he was the one who originally got the FBI interested in finding out what was going on, and how widespread it is."

"And now you're involved in this too?"

"Only relaying the phone calls. I am not going to do anything else." I was emphatic.

"I hope not," Ann said, "and the first thing you can do is give me a kiss. I'm starving, and I'm going to eat breakfast. The food they offered last night was basically lumps of lard masked by color, flavoring and texture. It would go straight to Peter's thighs, so I'm going to do my lose-a-hundred-pounds-in -seven-days workout while you make breakfast. After all, you are the woman of the family."

I put my arms around her and pulled her close. "In one hour Wendy is going to have a sex change, and maybe Peter would like to join her."

"Peter thinks that is a distinct possibility, unless... (she looked at the clock) it happens in the middle of Car Talk."

We kissed, made a promise to return to the same place in the afternoon, got out of bed and dressed.

I was half way through pouring the boiling water on the tea bags when my phone rang. I could hear the thumping music of the hundred-pound workout from our bedroom, so I couldn't ask Ann to answer it. I finished the tea-making as quickly and safely as possible, covered the teapot with the ugly tea cozy (aren't they all ugly?) and picked up the phone. It was Smith.

"Howya doing, Doc?" he asked.

"Fine."

"Hope I didn't wake you."

"No, I'm just getting breakfast together."

"Well, nothing happening here. I'll be away for the next couple of days, but I'll keep in touch."

"OK."

"Bye." He hung up. I called Jack and relayed the conversation to him.

Jack asked, "He said he'd be away? Where did he say he was going?"

"He didn't say and I didn't ask, but he said he would keep in touch."

"Was there any background noise to identify where he could be?"

"No, just the few words he said on the phone."

"OK. I suppose that means we can relax a little if he's going to be away. It will help us get things together."

"That assumes he's telling the truth," I said.

"And why wouldn't he?" Jack joked.

"I've no idea. I'll call if he calls." I smiled.

"Thanks." Jack hung up.

I assumed if Jack asked me if there was any background noise then my phone was not being tapped – yet. Although maybe he asked me that to try to head off any idea that it might be tapped. I stopped myself thinking like that. It would get me nowhere; I'd be better off making breakfast.

I stirred the tea bags in the pot, poured myself a cup and took it to the pan of oatmeal I was stirring on the stove. It was oatmeal weather. Outside it was cold, dull, with a slight drizzle falling in a light wind. NPR said it would all change tomorrow when we could expect it to be colder and duller but with the promise of November snow and strong winds. This would be great news for the local ski-hills, but depressing information for mere mortals struggling to survive at sea level. It was also early in the season for snow, but November has never been my favorite month of the year. It heralds at least four months of gloom in the weather, and maybe in my attitude. About now, I thought, I should be looking for a secluded cave to hibernate in until shafts of sunlight warmed my body on a bright day in March. I looked up from my stirring to the outside dreariness and watched the one hummingbird who stayed behind, when his friends had migrated to Mexico, sipping from the feeder I kept refilling all year. If I hadn't kept refilling the feeder would he now be sipping nectar from a bougainvillea in Cabo? Maybe he was asked to stay behind to keep the place clean until spring. Maybe he was injured and had to stay behind. Maybe he has agoraphobia. Maybe he is a she.

"Penny for your thoughts," Ann said close to my left ear.

I was startled but replied, "They aren't worth a penny."

"Well, they seem to be focusing your attention."

We both watched the hummingbird zoom away.

I said, "I was watching the hummingbird. He could be spending Christmas on a warm beach somewhere. Instead he's stuck here, next to his food source, until next spring."

"You told me once one of your dreams is to spend Christmas on a warm beach somewhere."

"Ah, but all your dreams shouldn't come true, then you wouldn't have any."

"You make new dreams."

"Oh, no. If you have any connections to Wales you are allowed a set quantity of lifetime dreams you dare not exceed. Fantasize beyond that and you might not be miserable any more. Then what would happen?"

Ann put her arm around my waist. I put my left arm around her and continued to stir the oatmeal. It was nearly ready. I turned off the heat and let it sit. With both arms I gave Ann a squeeze, a kiss, and realized how much I loved the woman. The miracle, especially with those Welsh connections, is she seemed just as happy with me.

I told Ann about Smith's phone call, my report to Jack, and my hope for a quiet few days. We had a few domestic chores planned for the morning. One of them was listening to Car Talk and Wait, Wait, Don't Tell Me from KUOW while we cleaned the house.

We had almost finished at 10:30 when my phone rang again. It was Dick and he was asking if I could help him out that afternoon and evening. He had to take his wife to urgent care. He said he would normally call Harry, but Harry was out of town, so would I pick up Shanty and take him to the two public meetings he had that day? The last one would be over by 7:00 pm. I lowered the phone, looked at Ann and asked her if it was okay.

"There's no one else?" she replied.

"Apparently not," I said, then shook my head, shrugged my shoulders, and mouthed, "I don't want to go."

"Do you have a choice?" she whispered.

"Not really. They'd do it for me," I whispered back. We both shrugged our shoulders resignedly.

I lifted the phone and said to Dick, "OK. I'll do it, but I am going to be so glad this is over on Tuesday." Of course, being a doctor, I couldn't let it go at that and asked, "What's wrong with Mary that you have to take her in on a Saturday?"

"She's had this cold and now she's feeling some chest tightness and wonders if she's getting short of breath."

"Sounds like you're doing the right thing," I said. "Give her my love and tell her I hope she'll be better soon."

"Will do, and thanks." Dick hung up.

"What's wrong with Mary?" Ann asked.

"Hopefully, nothing, but it may be something else," I answered in my best non-committal distracted voice.

"Thanks, doctor," Ann said.

"Oh, yeah. I suppose I didn't actually say anything did I?"

Ann shook her head.

I continued, "That's what comes of hanging around politicians all this time. I end up saying nothing and hope it sounds like something."

"It had better wear off soon. When do you have to leave?"

"I have to be in Shelton by 1 pm, with the candidate. As far as I know this is the last day he's scheduled to talk to any groups. After today all he has planned is phone-calling."

"Well, that's good. So, you have to leave here before noon. That doesn't give us much of an opportunity to get much else done. I've completed my sex change, and maybe that's enough for one day. I'd like you to call me Ann now, and not Peter, if that's OK with you?"

"When did that happen?"

"After Car Talk."

"Oh, good. I've completed mine too. I think mine must have happened around the same time." I took her hand. "Hello, my name's John, and I believe yours is Ann?"

"Correct."

"Good, we're back to normal again." I pulled her to me and put my arms around her. "But John, who doesn't like November, does feel a little disappointed he has to work and leave Ann here, so he would like to postpone the activities we had planned for the afternoon until maybe this evening?"

"Ann quite understands and looks forward to his return this evening. She may even have a surprise for him when he returns."

"John likes surprises."

John loved surprises, but not the one waiting for him later that day.

The election day polls would open in sixty-six hours.

15

I drove the well-worn path to Shanty's house on Hood Canal. Much of my initial enthusiasm and interest in his part of the political process had worn off. I was bored with the repetition of the questions, the presentations, and the driving back and forth the thirty minutes to his house. I'd tried to use the time constructively by listening to Spanish-for-linguistic-idiots tapes, but I kept getting stuck on the second one. I suppose the fact I was still using tapes in my car dated me, or at least my car.

I made a point to not turn on the radio and hear the same negative political advertisements. I had even soured on NPR and their attempts to keep up with the other stations and turn the election coverage into a horse race. My November mood didn't help very much and so I drove there with my brain on auto-pilot. There was very little traffic on that Saturday afternoon; most people had the sense to stay inside and pretend it was not November. I filled up with gas at Safeway in Belfair and drove the last fifteen minutes to his house.

He was looking tired too. At least all I had to do was sit through the boredom and repetition. He had to live it. He slumped into the passenger seat with uncharacteristic resignation and I pulled out of his driveway.

"Get any sleep last night?" he asked me.

"Pretty good. And you?"

"I don't know. I seemed to sleep all night – well after the Feds and you left – but I still feel exhausted."

"I think it's a miracle you haven't felt like this before. You've been like a machine. You've lived and breathed candidate Shanty for months now. You've put the rest of your life on hold. You're probably going to win on Tuesday, but it's been a big personal sacrifice. You've been cloistered away almost like a monk. You know, if I were a voter in your district I'd even vote for you now." I smiled.

"Wow! Can I use that in my next campaign speech?" He joked.

"Of course. I'll just take my usual percentage. But... you know... you've been great. You've worked hard. If every member of Congress worked as hard as you this country would leave all the others in the dust."

"Oh yeah?"

"Well, maybe not dust. At this time of the year it's more likely to be mud, especially around here. Also, look at the weather. It sucks all the energy out of you at this time of the year. I'm not surprised you're exhausted."

We both looked out at what we could see of the dull grey-green of western Washington through the wipers, the spattering rain drops, and the condensation at the edges of the windshield. After a while Shanty repeated the Pacific North West aphorism.

"The rain is good for us. We need the rain. The rain is good for us. We need the rain. We have to keep remembering that."

"That's what they tell us, and I suppose it's true. At least we're not like southern California. At least we have the rain. I just wish it would only rain between midnight and 6 am, Monday, Wednesday and Friday, all year."

"Then everyone would want to live here. This way anyone who is thinking of moving here, visits at this time of the year, and doesn't have webbed feet, will pass on through without stopping at a realtor, and never come back."

"You're right," I said.

Again we were both silent for a few minutes, then Shanty said.

"Thank you."

"What for?"

"For getting me out of my funk. It always helps to talk to you."

"Oh. Well, thank you too. It helps with my November funk too. And before I get to this next intersection, do I turn right or left? Where are we off to today?"

"Turn right. We're close to base today. Stop in Shelton at the office, and then it's a church near Union and up to Silverdale, the High School, for the next meeting."

"Silverdale? That's not in your district."

"It's a multi-district, multi-level, Republican forum. In other words it's a collection of those who are still standing at this stage of the campaigns. This way we are less likely to say something we shouldn't."

I smiled and turned right.

We chatted while I drove Washington Highway 3 south towards Shelton. He was still upset that should he be elected it was due to Smith's meddling. I told him I thought it was okay for him to be troubled about that. It was probably what to expect in a career in politics — he'd probably find it was the personality disorders who usually won and not the righteous, but maybe just this once good would triumph over evil — he'd find out on Tuesday. I even told him I'd support his campaign again if necessary. I also hoped he wouldn't find it necessary.

We arrived at his headquarters in Shelton just before 1:00 pm. He had a few items to pick up and attend to, so I found our favorite hole-in-the-wall Central American restaurant and bought two magnum vegetarian burritos. As I left, with both hands full of calories, I once again resolved to improve my Spanish beyond, 'Ola, dos burritos por favor...gracias' to maybe understanding what was being said back to me.

We weren't due in Union until 2 pm. Apparently, the candidate should never turn up too early (it implies he is not busy) but nor should he be late (maybe he doesn't care) so we had become experts at working with our GPS units and turning up at the optimal moment. We sat in his empty campaign headquarters, eating our burritos and checking our watches for the exact time to leave Shelton. His campaign manager, Alice, attended all his public appearances and was on her way there. She had ridden with us in the past, but often liked to take her own car. I suspected she liked the down-time to relax and not have anything political on her mind. Perhaps she was learning Spanish too.

At two minutes to 2:00 we drove into the Baptist Church parking lot in Union. It was now drizzling and I couldn't see the other side of the Hood Canal which I knew was somewhere in the gloom. At 2:00 pm precisely the candidate strode in to the Church.

There were six people in the congregation/audience, and this included Shanty's embarrassed campaign manager who was clearly upset by the situation. Shanty didn't miss a beat. He abandoned the podium and lectern, pulled up a chair and invited the audience, who were scattered among the pews, to come close. I accompanied his campaign manager to her car since I knew she would have to vent to someone.

"They said there'd be at least forty, and what do we have? Five. Who do they think he is? What do they think he's running for? The mayor of Union! I will be so glad when this is over. Roll on Tuesday." She looked at the heavens briefly for encouragement, but the drizzle prevented long gazes. She blinked her eyes, gathered her equanimity, put on her best sugary smile and asked,

"John, how do I look?"

"Butter wouldn't melt in your mouth. You look like any other political sycophant – totally unbelievable."

"Sycophant? And how would you define that, John?"

I thought quickly, "A creepy, fawning, groveling, flatterer?"

"That's me?"

I nodded.

"So, I look like a mix between a stewardess, and I don't mean 'flight attendant', and a sort of... Nancy Reagan?"

"I'm afraid so."

"Oh...I suppose that's good?"

"If you're in politics it's the badge you are supposed to wear, but after Tuesday you can be yourself again."

"Oh yeah?" She turned and opened her car door, turned back to me and added, "You know I think you've become even more cynical than me."

"Now it's my turn to thank you."

She laughed, stepped forward, gave me a quick hug, readjusted her smile, sat in her anonymous, grey, mid-size Dodge and drove north to where she would be waiting for us in another couple of hours.

I would have preferred to stay outside in my car, but my back was not enjoying the prolonged driving sessions , and the dismal drizzle forced me back into the church.

Shortly before 3 pm Shanty wound up the meeting with handshakes and smiles all around and we headed north in my car. I passed on Alice's frustration about the lack of audience participants. His only comment was, "I'm sure she tried her best, and by now, I'm wishing I could have run as mayor of Union. Who knows? More people might have turned up."

I replied, "You may be right. On the other hand maybe that was the total voting population of Union who attended your meeting."

"In that case, if I get in to Congress, and when I retire from there, I'm running for mayor of Union." He put his seat back, closed his eyes, and I drove along the south side of the Hood Canal to Belfair where I picked up Washington State Highway 3. There, I'd planned to stay on Highway 3 and head up to Silverdale. The GPS said we would be at our destination, Central Kitsap High School, at fifteen minutes to four, so in the spirit of not wanting to arrive too early, and the occasional vary-the-route-for-security idea that entered my mind, I took the left turn at the light to the Old Belfair Highway. This was a quieter, less frantic, curving road which was a lot more fun to drive, especially in my Subaru at about five miles per hour over the speed limit. I could probably drive it twenty over the limit, but that wouldn't be me. I was followed onto the Old Belfair Highway by a car which I noted in my mirror because only three of its four headlamps were working. The car followed me closely for a mile, and then gradually dropped back. It reappeared in my mirror on some of the longer straights.

I eased around the curves by the Gold Mountain Golf Course, slowed for the speed limit change along the straight into Gorst, and decided, since the GPS still said I would be arriving early, to take the back roads a little longer.

Instead of taking Highway 3 I stuck to the higher side-roads which those in-the-know used to avoid traffic jams during rush hours. On this Saturday in November there were no jams to avoid, but this route slowed me enough that I reached the Central Kitsap High School exactly five minutes before the meeting. There was not much parking left in the front of the school, but I noticed the frantic waving of Alice as she caught my attention and directed me into the space she had been guarding for us. I got out of the car, stretched and thanked her.

"Don't thank me, John. It's in the job description." She looked tired.

"That's a little cynical, maybe petulant?" I said.

"Why can't I be petulant if I want to be?"

"No reason, but you won't get any sympathy. Everyone will assume its PMS, except the press, of course. They'll assume you're pregnant."

She opened her mouth to say something, but just smiled. It was not the Nancy Reagan/stewardess smile, and then she laughed.

I smiled too, shrugged my shoulders, and walked to the passenger door. Shanty was still asleep, but stirred when I opened the door.

I said, "It's show time. You're on in three minutes."

"Where are we?" he asked.

"CK High School."

"High School? Oh, yes. The multi-candidate forum. I remember."

With that he moved his seat to the upright position, checked his hair in the mirror, got out of the car, and with Alice at his side strode through the doors of the high school.

As he disappeared into the school a car with only three of its headlights working drove into the full lot. I watched as it was directed to the overflow parking behind the school.

16

I considered my alternatives. I could stay in the car for the next hour while I got colder and the windows completely misted over. I could go and listen to the candidates and be warm, but bored, or I could go to Costco and spend money I didn't mean to. I opted for Costco.

I gave up my prime parking spot and headed for consumer heaven, or more precisely, I had to cross consumer heaven (the multiple stores of Silverdale) to get to the other side and the parking lot of Costco. Even at the end of the afternoon, with this miserable weather, the parking lot seemed almost full. Maybe the weather had driven people out of their comfortable sofas to the aisles and refrigerators of bulk-buying.

I checked in with Ann.

"I'm at Costco in Silverdale. Do we need anything?"

"What are you doing up there?" she replied.

"I dropped Will off at a multi-candidate forum at the high school."

"And you have to drive him back to Shelton afterwards?"

"I hope not. I may have to take him back to Belfair though. Maybe I'll ask Alice if she can take him back."

"I'll be glad when this is over. I want you back again."

"No kidding. I was thinking today that if you can buy lottery tickets for several drawings in advance, maybe we could send in our votes for several elections in advance."

"Why not? It would be democracy at work."

"Of course the scary thing is it may not make any difference."

"You may be right. Let's just stick to the Costco list. At least we can rely on that."

"OK. I have my pen and paper ready."

"Tomatoes...lettuce...small peppers...bananas...red wine – the one with a box of four...kitchen rolls..."

The list went on and I wrote the items down until she hesitated.

"Is that it?" I asked.

"I think so."

"It looks like we would've starved if I hadn't decided to come here today."

"I was thinking of making a Costco run tomorrow anyway, but your picking up the stuff is better. Have fun."

"I will. I hope to be home before eight. I'll let you know if I'm going to be later. Look after yourself."

"Will do. Hugs and kisses."

I rang off and hurried through the damp, cold, and murk to the welcoming lights and warmth of Costco.

I'd turned the radio on while driving to the store and listened to the weather forecaster say the rain would soon end but be replaced by cold winds from the north. There was also the possibility of snow as the change occurred. Maybe that's why the parking lot was full – there's nothing like the hint of impending doom to make people shop.

I was pretty good. I assembled all the items on the list in my shopping cart. I ate a few samples of cheese and salty meatballs as I walked around, but you can't go to Costco and just buy what's on the list. You have to buy something you didn't intend to get; something that would make life so much better if you slipped it in your shopping cart between the eggs and the frozen fish.

It was only $39.99 and came in bright yellow, light blue, or green. It promised to keep me warm and dry. It folded up into a small package I could keep in the car for days, like today, when I needed something extra to keep out the world. It was then I realized the black waterproof trousers which accompanied the jacket (I chose bright yellow) were $19.99 extra. I hesitated. Should I just buy the top? Should I throw caution to the wind? Should I buy a jacket for Ann too? I could call her, but I didn't want to be one of those people who go around Costco with cell-phones glued to their face. I decided. I couldn't quite bring myself to pay the extra for trousers I would rarely use, and if Ann liked the jacket we could always come back again. Having made that decision I felt morally superior for refusing any further urge-to-splurge.

And the final tally was under $200. After I paid I wondered if I should go back and get those trousers, maybe call Ann after all, but I resisted and instead took my newly purchased jacket out of its packaging, pulled the hood over my head, and headed for the wet darkness and my car.

My 1999 Subaru Forester pre-dated the remote control of things like doors, so I had to fumble for my keys, which were now under my yellow jacket, and actually stick the key in the rear door lock. The door swung up, I pulled the shopping cart under its shelter and was about to begin the transfer of my goodies when a voice near my ear said,

"Doc, don't turn round. It's me."

The only reaction to advice like that is to turn around, see who is close to you and say.

"Shit! It is you!"

"Yeah. I'm sorry. We shouldn't keep meeting in supermarkets. Look, can you open your car door. I need to get inside."

It was Smith and his customary expansive smile was brief, so I opened the front passenger door for him, but he indicated he wanted to get in the back seat. I noticed he was carrying a couple of small bags. I let him in and he lay down immediately. I closed the door and returned to the back of my vehicle.

"Sorry, Doc. I should have called," he said from the back seat.

I placed one box of groceries in the back of the car and replied, "I thought that was our arrangement. You call me once every day. What happened?"

"I think I'm being followed."

For some reason I found this annoying and said. "I know I'm being followed. Followed by you. When did you start following me? Was it at Belfair?" I was thinking of the car with one headlamp out.

"No, I figured you'd be at the high school shindig, so I followed you from there."

I placed another grocery box in the back, put the package of bananas next to the eggs, closed the rear door, opened the driver's door and got in behind the wheel.

I asked, "So, why did you follow me?"

"I've been staying at a hotel in Silverdale the last few days. Every two or three days I change hotels. Sometimes I stay a little longer to break the pattern. So, I go out for lunch today and it's so miserable outside I thought I'd treat myself to Thai. I ask for a booth, not a table, and sit so I can see the rest of the customers. The trouble is I can only see a few other customers – the dividers between the booths and the design of the place makes it difficult to see anyone else. This is good and bad. If anyone was following me it would be harder for them to monitor me too. So, I sit down and order my stir-fry, and another customer comes in and sits at a booth nearby. He's male, in his forties, and he sits with his back to me. Like me, he can sit at the window and look outside. He orders and I can just hear his accent. Like me, I can tell he's not from around here. He's from Jersey, or maybe Pennsylvania, so maybe I take a little more notice. My meal comes and I start into it and I'm munching away. I look outside and there's another guy walking along on the sidewalk – in this weather! He's got no umbrella but he has a hat and jacket and he walks along and looks in the restaurant. At some point I notice he makes a small move of his head and the other guy in the restaurant makes a similar move. The guy outside keeps walking and I concentrate on my food. I think to myself maybe I'm a paranoid SOB, but maybe that's what's kept me alive. I finish my food, get the bill and pay on the way out. I get in my car and I drive to Target. I check my mirror on the way there, but there's no way I can see if I'm being followed. I go to Target because I'd been there before and I know they've got a security camera which checks everyone coming in, and there's a monitoring screen in customer service. I wander over to customer service and look at the screen, and a couple of minutes later I see the guy who was outside when I was in the restaurant walk into the store. I move father into the store, buy a few items, pay for them, go to my car and head back to the hotel. But, there's something wrong here."

    He paused, expecting me to give him the answer.
    I said, "What was wrong?"
    "That's not how you follow someone."
    "It isn't?"

"No. They didn't need to be following me. They knew where I was all the time. They were just keeping an eye on me. They were hanging back too much – maybe so I wouldn't see them. The only thing that makes sense is they were tracking me, and the only way I know how was through my cell phone."

I let this sink in for a few seconds then asked.

"You haven't got your phone with you now, have you?"

"No, Doc. It's back in my hotel room and it's switched on, so they think I'm back there watching the soaps or something. I left the back way and my car is still in the parking lot there too."

"So, how did you follow me here?"

"How would you do it doc?" he asked.

I thought for a moment. "I suppose I'd take a cab. No, that wouldn't work... I don't know."

"You drive your other car. You keep another rental car close just in case. It can be a hassle at times, but you never know."

I think he was feeling pleased his efforts seemed to have paid off.

"But why are you following me?" I asked.

"You are my contact to the Feds. The deal is I give them what I've got and they look the other way when I leave. You know, you were there."

This made me regret even more my intermediary status.

"So, you've got the information with you?" I said.

"Yeah. I've got some real estate here in my bag – as the song goes. I think it will interest them."

During this conversation he had remained lying down on the back seat of my Subaru. I checked my watch and realized I should be heading back to the high school. I looked in my mirror and noticed the grocery cart was still behind the car, so I said.

"I have to get back to the high school, but I've got to move the grocery cart first."

As I wheeled the cart back to a collection area an obvious problem with his plan occurred to me. I returned to my car, put the key in the ignition, and hesitated.

"There's one concern I have," I said, "and that is what if someone is following me too?"

"Are they?"

"I don't know."

"Well, it wouldn't be the same people. They couldn't follow me and you at the same time."

I said, "There could be more than two of them. They could be monitoring me too."

"Do you think you've been followed?"

I could sense this was something that hadn't figured in his calculations.

"When I drove up from Belfair today I thought we may have been followed, and then I think I saw the same car drive into the parking lot at the high school, but that doesn't mean someone's following me."

"Christ! Look at that the other way. That doesn't mean someone is not following you. Damn!"

"Why don't you just go back to your car and leave the bag with me. I'll make sure it gets to the Feds," I suggested.

"I can't risk it if you're being followed too. Also, if that's true I have to think how long these people have been keeping an eye on me. I used my second car yesterday when I was at Shanty's. I used my phone then too. Shit!"

"If I'm being followed, or watched, don't you think it would seem odd if I've sat in this car for the last five or ten minutes talking to myself?"

"Doc, you're right. I need to disappear and you need to get back to your quiet life. I need to get something out of my car. It's two rows up. I'm going to walk there, get what I want and walk another two rows up. Pick me up there. Turn off your dome light so it doesn't come on when I get out, and get started."

I turned off the light. Smith opened the door, got out of the car and, staying low, headed away between the parked cars. I started the engine, backed out, and drove to the row he indicated. It took me about ninety seconds to do this – the traffic slowed me down. I drove slowly along the row. Smith appeared on my right. I stopped; he threw in another bag and lay on the back seat again. I drove to the end of the row, looked in my mirror and noticed a vehicle with one headlight out less than fifty yards behind me. I turned left at the end of the row, sped up and took the next right without stopping. The car behind matched my speed and maintained its distance behind me. I slowed back to normal Saturday afternoon commute speed.

"What was that for, Doc?" Smith asked.

"I'm being followed. There's a car with one headlight out behind me. I assume it's the same one I saw in Belfair, at the high school and now here. It sped up when I did, and is about fifty yards back." My mouth had suddenly gone quite dry.

"We have to assume there's more than one vehicle involved. It's also likely they know we're both in this car. Just drive normally to the high school."

That was my intention anyway. I stopped for a red light at the intersection of Ridgetop and Mickleberry.

The car following pulled up so close behind I couldn't see its lights in the mirror. I told Smith about this.

"Their plan must have changed. They're no longer interested in just keeping tabs on you. They want something else. Shit! I might just as well sit up – it won't make any difference now."

I put the car in gear, pulled away from the light and I could see in my mirror that Smith was now sitting and putting on his seat belt. The lights were green at the 'T' where Mickleberry hit Bucklin Hill Road and I took a right. The car following me had dropped back a little and I had a green light crossing over Silverdale Way, but we were nearly back at the high school.

"Don't go into the school," Smith ordered. "We'll be trapped if you go in there. Carry on."

I followed his instruction and stopped at the intersection between Bucklin Hill and Anderson Hill Road. The car behind came closer and gave me a light bump.

"Ignore that," Smith said. "Do you know the roads around here?"

"Pretty well."

"Then get us out of here."

I was about to say something when the bump from behind was repeated. I put the car in gear and turned right. I glanced in my mirror and noticed the car that bumped me was rapidly followed in the turn by another.

"I think there may be more than one vehicle following us," I said.

"It figures," was his only reply, but then he added, "It's up to you, Doc. You got to get us away from them...what's that up ahead?"

"You mean the roundabout?" It was an unusual roundabout. The circle had been placed so asymmetrically that traffic coming towards me hardly had to turn their wheel, but I would have to drive almost three-quarters of the way around it to get back to my lane.

"Take it on the left, Doc."

"The left!"

"Yep, pretend you're in the old country and do it now."

There was a pickup coming towards me, but it was still about a hundred yards from the roundabout. If I was quick I could do it. The car was already in third gear. I pushed the gas pedal to the floor and accelerated towards the roundabout. At the last moment I swung into the oncoming lane and made it back to my lane just missing the pickup. The car which had been following me wasn't quite as lucky. I heard a screech of tires, horns, but no sounds of a crash.

"Good move, Doc. He's backing up now, but the other one's still on us," Smith reported.

But by now I had a hundred-and-fifty yards between us and my Subaru was still picking up speed.

The light the other side of the Highway 3 underpass was yellow as I shot across the intersection with Frontier Road. Smith was looking back and reported.

"They ran the red light. Where's a cop when you need one?"

I glanced at my speedometer and noticed we had just topped sixty – not bad for an old driver in an old car going uphill. It wasn't quick enough. Smith reported from the back.

"The other car's there now and they're catching up."

I had no idea what vehicles were following me and knew my Subaru couldn't compete for speed with most new cars, but it could still outdo them at maneuverability.

There was an almost-ninety-degree bend to the left coming up. I moved to the right, slowed a little and took the turn by cutting the corner and moving back to the right. I seemed to have gained about ten yards by this, but the first car after me quickly made up the gap and moved to pass me on my left. I waited until it had almost passed me, moved to the center of the road, braked, and careened into a right turn on Olympic View Road. I was probably doing fifty at the time and for a split second thought I wouldn't make it, but I kept control and hit the gas pedal again.

A glance in the mirror showed one of the cars, the one with the missing headlight, made the turn and was only about seventy-five yards back. I looked again and it was catching up. I knew there was only one exit on this road which would get me back to Silverdale, and it was coming up on my right.

I couldn't take it. It's a turn you have to slow down for anyway, and if there's a large white RV, with an SUV in tow, wanting to turn onto the road you are on...I didn't risk it. I flashed past the turn and the next road sign. Smith noticed the sign.

"Doc, it just said 'No Outlet'. Do you know where we're going?"

"I hope so." I had the beginnings of an idea. I noticed the car behind was not getting any closer. It was probably waiting for the other to catch up. I was now doing seventy and there were not many bends left to negotiate. I slowed a little for the curve before Cougar Valley Elementary school, and then picked up speed. In my mirror I could see both cars would soon be close again. I took one hand off the wheel, felt for my cell phone and handed it to Smith.

"Turn it off," I said.

He took a couple of seconds to figure it out, turned it off and handed it back to me.

"We could have just thrown it out," he said.

"We may still need it."

In the mirror I could see the cars behind were now both closing on me. I pushed the gas pedal to the floor and slowly my Subaru reached eighty, but the cars following kept up with me. On my right was the impenetrable chain-link fence of Bangor Navy Base, giving no hope of escape. I flashed past the first sign to Olympic View Loop Road. I had less than three miles before the road I was on ended. I had less than a mile, and much less than a minute, to try to get my plan to work. It was going to be tricky.

I dropped my speed a little and the two following cars caught up. The one with the missing headlight came up behind me while the other tried to pass on my left. I swung my car to the left. There was a bump as I side-swiped the front of the passing car. The Subaru's steering went wild for a few seconds. I regained control and noticed the car I hit pull back, but only for a moment. I picked up what speed I could and started zigzagging across the road, and then stayed a moment longer in the left lane. Fortunately, there was no traffic coming at me. I could see the cars behind close on each other. I had about five seconds before I had to make my turn. As one they both moved into the lane to my right and accelerated. The leading car had just pulled ahead of me, when I braked as hard as I could and turned left on Olympic View Loop Road's second access. We almost didn't make it. I slid off the road, and for a moment it seemed the Subaru would tip as its wheels tore into the shoulder, but it regained its balance. I took the next left, counted driveways and took a right. I made sure I was in the right driveway, turned off the lights, and coasted. Less than ten seconds later both following cars raced past the end of the driveway behind me. It wasn't going to take them long to figure out what happened. My only advantage was they didn't know which driveway I'd taken.

I risked a short flash of my sidelights to make sure I wasn't going to hit one of the trees which lined the driveway, corrected my steering a little and pulled to a halt using the hand-brake. I hoped my car was not visible from the road, but I wasn't going to take the time to check. I looked back towards the road and a vehicle drove past the end of the driveway. If they searched logically, and I had no reason to think they wouldn't, they would start checking from two directions, going down each driveway in turn. At best we had three to four minutes.

"Where are we, Doc?" Smith asked.

"We're at a friend's summer cabin on the Hood Canal. They aren't here at the moment."

"We're going to make a stand here or something?"

"No, just do what I say. We haven't got much time. Get your bags and follow me."

I realized I had a car full of food which could be useful, but I put the idea out of my mind when I saw the headlights of a car turn into the driveway. I grabbed one item out of my glove box – a small flashlight.

"Follow me," I said.

With me leading we walked quickly to the other side of the house.

"Stay here a second," I told Smith.

I walked onto the porch, which on a summer's day afforded a drop-dead view of the Olympic Mountains and Hood Canal, and felt for the key above the patio door. I unlocked the door and replaced the key. I rejoined Smith and led him down a short, grassy slope. There was very little light to guide us and I couldn't risk using the flashlight.

"Now keep close," I said.

"Where are we going?"

"Down the cliff."

I hoped that whoever was following us would check out the house and find the unlocked door before looking further, but there were no guarantees.

At the southern end of the small slope a dense undergrowth of head-high bushes appeared to block our way, but I knew this was the access point to a trail which led down the sixty feet to the water's edge. In mid-summer, during the day, when there had been no rain for a month, the trail was tricky, but at night-time, in rain in November it did not want to be disturbed. The only positive discovery was the owners had taken the time to cut back the vegetation which threatened each year to smother the trail. Out of sight of the house I risked an occasional beam of flashlight, but we still slithered, slid, and fell down most of the trail. In places where the trail was steeper and had been replaced by decking, steep steps, and hand rails, we could move more quickly, but we were bruised and soaked by the time we made it to the narrow beach.

I risked a stab of light from my flashlight and revealed the inflatable dinghy tied to an overhanging branch above the high-tide line.

I knew it 'd been used in the meantime, but it was back where I'd left it in August.

I allowed myself a brief moment of relief, then indicated to Smith to help me turn it over and move it to the water. We slid and carried it until it was floating and stable beyond where the small Hood Canal waves were hitting the shore. Smith sat in first. I pushed us out a little further, took the oars and rowed away from land and to Dick's sailboat, Roho.

She was resting at her moorage, where Ann and I had last seen her, after our sexless "honeymoon" in August.

I could just make her out in the gloom. As we approached I could see she was pointing south, which meant the tide was still going out. I adjusted my rowing so we reached her bow first and held onto the buoy to which she was moored.

Dick, like all good sailors, had two lines holding her to the buoy. These were both clipped on with stainless steel carabiners. It was a simple system, but it seemed to take me forever to find and loosen them. Trying to detach the lines while sitting in the dinghy was difficult, but eventually I succeeded and both sailboat and dinghy began to drift north with the current and away from our pursuers. I secured one of the lines from the sailboat to the dinghy and looked back at the cliff-face we'd come down.

I could see a flashlight bobbing on the lower half of the trail. The light reached the bottom then scanned up and down the beach.

"Get down!" I said. We were over two hundred yards away, but when the flashlight turned to the water I tried to lie down as much as possible in the dinghy.

The beam paused for several seconds in our direction.

I didn't think we could be seen at that distance, but the white hull of the sailboat would have been visible.

We had escaped, but for how long?

17

We continued to drift north with both the sailboat and dinghy rotating slowly in the current.

We'd escaped from our pursuers, but now we were getting colder by the minute. If we didn't get on board the sailboat soon we wouldn't be able to – we would be disabled by hypothermia. Already my hands were finding it hard to grasp the gunwale of the sail boat and I was shivering uncontrollably. Smith was better off than me and seemed to be moving easily. He was a couple of inches taller, younger, and about fifty pounds heavier, which probably made the difference. We'd both been up to our thighs in water, and we both had on rain-jackets with only one layer underneath. Neither of us had expected to go boating on a cold, wet evening in November.

Holding on to the sailboat I pulled us around to the stern and with difficulty pulled down the swim ladder. I tied the dinghy to it and told Smith to climb into the cockpit first.

He managed to get a grip on the upper rung of the ladder and pull himself up. I tried to push him, but found my efforts were better directed at keeping the dinghy close and stable to the sailboat. A couple of times he slipped before he made it into the cockpit. I threw his bags up after him, and it took me another two minutes of gripping and sliding before I joined him. A few more minutes in the dinghy and I wasn't sure my body would have had the strength to move.

Dick had installed a combination lock on his companionway access. I could remember the number, but it was too dark to see. I thought of my cell-phone, hesitated for a few seconds, but realized if I didn't turn it on and use its light to see the lock, we wouldn't survive. Then I remembered the flashlight I had in my pocket. I located the lock, but found I couldn't turn the numbers to the correct combination. I asked Smith to try it. As I held the flashlight he opened the lock and together we removed the companionway boards and climbed down into the cabin. It helped I knew the boat well and could find my way in the dark. I fumbled for the master switch, turned it, and put on a single interior light. Together we looked around to see what we could use. We found towels, hats, sleeping bags, and rubber boots.

Dick had finally given up his beloved kerosene stove and oven at the beginning of the year and installed a propane replacement. The propane tank was stored at the stern in the lazarette. I prayed whoever had last used the boat had not turned it off there, and was relieved to be able to light the stove without another trip outside. I also lit the oven – the only form of heating on the boat. Dick had always kept a few cans of soup and stew on board. Usually, they were of questionable safety (their external metal rusted rapidly in the humidity and salt environment) but the clam chowder I found seemed to have been a relatively recent addition to the larder. Only a few rust stains had penetrated its label. I opened the can and poured the contents into a saucepan. I could feel the cabin warming, but now I had to get myself warm. I was still shivering. It would come in spasms and I had to concentrate to pull off my wet jeans and dry my legs with a towel. I put on a wool cap under the hood of my jacket and returned to the stove in my underwear. The soup was hot enough to drink and I poured a cup for each of us.

I was still shivering, which made drinking the soup, and even holding the cup, difficult. I looked around the boat to see if I could find any extra clothing. At the back of a locker I found a fleece jacket, a sweat shirt and sweat pants (which I immediately put on) and four pairs of socks. There were two pairs of waterproof jackets and trousers in the hanging locker, and a couple of bulky offshore life-jackets which would provide good insulation. I was going to put one on, hesitated when I thought it better to wait until I had to go outside, then realized I needed to be outside anyway.

We were slowly drifting north with the outgoing tide, but I'd no idea how long it would last, or if our course would be reversed when the tide turned. There was also the possibility of running aground or bumping into something else. I knew if we drifted far enough north we ran the risk of tangling with the marines who guarded the restricted waters off Bangor Submarine Base. I'd heard they didn't take kindly to anyone trying to steal one of the Navy's expensive Trident submarines. Rumor had it they assumed anyone who didn't have permission to be in their area was a kleptomaniac international terrorist. Part of me would have taken the risk, but I knew Smith wouldn't have wanted to end up in federal hands. I hadn't asked him what was in the bags we had brought with us, but I suspected whatever the contents they would not have helped endear ourselves to the military.

I put the key in the ignition, turned it, and pressed the glow-plug button. Dick may have upgraded his stove, but his old Westerbeke diesel required at least sixty seconds of pre-heat before it decided to wake up, and even then you had to be nice to it. Apparently, I wasn't being nice enough. It took another minute of heating before the motor started to react, first on two cylinders and finally on four. I left the motor to warm up. So far I had managed to start her from the relative comfort of the cabin, but now I had no choice but to climb out to the cockpit and figure out the next step. I tightened the hood of my jacket and the life jacket straps and climbed back to the cockpit.

The brilliant lighting of the docks at the Navy Base was probably about three quarters of a mile away, and we seemed to be almost still in the water. From the reflection of the lighting I could see the tide was still moving out but a mild breeze from the north was counteracting this. Apart from that I could see the lights of a few houses to the east of me and total darkness to the west. For the moment we were safe.

Back below I checked on Smith. He'd been uncharacteristically quiet and was sitting on a berth finishing his soup. I explained our situation.

"I think the first thing we have to do is steer clear of the Navy Base. I don't really want to end up there and I suspect you don't either?"

He nodded.

"So, we have to go west and stop before we hit the Toandos Peninsula, which is only a couple of miles away, then head north. I think we should aim for Port Ludlow or Port Townsend. We should be able to get help there. The only problem is it's completely black out there, apart from the Base, so I need to look at the charts and see where we should be going."

"OK, Doc, and thanks."

"What for?" I was surprised.

"Getting us out of there."

"Let's see where we end up before we congratulate each other. We may be out of the frying pan and into the fire."

I hadn't had time to think about it much, but since the car chase and our climb down the cliff, he hadn't been his usual, pushy self. Our roles seemed to have reversed. Now I was determining our future and he was following.

I found what I wanted under the mattress of one of the bunks and pulled out the chart book to see if it would help us. Like most fjords Hood Canal is deep with steep banks and minimal beaches. We may not have been able to see where we were, but if we went due west and watched the depth sounder we would be safe. I turned on the instruments and read we were currently at thirty-two fathoms. The middle of the channel at this part of the Canal was over fifty fathoms. We could go west until we reached twenty fathoms, then take a heading a little east of north of about twenty degrees. This should bring us in sight of the flashing buoy at Brown Point. Then all we had to do was head a little more north until we could see the Hood Canal Bridge. It seemed simple.

I switched on the navigation lights – we might as well be legal – and climbed outside again. I checked to make sure the dinghy was safely attached and no lines were in the water to wrap around the propeller. I put her in gear, noted the heading and turned west leaving the lights of Bangor behind me to my right.

I had to assume there would be no major cross-currents at that part of the Hood Canal, so I kept her speed to four knots and watched the depth meter. The Canal bottomed out at fifty-nine fathoms; slowly the depth came up to thirty-four, then rapidly changed to twenty. I looked at my watch. It had taken just under twenty-five minutes to get to this point. I turned north, corrected my course to twenty degrees, and allowed myself to relax a little.

I rechecked my watch. It was 9:15 pm. Two hours ago I'd been sitting in my car, worlds away, at Costco. Ann would be expecting me home soon and Shanty would have wondered why I hadn't been at the high school to take him home. I considered using my cellphone, but I wasn't sure if it could be monitored. Could someone listen to my conversations? It seemed as long as it was on I was broadcasting my position to someone. I decided to leave it turned off. I secured the tiller as best I could with the rope and bungee-cord device Dick had devised for this and went below.

Smith was standing and warming himself by the stove.

"What's up, Doc?" he asked – some of his personality was returning.

"We're heading north," I replied.

"On auto-pilot?"

"Not exactly. I'll have to go and check in a minute or two."

We divided the last of the chowder and I carried my bowl with me back to the cockpit.

The "self-steering" device was already "failing" and we were on a heading which would have taken us back across the canal. I readjusted the course and realized I would have to stay at the tiller until we had more sea-room to play with. To my right, the east, the dockside lights of the Navy Base glowed through the dark and drizzle, but apart from that I had no way of knowing where I was, apart from my compass heading and the depth sounder. Somewhere on board there was supposed to be a hand-held GPS.

It was cold and getting colder. The breeze was coming right at us down the canal and seemed to be getting stronger. I checked our speed and it had dropped to three-and-a-half knots. We were being slowed by the wind, so I increased the engine speed until we picked up to four knots again. With the tide about to start coming back in it would slow our speed further. For the time being there wasn't much we could do about that.

I managed about ten minutes outside before I knew I had to go below to warm up or I would be in trouble. Smith was sitting wrapped in a sleeping bag.

"No point in getting cold," he said, indicating the sleeping bag and asked, "Back so soon, Doc?".

"It's cold out there. I had to take a break."

"Let me spell you, Doc. We'll take ten minutes down here and ten up there. OK?"

"You up to it?"

"Do we have an alternative?"

We didn't. Smith wrapped himself as best he could. I gave him my wool hat and the remaining fleece jacket and he climbed into the cockpit.

"Can you see the compass?" I asked.

"Yes."

"Steer as close to twenty degrees as you can."

"OK."

"And check the depth gauge. If it goes to less than twenty let me know."

"OK. It's...it's twenty-nine right now."

I had no idea if he'd steered a boat before, but I could feel the boat move a little to right and left as he figured out the steering.

I had ten minutes before I was due out again. I refilled the saucepan with water I found in a bottle in the cooler and turned up the gas. I rummaged in the electrical box where Dick usually kept his GPS, but it was not there. Eventually, I found it hiding under a pillow in the V-berth. I switched it on and the battery meter showed there were about two-thirds of power left. I confirmed our course and speed. I converted the hot water into hot chocolate and it was time for my shift.

I took my cup with me and relieved Smith at the tiller. I checked our depth, course and speed, then looked around. The lights of the Navy Base were still visible behind us and to the right, and coming up on our left was the flashing red buoy of Brown Point. It was impossible to know how far away it was. I thought about checking our position with the GPS, but that would have meant a trip to the cabin. In the meantime I changed the heading to fifteen degrees. I'd check the chart after my next shift. In theory this would bring us closer to the straight line between Brown Point and the Hood Canal Bridge some ten miles away.

I hadn't thought it could get much colder, but I was wrong. The wind was picking up and I could see the occasional white-cap form from the reflection of the cabin light on the water. I vaguely remembered a forecast of cold wind and possibly snow, but couldn't remember the details beyond that. So far Dick's boat, Roho, was handling the sea and weather well – she was probably glad to be free of her mooring. Dick had once told me she had a sister-ship which had sailed around the world. I would be happy if we made it the eighteen miles to Port Ludlow.

At the end of my shift I was ready to get back to the shelter of the cabin. Ten minutes standing at the tiller in that weather was all I could bear. Maybe with better clothing I could have stood it for longer, but we were already wearing every stitch of clothing we'd found on board.

I reset Dick's "autopilot" and went below.

"What direction?" Smith asked as he climbed the steps, "Same as before?"

"Close. Let's make it fifteen degrees."

"She's pointing at forty," he shouted down. "This thing is useless." Again I felt the boat move as he corrected the course.

He was right. We had to find another way of keeping our heading constant and ourselves out of the elements. I looked around for something which might work and found a boathook in the V berth. If I lashed it to the tiller it might be long enough for us to steer from the relative shelter of the companionway. At my next shift I tried to set up the system. It wasn't ideal, and there was more play in the steering than I wanted, but considering the drizzle, the wind, and my soaked gloves I managed to set up a workable tiller extension. In the wind and rain we couldn't really see where we were going, so looking ahead wasn't necessary until we were closer to the Hood Canal Bridge. We could also steer using the GPS. However, despite increasing the engine speed, we had dropped again to three-and-a-half knots. I compared the speed on the GPS too and this indicated a little under three knots. It seemed the tide had turned and was now beginning to push against us. I opened the throttle to bring the speed up to four knots as measured by the GPS. According to my estimation we would reach the Hood Canal Bridge by about midnight.

For the next hour we spoke little as we continued northward. My addition of the boathook to the tiller made life more bearable. One of us had to sit on the companionway steps and steer according to the GPS heading. It took a while to get accustomed to looking south, traveling north, and steering backwards, but we were sheltered and had both warmed up. However, we were both feeling the effects of fatigue and the pleasant, but dangerous, sensation of feeling warm and tired again.

I had intended to carry on when I reached the Hood Canal Bridge, but I wondered if this was the right plan. It's a floating bridge and there are only a few ways of getting through it. Back in the summer we'd followed a boat through the middle section, which opened by request, but at both ends there were fixed parts of the bridge. Looking at the chart it was only the east side of the Bridge that would give us sufficient clearance to sail under. And then what? We hadn't decided what to do. We hadn't talked much at all and there was a lot to discuss. I'd driven over the Bridge many times, and when it's windy, and there's an incoming tide I'd seen the watery turmoil this produced. I wasn't sure how we would cope sailing under the east side. There might be more wind and tide than we could deal with. Already, at times a stronger gust would hit us. The bow would rise and smash into the waves. The boat speed would drop and slowly pick up again when the wind eased a little. The fifteen horsepower motor was designed for getting in and out of marinas, not ploughing through waves in twenty miles-per-hour winds.

What we needed was to take a break – Squamish Harbor looked like it might work. At least, looking at the chart, it seemed the only place to shelter from the wind. It was to the west of the Bridge and on its north side lay a hundred feet of Hood Canal cliff. However, that's all it had. There would be no moorings, bright lights, bars or other signs of civilization. It was probably much as it had been when it was named. On the chart it looked like it was shallow enough for an anchor to hold, and deep enough we wouldn't run aground. I told Smith my plans and showed him on the chart what I intended to do.

"So we go in between these buoys?"

"That's the idea."

"How close to them do we get?"

"Not too close. They're both numbered. It looks like one is numbered '4' and the other '6', and they are both flashing red, but they seem to be close to hazards we don't want to be close to. So, if we can try to keep them about the same distance away it might be good. Then it looks like we go slowly until we get to six fathoms and drop the anchor. What do you think?"

"I agree. We need a rest, and maybe in the morning we'll have a better idea of what we can do. Where are we now?"

I checked the GPS and it looked like we were a little bit west of our intended course, but closer to Squamish Harbor.

I slid the companionway hatch open and looked out. In the distance I could see the glow of lights from the Bridge, although it was still over two miles away. To my right I thought I could see a flashing green marker which I'd noticed on the chart, but I wasn't sure. We'd kept a light on in the cabin since we didn't really need to know what was going on outside, but now it seemed we would need our night vision. I closed the hatch, switched on the red navigation-station light, turned off the cabin light, detached our makeshift steering device and climbed into the cockpit.

Maybe it was the contrast between the cabin's warmth and the cockpit weather, but it felt even more miserable to be standing outside again. The wind and the drizzle were icy and my face and hands rapidly became stiff and cold. However, as I looked around I could see both buoys marking the reefs and shoals at the sides of the wide entrance to Squamish Harbor. I changed direction and aimed the bow between them.

The wind was now coming at us from the right and the motion of the boat through the water changed. She picked up a little speed since she was no longer directly battling the wind, but she rolled more with the waves on her starboard beam. With the wind threatening to push us sideways, and the tide coming in, I thought it would be safer to be closer to buoy '4'. I aimed her just a little west of due north so we would end up at the northern end of the bay. I hoped this would bring us the shelter the chart promised.

At the end of my ten minutes I called to Smith.

"We both need to be up here now. I'll go forward and drop the anchor while you steer her, but I want to check the GPS first."

"OK," Smith answered.

He took over steering and I went below. According to the GPS we were just where I wanted to be. I checked the depth sounder and we were in twelve fathoms of water. If we aimed at a course of about 270° we could wait until we reached six fathoms, and then drop the anchor.

It was not a great plan, but it was the best I could think up. The anchor may not set, it might get stuck, and I didn't know how quickly the water shallowed.

I talked to Smith about the plan. He changed the course to 270° and cut the speed to two knots. The wind lessened, so at least one aspect of the plan was working . The boat was rocking less, and the further we crept forward, the calmer boat, water, and crew became.

I clambered forward to the anchor. With my small flashlight in my teeth I untied the anchor tethers. Smith called to me when we reached six fathoms and put her in reverse. I shone my light on the water and when I saw we'd stopped, told him to put the engine in neutral. I released the anchor. We put her in reverse for ten seconds then waited in neutral again. I estimated I had paid out about a hundred feet of line before I tied it off and waited. The line went taut, the bow of the boat dipped a little with the tension, pulled back up a little, dipped again and held. It looked like the anchor was set. I let out another twenty feet of line, tied her off and waited. Again, it looked like the anchor was holding. I thought about letting out more line, but was concerned about the boat swinging to shallow water if I gave her too much.

I went below, checked the GPS for a couple of minutes to see if we were holding. The reading didn't change so I relaxed a little. There was probably another anchor on board, which I could have used for extra security, but I'd had enough. At some point you realize you can't make everything perfect.

18

I reached out from the cabin and turned off the engine. It seemed unnaturally quiet for a few seconds until we became accustomed to the sound of the wind in the forest at the edge of the fjord. Apart from the occasional gust, when the boat swayed at anchor, we were relatively sheltered from the storm. The companionway entrance could be closed by three boards. I put in the bottom two and left the top one out for ventilation. We had a propane-fuelled oven heating the cabin and I didn't want to die from carbon dioxide poisoning. There was plenty of ventilation to ensure we had a good turnover of the interior air, but I didn't want to take any chances. I took off most of my outer clothes and found I was warm with only a shirt and fleece on.

Smith had busied himself heating a pan of water with which he made hot chocolate for both of us. We sat down on opposite sides of the table facing each other. I started.

"I think we're OK here for a few hours. I reckon the tide should change again at maybe four or five in the morning. It's probably light around seven or eight and that's when we can move on. What do you think?"

"That seems about right, Doc."

"Right, but what are we doing here in the first place?"

"It was you who got us on this boat."

"You know that's not what I mean," I said.

"You mean who was after us back there?"

"Exactly. Why are we running, who are we running from, and where are we running to?" I asked.

"I know why we're running. Those guys back there in those cars weren't messing around. I don't think they wanted to just chat with us. I think they were after what I have in my bag here, and if they walk over us to get to it they wouldn't care. By now they may even have orders to either get hold of, or destroy, what I have. But I have to level with you. That might include destroying me and anyone around me."

"Ah...I didn't want to hear that."

"Sorry, Doc, but that's what I think."

"Maybe I was trying not to think about that. I was afraid that's what you'd say. At least they can't get at us here."

"I hope you're right. I assume this boat has no vessel identification signal it's sending out?"

"I don't think Dick has anything like that. We may not even show on anyone's radar. He has a radar reflector, but I don't know how effective it is. I don't really want to go outside and bring it down, and I don't think anyone would have been tracking us on radar."

"You're probably right," Smith stood. "However, I've already made assumptions that proved to be incorrect, so we can't afford to take risks. Is it easy to take down?"

"Yes."

"Where is it?"

"It's attached to the starboard spreader by a line which is tied off at the bottom end of the shroud."

"You mean about there?" He pointed through the boat's side to where the radar detector was attached.

"Yeah."

"Well, I've still got my gear on. I'll go."

"Take a knife and cut the line. It'll be quicker."

He took a kitchen knife, removed the companionway boards, climbed on deck, and was back in the cabin within two minutes. He handed the radar reflector to me. While he replaced the boards I took apart the spherical reflector and laid it flat on a berth.

"I think we should also go back to red light and not display the anchor light," I said.

He agreed.

I changed the lighting. By the time we sat down again it had taken us less than five minutes and we'd done our best to make the boat as undetectable as possible. I sipped my hot chocolate and asked.

"Do you think it would be safe to use my cell phone now?"

"I don't know."

"My wife's going to be wondering what happened to me. She's probably already made some phone calls."

"I think it's probably better if you don't use your phone until we know what we're doing."

"Then what are we doing?" I said.

"We're going to be staying here for a while?"

"Yeah. Until it gets light anyway."

"Then what do you have in mind?"

"Port Townsend is probably less than fifteen miles away. Port Ludlow is even closer and the weather is lousy, so maybe that's where we head for. Both have marinas we could sail into and get help. I was thinking that would be our best plan."

"I think you're probably right," Smith said. "I don't think going back to where we left your car is a good idea. It's too isolated and I assume there's nowhere else we could get help?"

"There are some smaller marinas, but I don't know much about them."

"At some point we are going to have to let someone know where we are and where we will be. I assume your FBI friends will come running if you call them."

"I hope so. Why don't I call them now?" I suggested.

"Because I'm not sure who is after us and what resources they have at their disposal."

"What do you mean?"

"This whole thing has gone to shit. It hasn't played out like I expected and I'm beginning to wonder if there isn't someone else involved now. I haven't felt comfortable about this whole thing. For some reason it hasn't been right from the start – even before I heard Preston had died, or been killed. It didn't seem like the work of the people I'd been dealing with for the last ten years."

"Well, who do you think it is then?"

"You're going to think me paranoid, but I'm thinking government."

I raised my eyebrows and grunted.

"Yeah, I know. The government is the bad guy in every conspiracy theory we've ever heard, but it would fit. Even if it isn't the government it's better to assume the worst. The point is if you call and get your FBI friends to help and they come running, someone else may be running faster."

"You think so?" This was a totally alien way of thinking. I paid my taxes and in return I believed in a benign form of government. Well, maybe not benign, but at least not too toxic, and yet Smith was obviously not discounting this possibility.

He continued, "I think it's possible, Doc. I don't think it's the FBI, but it could be. Your two friends I met at Shanty's house are probably straight, but they seem to be running whatever operation they're doing on a shoe-string, and I can see why. They probably don't trust anyone in DC any more than you or me. It turned out to be dumb luck to concentrate on Shanty's campaign, and they don't seem to have any back-up, so if we call them I don't know if they can call on a wider selection of agents to help."

"But we can't stay out here on a boat forever. At some point we'll have to make contact either by phone or when we get to land."

"How about we get on land, walk away from the boat, then call for help and see who turns up?" Smith suggested.

I thought that over before replying.

"It might work. Of course, there are only a couple of options to where we're likely to land, so we couldn't be certain of not having a reception committee waiting for us wherever we go."

"I know. But, like you said, we can't stay out here forever. At some point we have to make a decision and commit to it."

I nodded agreement and said, "I suppose we could try for one of the marinas further south in the Sound, like Edmonds or Kingston, but I think it would take a lot longer to get to one and, at least to begin with, we are both going to be outside sailing tomorrow. We're going to get cold."

"Then we'd better get some sleep now. Agree?"

"Agree."

We finished our drinks and both agreed bladder emptying could, just this once, take place in the correct cabin receptacle in the head, and not outside in the usual male way over the stern of the boat. I turned off the propane oven, rotated the battery control so only the house battery powered the red lighting, and pulled myself into a sleeping bag. Smith had done the same in the V berth at the front of the boat, and I lay down on the broad seat in the cabin.

I checked my watch. It was coming up on 1:15 am.

19

It was a restless night with sleep not coming easily. The sudden squalls that rocked the boat seemed to get more frequent and it was hard not to think of the challenges dawn would bring. But I was warm and dry and must have fallen asleep a few times. I was woken by the sound of clinking cups as Smith filled them with hot water from the stove. It was 6:15 am.

"Good morning, Doc. Good to see you're awake. I was going to give you a few more minutes then give you a nudge. Coffee and oatmeal OK? Sleep OK?"

"Better than I thought I would, I think." I replied.

"Mm...brain not woken up yet perhaps?"

"Apparently not."

"Well, no chance of another hour or two in bed today."

"No chance."

I unzipped my sleeping bag and reluctantly left its warmth for the cabin, which had cooled enough in the night for us to now see our breath. I used the head, and came back for my oatmeal.

Smith said, "I believe in Scotland they call oatmeal, porridge. Is that correct?"

"Yes, and 'doing porridge' means spending time in prison. I was told it's because that's all you get served for breakfast there, or because life there is bland and boring, like porridge."

"I think the breakfast reason is more likely. The bland and boring sounds too philosophical to me."

I shrugged my shoulders and concentrated on eating my oatmeal and drinking my coffee. I re-lit the oven to give us more heat, and then braved a look outside.

The wind speed must have increased during the night. I could hear it howling through the trees on the nearby cliffs. It was now coming from the north-east and meant we weren't as protected in the small bay, but the waves still didn't have much distance to build up height, and Roho was riding comfortably at anchor.

It had stopped drizzling.

It was snowing.

I reported my findings to Smith.

"Snow. Does that change our plans?" he asked.

"I don't think so. I think we should try for Port Ludlow as soon as it's light. I need to figure out how we're going to do this."

We stuffed the breakfast dishes in the sink and spread out the chart on the table. I switched from red to regular cabin lights so we could see the chart. Most of the Hood Canal Bridge is floating with just two raised fixed spans at each end to allow boats to pass. Because of our mast height I confirmed we would have to go under the east side of the bridge, but it was hard to know if the wind would help with this. The banks of Hood Canal were not as high there, and we wouldn't know the effect of this, or the main body of the bridge, on the direction of the tides and wind until we were there. I also didn't know how close we could get to the bridge to see if it was possible to make it through because of the snow reducing our visibility.

There was one other major sailing unknown. We were on a sailboat and sailboats do better under sail, not under power. She would handle much better with sails up than she would without, but it was possible they might slow us down going under the bridge. I discussed this with Smith. We had about an hour before it would be light enough, and safe enough, to pull up the anchor. In the meantime I suggested we put up the sails as soon as possible, and then come back into the cabin to warm up before we set off. We were going to put up minimum sails. This meant a small storm jib for the front sail, and we would reduce the surface area of the mainsail by two reefs. I had no idea if this was still too much sail, but I couldn't see any alternative.

One Christmas day, shortly after I moved to Washington State I went for a walk in Manchester State Park. It had snowed the previous night and there was snow on the beach. It seemed so strange. I'd always associated beaches with sun and summer. For some reason my brain thought the snow shouldn't have been there then, and for the same reason it shouldn't be collecting now. It was wet snow, but it was beginning to stick, and made it harder to hank on the storm jib to the forestay. Eventually we succeeded and left it flapping while we paid attention to the mainsail. Smith pulled on the main halyard and I allowed the sail up enough to tie in the second reef. We left it and retreated to the cabin stiff and cold. It had taken us twenty minutes to put up both sails and we were played out by the time I replaced the two lower companionway boards and sat down. We didn't need to make any comments. We knew we didn't have anything left in reserve. Reaching Port Ludlow would be all we could expect to do, and we might need luck to get that far.

It was warm in the cabin and we drank more coffee to prepare for the ordeal ahead. I started the engine again. I thought we would probably need it and it also helped keep the cabin warm.

By 8:00 we decided it was light enough to move. We both climbed up to the cockpit and looked around. The snow was still falling and now that we could see better it seemed to be flowing almost horizontally. The grey and green cliffs to our north could be distinguished, but any other features were whited out by the snow. I estimated visibility to be about four hundred yards. It was also disorientating. The movement of the snow and the boat was harder to tolerate when we had nothing to fix our eyes on, and I was already feeling a little queasy. We needed to get going.

Smith went forward and I noticed he had wrapped his shoes in plastic supermarket bags to try to keep them dry. He pulled the anchor up with no difficulty. I put her in gear and we moved east out of the bay.

The further we moved from the protection of the cliffs the stronger and steadier the wind became. I headed east until we could see all the bridge. The bridge runs across Hood Canal from north-west to south-east and the wind from the north-east was hitting it at a right angle. We were on its sheltered side so were not taking the full force of the wind and waves. I tightened up the jib and mainsail and made a course parallel to the bridge. I stayed about two hundred yards away where I hoped there was enough shelter and not too much wind. She heeled to about fifteen degrees and sliced eastwards through the sheltered waters.

One of the decisions we had made before we set off was to go straight for the passage at the east end. While we had thought it would be prudent to check this out by cautiously approaching and reconnoitering, we agreed we didn't have the luxury of being able to do this. The longer we spent outside the less likely we would have the strength to make it to Port Ludlow.

I could see the steel girders of the bridge appearing through the snow. It looked lower than I thought it should be for us to sail through, but the chart said it was possible.

I tightened up the main and jib and pointed her at the far end of the bridge span. The closer I got to the floating part of the bridge the less wind filled the sails, so I was concerned about losing speed. I pushed the throttle all the way forward and heard the diesel respond. I glanced at the speed and we were making about six knots.

As we came out of the shelter of the floating bridge into the open water the wind suddenly increased, hit us broadside and we heeled to forty-five degrees. Smith and I both grabbed on to the life-lines as she recovered to twenty-five, rounded a little into the wind and passed under the roadway. A minute later we cleared the bridge but were heading directly towards a rapidly approaching beach.

We had no choice but to tack.

"Ready about?" I shouted.

"Ready," Smith replied.

"Lee ho."

Smith released the jib, I pushed the tiller away from me and the boat swung around into the wind. I ducked my head as the boom swung across and banged into place. The mainsail filled but the jib had not come round. One of the jib sheets had jammed under the edge of the forward hatch vent. The sail was pushing the bow around and the boat was again leaning at forty-five degrees, heading directly for the floating part of the bridge. I tried to control the tiller with one hand and released the main sheet with the other. This brought her back up to a more respectable twenty degrees, but we were still heading on a collision course towards the bridge. Smith disappeared into the cabin and I was faced with a choice. I could take the safe way out and turn south to bring us to the sheltered side of the bridge, and we could attempt this all over again, or I could try to head her back into the wind and away from the bridge. Anyone who knows me would expect me to choose the safer way. I would have done, but at the moment of decision, the front hatch flew open briefly, Smith's arm reached out and released the jib sheet. Without the pressure on the sail I managed to point her more into the wind and to safety. I tightened up the mainsail. Smith came back and winched the jib tight. I shouted a thank you into the wind. He shrugged and watched.

With the engine still running flat out we headed slowly away from the bridge and as we left the relative shelter of the east end of the Canal the wind direction moved more favorably in our direction and we could relax a little. But it was a rough ride. The remains of the force of the outgoing tide and the opposing wind created standing waves near the east side which the boat rode, then plunged, or cut through, burying her bow in the water at times. As we moved further towards the middle of the bridge, and we encountered the full force of the wind, we could see waves hitting the floating pontoons and splashing onto the roadway. They also created an unpredictable undulating back wash of foam and spray through which we were now thrusting and dipping, but the further we moved away from the bridge the steadier the boat became. I cut back the motor.

It was good to get away from the maelstrom on the north side of the bridge, but the bridge had given us a landmark. Now we had none. All we knew was it was snowing, we were moving under sail and motor at five knots, and we were near the top of Hood Canal.

Somewhere in front of me was Hood Head, a rocky promontory I did not want to run in to, and beyond that were Foulweather Bluff and the opening to Puget Sound. I guessed it was about fifteen to twenty minutes since we pulled up the anchor and maybe five minutes since we cleared the bridge, but despite the activity of holding on and steering I was already feeling very cold. Smith had stayed with me in the cockpit, and found a little shelter from the weather by standing on the companionway steps. If we were to get out of this alive we'd have to take shifts on the tiller again.

I called to him, "We need to go about. OK?"

He nodded and came into the cockpit with me. I called out the orders, pulled the tiller towards me and she came around. This time the jib sheet didn't get stuck and we made the turn without incident. I asked Smith to tighten the jib as much as possible and I did the same with the main. This way we headed as much into the wind as we could. It made for a rougher ride with the bow dipping into the waves and spray hitting us, but it would give me a little time to figure out our next moves. I asked Smith to take the tiller, showed him what I wanted, and went below.

I'd been feeling queasy and had a slight headache from the disorienting effect of the horizontal snow and waves in the cockpit. In the cabin it was ten times worse and it was all I could do to avoid vomiting. I checked the chart and the GPS. We were now heading east and the GPS reading showed we were at a longitude of 122° 37' W. If we tacked again when we reached 122° 35' and then sailed a course of 312 on the compass we should be able to turn west towards Port Ludlow when we got to 47° 57' N. There was a compass rose on the chart which indicated the magnetic north deviation in the area. I tried to figure out if it was in our favor, but my brain wouldn't work with the nausea and headache. I wrote the numbers down on a scrap of paper and returned to the cockpit.

As I looked out over the stern I could see the inflatable dinghy we'd used to get on the boat the previous night was still attached to us. It was half full of water. I wondered why it wasn't completely full, but as I watched it jumped a wave and water splashed out of it, only to rush back in when it didn't jump the next one. It was slowing us down, and I thought about cutting its line, but then again, if we had come this far with it following us it couldn't be causing too much of a problem.

I told Smith of the plan and asked him to tell me when we got to the turning point and sent him below to warm up. He didn't argue with me. Less than ten minutes later he came back to the cockpit.

"We're there," he said.

I nodded.

"Ready?" I asked.

He nodded and we turned. We tightened up the sails and again headed into the wind, close-hauled, on a course of 312, or as near as we could steer in the weather. After a couple of minutes I went below after agreeing we would change every ten minutes. Once again I looked at the chart and it seemed the magnetic deviation would work in our favor. We might be heading more east than I anticipated, but the wind was pushing us west. I hoped they balanced out. I also figured out if we maintained over forty fathoms under our keel we should be safe. I checked the GPS. We were on course, and making three and a half knots, but the battery indicator showed we only had one of five bars of power left. I looked around for replacement batteries but this only made me feel even more nauseated. I turned off the GPS. I'd turn it on in one hour, by which time we'd be nearer the top of the canal. I drank a glass of hot water, hoping it would warm me up, but my stomach revolted and I vomited into the sink. My ten minutes were up and I returned to the cockpit.

Keeping the boat's bow on track required constant attention to the tiller as she bucked and cut the waves, but even this activity, which would have had me sweating on a warm day in summer, didn't slow down the freeze which crept over me every ten minutes. Much as I hated the sea-sickness it was preferable to the stinging salt spray, the cold and the snow in the cockpit.

I returned to the cabin and washed the salt spray off my glasses. This time I lay down on a berth, shivering, and closed my eyes. I was already exhausted.

I remembered a time in college when a group of friends had sailed a small boat from Cardiff, across the Bristol Channel, to a port somewhere in Somerset. Getting there on the Saturday seemed fine, but it probably didn't help we had too much Somerset cider that night, one of the women in the overcrowded boat had a bladder infection and had to pee every hour, and a leaking diesel line added its aroma to the cabin, so before we left the small harbor the next morning I was throwing-up. I threw up every five to ten minutes for the rest of the four-hour crossing. My friends held onto my legs as I leaned over the gunwale and watched the ocean whisk my bile away. At one point I remember wishing the ocean would take me away and end it all.

Memories of that trip came back to me every time I got sea-sick. I tried to push them away and thought of this trip and what had happened. I'd driven over the Hood Canal Bridge many times, and sometimes in windy weather, but had never experienced waves and spray reaching the roadway, probably because when that happened the bridge was closed to traffic. It then occurred to me that I hadn't seen any vehicles on the Bridge. There weren't likely to be many on a Sunday morning in November, but there were none, so it was probably closed to traffic. No big deal until I thought a little more.

Our plans called for getting the cavalry to rescue us once we got to Port Ludlow. We were going to call when we were on dry land. What if the cavalry couldn't get to us?

I sat up quickly. I shouldn't have done because I just made it to the sink before I vomited again. I climbed up to the cockpit to Smith. I explained the situation as quickly as possible and said.

"I think we need to make the call now."

"Who're you gonna call?"

"My wife. She'll get things moving."

"Now?"

"No, when I next go below."

He nodded, relinquished the tiller to me and went below. I noticed he was talking and moving stiffly and slowly. It never occurred to me I was doing the same.

The depth gauge showed forty-seven fathoms which was reassuring. It was still snowing, but as I looked around I had a brief sighting of land to our right before the snow obscured it again. I noticed the wind direction was becoming less reliable, so I wondered if we were getting closer to Foulweather Bluff and the open water beyond. I eased the sails a little and pointed her a little more west. This made sailing minimally easier. After ten minutes I went below. Again I found myself shivering and nauseated. Again I vomited into the sink, but there was very little left in my stomach. I remembered to turn on the GPS. I checked our position, fumbled with my cell phone, eventually turned it on too, and called Ann.

"Where are you? Are you OK? Where've you been?" She asked.

I was surprised how hard it was to move my lips.

"We're in Hood Canal...on Dick's boat...get something to write with."

She was a nurse and used to getting things done. She got the pen.

"OK. Where are you?" She asked.

I looked at the GPS and said, "122° 38' west...and...47° 56' north." Concentrating on the GPS screen made me start retching again.

"Are you OK?" She asked.

"Yes...just a little cold...tell Jack and Miller we will be at... Port Ludlow in less than two hours. We'll need help. The Hood Canal...Bridge is closed. Meet...us in Port Ludlow."

"Jack's here. I'll tell him."

"Good...I love you. Gotta... go."

I turned off the phone, put the GPS down, tried to stop retching, failed, and looked at the chart. With a lot of difficulty I read the chart and found we were just a little west, or was it east, of where we were supposed to be. Time was up for a shift change. I pulled myself into the cockpit.

The first change I noticed was the waves. I didn't really need a GPS to tell me where we were. Until now we'd been relatively sheltered from the wind by the cliffs of the canal. The waves had very little distance to build up height before they reached us, but as we cleared Foulweather Bluff, even though we couldn't see it through the snow, we were hit with waves which had the width of Puget Sound to build up size. We were heading more-or-less north, and the waves were hitting us on the side, so the wind must have backed more to the east. We were rolling, pitching, shuddering and corkscrewing our way through the waves. Occasionally, one would break close and threaten to engulf us, but Roho rode to meet each one, heeled one way, righted herself, and heeled the other as the wave passed under us. She looked like she could carry on like this all day. I knew we couldn't.

Tiring as it had been before to maintain a course, handling a boat in this weather was exhausting. I didn't think we could get any more exhausted – I was wrong.

Somewhere to our west were Tala Point and its cliffs. Behind them was the relatively sheltered inlet leading to Port Ludlow. I released the main and turned west. Immediately, the motion of the boat changed. The wind was now behind us, pushing us to shelter.

We were now pitching forward as a wave came up behind us and leaning back as it moved away in front of us. Smith started to come up to the cockpit but I asked him to put in two of the companionway boards first. A few waves had tried it, and one might succeed at breaking into the cockpit. I didn't want to get pooped. Water would drain out of the cockpit, but it would not drain out of the cabin. The weight of water might push us down and, in nautical terms, we would be pooped. In layman's terms we would be screwed.

Sailboats don't usually like to handle winds coming directly from behind. They want to keep moving to one side or another for the sails fill as they are supposed to. Despite the small sails we had up, they were still too much for the conditions and we were in danger of the bow being forced down into the waves. I released the jib so it flapped noisily and this seemed to smooth out the ride. The other factor which helped was the still-attached dinghy. It was slowing us down, but its drag effect helped me keep the boat on course.

Out of the swirls of snow I could see cliffs coming down to the sea on my left and then the headland, Tala Point, appeared. It looked like we would clear it by about two hundred yards on our present course and that should be sufficient to find the deeper water and avoid the shallows that extended from it to Colvos Rocks a mile and a half away.

As we got closer I watched the depth gauge. It rapidly went from twenty fathoms to six to four, to three and back to seven before slowly increasing to ten. We'd made it over the shoal. It was too dangerous to gibe so we tacked 270 degrees and headed towards the calmer waters of Port Ludlow.

It looked like we'd made it.

It was then we spotted the other boat.

20

It was a cabin cruiser. It was about six hundred yards away and looked to be thirty feet long.

Again my mind said it shouldn't be there.

No one but an idiot would take out a boat in this weather. The waves, even in the shelter of Tala Point headland, were still rough enough to prevent a boat like that being able to get up on a plane, but she was coming straight at us through the snow. Smith reacted first.

"Turn around and let's get out of here."

I didn't move. I couldn't get over the fact that it shouldn't be there.

"Doc, turn around. We need to move." He nudged me.

That broke the spell and I understood. We jibed and tightened both sails so we would once more be heading out into the storm on Puget Sound, but it wasn't that easy. As the wind from the east flowed around Tala Point it changed direction to north-east. This meant we had to aim more to the north-west, across the entrance to Port Ludlow bay. We picked up a little speed. The boat engine had been running since we left Squamish Harbor so Smith pushed the throttle forward. With sails still reefed and motor assistance we crept up to six knots.

I looked back and initially couldn't see the other boat. It had been lost in a flurry of snow, but when I looked again it seemed to have changed direction to follow us. It probably had a higher hull speed and was closing the gap between us.

"Who do you think it is?" I asked

"We have to assume it's the same people who were after us yesterday."

"Couldn't it be someone coming to help us?"

"Maybe. Let me take the tiller. You call your wife and find out."

I went below to the cabin and back to retching. I lay down, closed my eyes, let the nausea settle a little and made the call.

Ann answered. "Where are you? I'm worried sick about you."

"We're..." I had to think, "... near Port Ludlow."

"Good. We'll be there in fifteen minutes. They're just letting us over the bridge now."

"I thought the bridge was...closed."

"Not to us it isn't"

"Oh."

"You don't sound so good?"

"It's just sea-sickness and I'm...I'm a little cold."

"We'll be there soon."

"Someone was following us."

"When?"

"Yesterday."

"I know."

"You do?"

"Yes."

I finally realized I was there to ask a question. "Have you sent out a...a...er...boat to meet us?"

I could hear her repeat the question to someone else. She came back and answered, "No."

"Oh."

"Then I'd better...help out."

I ended the call, lay there for another minute and realized I needed to tell Smith the news.

I pulled myself into the cockpit and told Smith that the boat following us was probably not friendly.

I looked behind and it was a hundred yards closer. In front of us I could see the mainland appearing through the snow.

We tightened up the sails as much as possible and, once free of the shelter of Tala Point, we managed to head almost north-east, but away from land.

We were back in the heavy waves of Puget Sound again, only this time the seas were more erratic as the backwash from the land sometimes gave us relatively short and steep waves and occasional larger breaking waves. It made for a rough, inconsistent ride and looking back at the cabin cruiser I could see they were having an even tougher time, but they had closed the distance to three hundred yards.

Something made a connection in the fog of my memory and I went below to check the chart again. I looked at it, and the GPS, and couldn't figure anything out. I vomited once more then heaved myself up to the cockpit.

The water was so rough we almost missed it, but there, fifty yards to our right was a red marker buoy with the number '2' written on it. I checked the depth gauge. It read four fathoms then started increasing to ten, and twenty. We had just crossed back over the shoals between Tala Point and Colvos Rocks. I had no idea of which side the buoy should have been on – at least we hadn't hit anything. And where were we going? I hadn't thought about getting anywhere apart from avoiding our pursuers.

Perhaps I should think about that?

I went below again to look at the chart. I seemed to have trouble moving my legs and arms. They moved so slowly, but I got to the chart, checked it out, and came away with the number 312 in my mind. I was about to go to the cockpit when I heard a loud bang, followed by another two. It sounded like something had hit the side of the boat. I checked forward and couldn't see any problem in the V berth, but as I walked back to the companionway stairs I noticed my boots were sloshing through water. I wondered where it came from.

I found a lot of difficulty moving up the companionway steps.

I looked beyond Smith and it appeared the other boat was no longer catching up. I told Smith there was water in the cabin and I'd no idea where it was a coming from. I shook my head to try to clear the fog which was slowing me down.

"They're shooting at us," he said. "They must have hit the hull. Get pumping."

It took a few seconds for me to realize the implications of what he said and then adrenaline kicked in, or maybe it just oozed in. I remembered where the Whale Gusher bilge-pump handle was in the lazarette. I stuck it in the hole under the port side cockpit seat and started pumping.

Smith asked, "Where are we going?"

Numbers came in to my head. "Steer 300. That should get us to Port Townsend."

I remember he gave me a strange look when I said that. We couldn't get back to Port Ludlow, so the only alternative I could think of was Port Townsend. He eased off from our current course to 300. This was a marginally more comfortable direction. The wind was coming at us from our right and she was still making six knots, but she was not sailing as well. She was rolling more and Smith seemed to be having trouble steering.

I glanced into the cabin and could see that whatever I was pumping was not enough to stop her filling up. I tried to pump harder but all I did was make the handle come out and it took another minute to put it back in place.

I looked behind and we were still being followed. The cabin cruiser was still about three hundred yards back and had turned when we had made our course change. The result was she was on a parallel course to us, but more west and nearer the mainland. I looked around and the snow was still obscuring any sight of land. It was then I realized what Smith already knew. We were not going to make it to Port Townsend.

No more shots came after the three I heard hitting the hull. It was impossible to have an accurate shot with both boats fighting the waves, but all the shooter in the cabin-cruiser had to do was hit our hull and wait. It must have been obvious to them we were taking on water. I could feel the boat settling lower despite my pumping.

For some reason I looked at the depth gauge. It read fourteen fathoms, then ten. This didn't seem right. I looked to starboard, and then to port, and as I did we sailed by another buoy. It was less than twenty yards away and ten seconds later was nearly invisible in the waves and spray. The depth gauge read fifteen fathoms, then seventeen.

We had just missed hitting Klas Rock. I'd seen it on the chart when I'd checked earlier.

I looked back to see where the cabin-cruiser was. She was still following us.

Then she wasn't.

Despite the sound of the wind, the waves, and the motor I could hear the crack as she hit Klas Rock. Smith turned to see what had happened too. She was stuck on the rock, and I could see figures moving about on her decks. She stayed upright for maybe half a minute, but waves continued to pummel her pushing her onto her side and off the rock. She drifted westward sinking as waves engulfed her. Her bow lifted briefly above the waves and then she disappeared. I couldn't see if anyone had managed to get off before she sank. I stared back, but the snow closed around us again.

We were alone once more, but we were sinking.

We couldn't make it to Port Townsend, or to Port Ludlow. After trying so hard it seemed a shame we would die out here. I started thinking back to how I'd wanted the waves to carry me away all those years ago in the Bristol Channel. I'd felt like dying then, but I didn't feel like dying now. I wasn't sure I was feeling anything.

I was just about to lie down and have a quick nap, but somewhere in my brain a glimmer of an idea took fire and I said, "Mats Mats Bay."

"Mats Mats Bay?" Smith asked.

"Mats Mats Bay. It's just...west of here."

"Can we get to it?"

"It's west of the rock the boat hit. There's a narrow...entrance and it opens to a small... bay. Never been in there, but it might work."

"Let's do it. Keep pumping."

This time Smith gibed the sails. The boom swung over and with a following sea we headed for the mainland. I did my best to keep the pump going, but I was going slower and slower.

"Is that it?" Smith asked.

I looked up to see land less than a quarter of a mile away. There was a gap in the wooded slopes leading down to the water and it looked like a boat might be able to sail through it.

I nodded. I hoped I was right. I kept trying to work the pump, but my hands wouldn't do what my brain thought they should. It was too much effort and I lay down on the cockpit seat and closed my eyes. Smith kicked me.

"Stay awake you ass-hole. We're nearly there. Get up." He kicked again harder.

It had the desired effect. Slowly I got myself into a sitting position to see where we were. The wind was funneling down the narrow channel into Mats Mats Bay. Douglas Firs seemed to surround us on all sides and then we sailed into the bay's open water. Smith aimed the boat at the nearest shoreline on his right, and with sails now flapping aimlessly, but the engine pushing her at full throttle, ran the boat aground. He cut the engine.

I wanted to lie down again, but he pushed me against the cabin bulkhead and propped me up. I could see we were fifty yards from shore – a distance we could have swam and waded in a couple of minutes in the summer, but not in this snow storm. Neither of us would have made it. Smith brought the dinghy from the back of the boat alongside the cockpit. He tried to empty it of water, but it was too heavy. He looked around, noticed the pulleys of the main sheet, detached them from the traveler and tied them to the ring on the bow of the dinghy. Using this he managed to pull the front of the dinghy out of the water and empty most of the water out of the stern. He released the pulleys, attached the bow and stern of the dinghy to the boat, undid the lifelines and told me to get in. In some ways it was now easier to get in the dinghy. Water was lapping at our feet in the cockpit and the top of the dinghy and the gunwale of the boat were at the same level. Smith pushed, cajoled, and kicked me towards the dinghy. At the last moment he asked.

"Where's your cell phone?"

I tapped the breast pocket of my waterproof. He nodded and rolled me into the dinghy. He placed the oars next to me and threw in his bags, which he rescued from the cabin. He sat in the dinghy, released the lines holding her to the boat, and rowed for shore.

21

The nurse later told me it got down as far as 83. That was my temperature, measured rectally in degrees Fahrenheit, when I arrived at the ER. The paramedics had found a vein, started an IV, covered me with a blanket, and whisked me off to Jefferson County Hospital in Port Townsend.

I don't remember any of it apart from Smith lying on a gurney next to me and waving away any treatment they offered. I'm still not sure if he was in the ambulance with me or in the hospital. It's still a jumble.

The doctor told me I had a 'J' wave on my EKG and it was the first time he had ever seen one not in a textbook. I couldn't remember if that was good or bad. Since I was alive it had either passed or didn't matter, but as a general rule it's probably better to avoid being a "textbook case".

I'd come back from beyond feeling cold, and not shivering, to feeling colder than I had at any time in my life. I was aching from shivering so much and it was not until I had been in hospital for a day that the rigors stopped. I was exhausted and all I could do was eat and sleep.

Slowly they re-warmed me, and slowly my brain began to function. I asked questions I don't remember asking, and received answers I don't remember receiving. I found myself in tears at times. Eventually, I started to put things in the right order and to remember who and where I was as the fog in my brain started to lift.

All this time Ann stayed with me and helped me back into the world. She held me when I cried, fed me when I shivered and couldn't hold a fork, and hugged me when I needed it.

I'd been in the hospital just over twenty-four hours when they came to talk to me.

It was Miller, whom I was glad to see, and two of his colleagues. I know their names now but at the time I couldn't remember. Their titles meant nothing to me, but I think they were deputy directors, whatever that meant. I called them Black and White. Both were about Miller's age and looked tired. I figured they'd probably flown in from DC. As the interview progressed I was left with the vague feeling that Miller didn't really want to be there with the others. They found chairs and sat looking at me.

"Feeling better, John?" Miller asked.

"I'm getting there. I get to go home tomorrow so I must be feeling better."

He introduced me to his two colleagues. Black asked Ann to leave. She refused.

"I'm staying. He's my husband, my patient, and I am going to be here."

They didn't push it. They knew when they wouldn't succeed.

Miller risked a hint of a smile in my direction and continued.

"John, we would like to ask you some questions. Is that OK?"

"Sure."

"Well, we have a pretty good idea of how you ended up on that boat, but can you tell us what happened?"

I gave them an account of my encounter with Smith in the parking lot, our flight from Silverdale and how we got onto the boat. Miller stopped me a couple of times when he needed some clarification. I asked.

"What happened to my car?"

"I'm not sure."

Ann said, "It's drivable. I asked Dick and Harry if they could take care of it."

"It was full of food," I said.

"I know. And it's been colder than the inside of a refrigerator, so it'll be OK, John," Ann replied.

I think it was being brought up in post World War Two England that made me never want to waste any food.

I started to ask if Dick knew what happened to his sailboat, but Miller said.

"John, we can talk later, but let's get back to after you got on the boat."

"Well, basically, we decided to get the hell out of there. We headed north on Hood Canal, but it was cold and windy, so we anchored in Squamish Harbor overnight."

"Where's that?"

"Just south of the bridge, on the west side."

"Whose idea was that?" Miller asked.

"It was mine, I think. I was in charge of the boat and I thought we'd be better off navigating through the Hood Canal Bridge in daylight."

"Couldn't you have tried to dock somewhere else?"

"Like where?" I asked.

"I don't know. Isn't there anywhere else?"

"Well, I thought about the Navy Base at Bangor, and maybe we should have gone there, but at the time we just wanted to get away...and...they have a reputation of not welcoming stray boats."

"So you sail north along Hood Canal."

"We motored. The wind was coming right at us."

"OK. So you motored north. Why didn't you call your wife or me or Agent Straw?"

Calling Jack, "Agent Straw", was interesting and was obviously done for the benefit of Black and White. I wondered if Miller was in trouble for not passing information about what he was doing up the chain of command. I answered.

"I was going to call, but it seemed that they were tracking where we were by monitoring cell phones. So, I couldn't call until I knew where we were going and were close to help."

"Why would you think that?" Miller asked.

"I was followed from Belfair, and I think to the High School and Costco. Smith may have been followed too. It seemed a logical way of tracking us."

"Was it Smith who suggested your cell phone was being monitored, and did he advise about not using it?"

"I think it was. Why don't you ask him?"

"I haven't had a chance to talk to him yet."

"Well, he was here in the hospital, or was it the ambulance? I'm not sure."

Miller replied, "Smith came with you in an ambulance to the hospital. He was seen in the ER, but disappeared. We have CCTV showing him walking out of the hospital. We've asked the local police and the State police to keep an eye out for him. We'd like to talk to him."

"So, you don't know what happened then?"

"No, that's why we're here."

"Oh."

"We want to know what happened to you."

I recalled something Smith brought on to the boat. "Did he give you any information? He brought a couple of bags with him and I vaguely remember him taking something off the boat."

Miller glanced at his colleagues before replying. "He left a bag at the hospital here with some CD's in it. We'd like to talk to him about those. But, for the time being tell us more about your trip up here."

"OK. Well morning came and that was yesterday?" I asked Ann.

She nodded.

"We sailed and motored up the rest of Hood Canal. I was having a hard time of it. I was feeling very cold and was sea-sick. We thought we were about two hours from Port Ludlow and decided we would call and tell someone where we were and what was happening. I called Ann."

Miller said, "We know about that. Ann called us and we headed towards Port Ludlow, but you didn't make it there?"

"No, of course not."

"Why of course not?"

"You don't know?"

"No."

"I suppose there's no reason why you should."

"What happened then?"

I continued, "We turned to get into Port Ludlow bay, but we couldn't head any further south because there was a boat between us and the port. We had to turn and run?"

"Why?"

I looked at the blank faces staring at me.

They didn't know.

"The other boat. You don't know about it do you?"

Miller looked at his colleagues, then back at me before saying.

"What boat?"

"It was a cabin cruiser of some sort. The weather was dreadful. We shouldn't have been out there. It was dangerous and there shouldn't have been another boat out there either. So, we headed back away from them, just in case. I called to see if it was something you had ordered. You know...a boat coming to meet us, but Ann said you hadn't, so we kept running from them."

"Did they catch up with you?"

"Partly, at least to begin with, but when they got out in the Sound they were having as hard a time as we were just trying to avoid being capsized. They shot at us though."

"What?"

"They shot at us."

"They did?"

"Yes."

"Did they hit anything?"

"They didn't hit us. They hit the hull. I'm surprised they could hit anything with the seas like that."

"What happened to them?"

As much as I could remember I told them about the chase over the shallows near Colvos Rocks and then coming close to Klas Rock.

"I seem to remember being close to the buoy that marks the rock. We missed it, but the cabin cruiser wasn't so lucky. They hit the rock and the boat sank in less than a minute or two."

"Did you look for survivors?"

"No. We were sinking. I remember water in the cabin. I think we were lucky to save ourselves."

"How many people did you see on the boat?"

"Three, maybe four. I can't be certain. I wasn't thinking straight, and I only saw people after the boat was on Klas Rock."

"So you chose to go into, what's it called Mass Mass Bay, not Port Ludlow?"

"Mats Mats Bay. I don't really remember why, but I think we wouldn't have made it anywhere else. We were sinking."

"What was Smith doing during this?"

"He was at the tiller."

"He knew how to handle the boat?"

"We'd taken turns at the tiller most of the time, but I was sea-sick and he seemed to be OK. I was also getting colder and had trouble moving and thinking. To begin with I didn't recognize it, and looking back I can now see I was not functioning well. He seemed to manage fine at the tiller."

"OK. So, you get into Mats Mats Bay and then what happens?"

"I don't know. I really can't remember anything much about that. I vaguely remember Douglas Firs."

"Douglas Firs?"

"They lined the entrance to the bay."

"Oh."

"But after that I don't remember much until I woke up here. You tell me what happened. How did I get here?"

"Someone, we assume it was Smith, called an ambulance and they brought you here. We found the sailboat in Mats Mats Bay, but it was half under water and we haven't got around to checking it out yet. We asked the sheriff and the Coastguard to work on that. About half an hour after you got here your wife received a phone call, on your cell phone, from Smith, saying you were here. We got here as quick as we could after that."

"So, Smith did the right thing? He may have saved my life?"

"Apparently."

"But he's not around for me to thank?"

"Correct. We don't know where he is. Do you?"

"No. He didn't tell me of any plans."

Miller looked at his colleagues. White asked me.

"Doctor, Smith left some CD's here. Do you know why?"

That was an interesting question. I assumed Miller had not discussed all the details of the meeting he attended when Smith, Jack, Shanty and I met at Shanty's house.

"He didn't talk much about it but I think he was hoping he could give up that information and in return he would be left alone. I think he wanted to give up whatever he was doing."

"You mean he wanted to go straight?" White asked.

"I don't think he said it in so many words, but I think he wanted to give up playing politics, or however he thought of his activities."

"Do you remember a deal or any similar thing being offered to him? I believe you met him with Agent Miller at a politician's house?"

"Yes. It was at William Shanty's house on Halloween. Smith turned up. I think he was interested in turning king's evidence."

"Kings evidence?"

"Oh, you know, state's evidence, but I'm not sure how he'd do it. I suppose leaving the CD's was one way of his doing that."

"Do you know if Smith had more than one copy of these CD's?"

"No."

"Do you know what's on these CD's?"

"No."

"Do you have a copy of these CD's?"

"No."

"Good...one last question. Do you remember Shanty, Smith, Agent Miller, or Agent Straw talking about a way of, shall I say, entrapping someone who might be manipulating political campaigns?"

So Miller could be in trouble.

"Entrapping? How?" I replied.

"I'm not sure. There are probably a few ways of doing it. Do you have any ideas?"

"No."

"Well, do you recall any conversation between Miller, Shanty, Smith and Straw about something like that?"

My memory said "yes, of course I do," but my mouth said, "No. I'm pretty sure I'd remember something like that."

He looked at me for a few seconds before saying, "Thank you. Please let me know if you recall any information about it. I have no more questions. Miller, do you?"

"Well, a couple. First, can you tell us any more about the boat which sank? Second, who do you think was after you?"

"The boat was white, probably about thirty feet long. It was an older design, maybe from the 70's or 80's. Any more I can't be sure of. The snow obscured it, and it never got closer than about three hundred yards, maybe more."

"And it seemed to be coming out of Port Ludlow?"

"Yes."

"Well, we'll have to inform the Coast Guard and the Sheriff. And this was on Klas Rock. K-L-A-S?"

"Yes."

Miller made a note.

"And my second question. Do you know who was after you?"

"I haven't a clue. I don't think they were after me. They were after Smith. He didn't think it was the people he'd dealt with in the past."

"Did he say who he thought was after him?"

Should I say it, should I not? I should.

"He thought it was the government."

"Government?"

"When I wanted to call from Squamish Harbor he said I could call for help and someone might come running, but someone else might come running faster. So, we didn't call that night, and when we called the next day, someone did seem to come running faster – in that boat. I'm not saying it was the government, but if they were tracking my cell phone that closely, it was someone with resources. At least that was his argument. I haven't a clue who was after us."

Miller looked at the other two, shrugged, rose, shook my hand and took his leave. The others followed him.

The door closed after them and Ann said, "I don't think they believed you."

"What's not to believe?"

"They just seemed skeptical."

"I told them all I know, or at least all I could remember. I think they're just congenitally skeptical."

"You may be right, but I think we haven't heard the last of them."

Ann, as usual, turned out to be right.

22

It was Tuesday and I wanted to walk out of the hospital using my own foot power. There was no medical reason I couldn't, but I was wheel-chaired, according to the rules, to the waiting grey Ford Explorer of Jack, Agent Straw. Ann sat in front and I sat in the back for the hour journey home. At least, that's where I thought we were going, but as soon as I clicked in to my seatbelt Jack asked me.

"John, I've just had a call from Miller. The sheriff is bringing in a body they found on a beach. They're taking it to the Coastguard station. Miller wondered if you could be there too to see if you can identify the body."

"I can't see why I would recognize anyone," I replied, thinking it was a strange request.

"Nevertheless, he would like it if you were there."

"It sounds like an order. Is it?"

I could see from watching his eyes in the rearview mirror that Jack was clearly uncomfortable about this and he replied, "I guess it is... Miller is under scrutiny over this and has been asked to get you there."

Ann said, "So, John is a suspect?"

"Not exactly."

"A person of interest then?" she persisted.

"Put it this way. I have full faith in John and so does Miller, but there are some in the Bureau, to name no names, who have their heads up their asses. Sometimes the Bureau can't see the forest for the trees and they may be priming Miller to take the blame."

"Blame for what?"

"Who knows? They just don't want any blame from any congressional panel, or any investigative panel, to land on them."

No one spoke for a few seconds then Ann said, "If they have their heads up their asses the correct metaphor is not that they cannot see the forest for the trees; it should be they cannot see their rectal wall because of the shit."

I laughed. Jack smiled, and said, "And there's a lot of that around in DC as far as I hear."

A minute later we arrived at the Coastguard station gates where Jack showed his ID. We were waved through and drove the hundred yards to the dock where a Jefferson County Sheriff's boat had tied up. In its cockpit was an obviously full body bag on a stretcher. This had been attached to a block and tackle and the boat crew was checking the balance as it hovered over the transom.

The day was grey, windy and cold, but dry. Waiting on the dock was Miller and the two senior G-men, Black and White, who'd interviewed me in hospital. Jack and I got out of the car and nodded our greetings. Only Miller spoke, "It's good to see you up again, John."

I nodded and smiled.

An electric winch whined, the body bag lifted into the air and landed at the edge of the concrete dock. Miller signaled for it to be moved further in and the bag and stretcher slid another yard away from the water. The sheriff's deputy climbed up from the boat, approached the body bag, disconnected the tackle, and unzipped the top.

He said, "This one's not too cut up," and stood back. We moved forward for a better look.

I'd seen dead bodies before, but there's always a little more apprehension when the corpse is lying in the cold wind on a dock than in the more controlled "marble slab" of an autopsy room. I didn't recognize him. The skin on his face was blue-green, waxy and swollen, and the dullness in his eyes was partly hidden by his swollen eyelids. There were strands of seaweed over his face. His dark, curly red hair was plastered to his forehead. A little bloody fluid trickled out of his left nostril and the right side of his face looked like someone had taken rough sandpaper to it for an hour or two.

"You found him on a beach?" I asked the deputy.

"Yeah."

"Face down?"

"Yeah."

"That's probably what happened to his face. It got rubbed in the sand. Any other injuries you noticed?"

"There was a cut on the back of his head."

"Anything else?" I asked. I wasn't quite sure why I was asking the questions, but no one was stopping me.

"His clothing."

The deputy returned to the body and pulled the zipper down another foot. He pushed back the man's yellow waterproof and wet fleece jacket with his gloved hands to show what the corpse was wearing.

It was a white clerical collar over a black clergy shirt.

The FBI agents moved forwards for a closer look.

"Jesus!" It was Miller. "That looks like Riley." He moved closer and reached out to touch the body. The deputy stopped him and handed him a pair of disposable gloves. Miller put these on and moved the face and head from side to side.

"I'm not sure, but this could be Riley."

"Who's Riley?" asked White.

"He's the one who came to see me with Preston. I told you about him. I'd never seen him before that day.

Do any of you recognize him?" He asked looking at his colleagues.

Jack and his two seniors leaned forward for a closer look. I stayed back and watched the scene play out. The three examined the face more closely. I watched their faces. For a fraction of a second a worried look crossed White's face. I almost missed it. It was a hint of a frown and a slight hesitation of his movement. He was the first to speak.

"I've never seen him before. What about you?" He looked at Jack and Black. They both shook their heads. Almost as an afterthought he asked me the same question. I shook my head too. He turned to Miller.

"Tell us more about who you think this is," he said, indicating the body.

"Like I told you I met..." Miller began, but turned to me. "John, I'm sure you must be tired. Agent Straw can take you home now as planned." He added, "We may need to talk to you again, but that can wait a while."

I realized I was the gate-crasher at their gathering and walked back to the car, relieved I was now being disinvited from their stag party. Jack and Miller had a brief conversation which was not meant to be overheard by me. Jack returned to the car and drove out of the Coastguard station.

We cleared the last roundabout out of Port Townsend before Ann asked me, "Did you recognize the body?"

"No. Miller did though, and...I'm probably wrong, but I think White may have recognized him too."

That got Jack's attention.

"Who's White?" he asked.

I leaned forward and replied, "White is the taller one of those agents from DC. I couldn't remember their names after they interviewed me so I call them Black and White."

"Well his real name is..."

"Ah, ah. I don't want to know," I interrupted. "The less I know the better. At least that's what I'm beginning to think."

"Uh. Maybe you're right. But what makes you think he recognized the body?"

"He may not have, but he seemed to react when he looked at the body after Miller had said it could be... who was it? Riley?"

"That was the name."

"Well, I'm curious. I probably shouldn't be, but who is, or was, Riley?"

Jack hesitated before replying.

"Riley is the priest who accompanied Preston when he visited Miller. That's what started this whole thing off."

"Preston was the senator who was killed?"

"Yes."

"I remember. Smith asked about that when he was at Shanty's house. Preston was the one who came to Miller and sort of confessed?"

"Yes, that's right."

We drove on in silence for a couple of minutes. I looked out of the window at the passing grey scenery and the gaudy political signs lining the edges of the road at each intersection. Then I remembered and leaned forward.

"It's election day isn't it?"

"Yes," Ann replied.

"Anyone talk to Shanty? What did he do after I left him at the school? I hope he wasn't too upset?"

Jack said, "I talked to him yesterday and filled him in on what had happened. He said he'd get in touch with you and I was to pass on his thanks for the work you'd done to help him."

"Oh." I leaned back. "We'll have the results this evening, I suppose."

"Yes," Ann said.

"You both vote by mail?" Jack asked.

"Yes. We mailed them in a couple of weeks ago... I didn't vote for Shanty, Jack. We're not in his district, but I hope he wins, especially after I've seen all the work that goes into it."

I returned to looking out of the window. We crossed over the Hood Canal Bridge. The water on both sides seemed calm and it was hard to remember why I made the decisions that eventually took us to Mats Mats Bay.

I asked Ann, "Does Dick know what happened to his boat?"

"I don't know."

Jack said, "He knows. I talked to him yesterday too. He didn't seem too upset, although I didn't give him all the details and you can never tell on the phone. The police report will probably say it was stolen and wrecked. He said he had insurance."

I wondered how much respect Dick had for his old sailboat. It was somewhat of a love-hate relationship. He loved it and it hated him back. It always seemed to need something done to it, and the smell of diesel permeated its every fiber, even though the bilge fuel-tank leak had been fixed years ago. She was built like a tank, and for that I'd been grateful. I'd proved she could handle any weather, even if there was rarely any need for that in Puget Sound. Dick had sometimes verbalized the dream of owning a lighter, brighter sailboat. Now, it looked like he might be able to, or would he just spend the money on sailing vacations in the Caribbean?

Maybe he'd try to resurrect her from the shallows of Mats Mats Bay.

    I leaned back in the seat. The rocking of the car, the heat, and my lack of sleep caught up with me, and as we approached Poulsbo I fell asleep

23

I woke to the murmur of Jack's and Ann's conversation and the change in the rhythm of the car as it negotiated the streets close to our house. I closed my eyes again, but a sudden change in tone of Ann's voice brought me fully awake.

"What the hell are they doing?" I heard her say.

The car stopped abruptly.

Jack opened his car door and said, "Stay in the car."

All I could see was his back as he walked towards our house.

"What's happening?" I asked.

"Look!" Ann replied, "Someone's emptying the house."

She was right. An unmarked white van had backed into our driveway and two men and one woman were ferrying items from the house. They all wore short rain jackets with the letters FBI across the back. I could see Jack was having a heated discussion with one of the men. Ann couldn't take it anymore, got out of the car and ran towards the house. Jack noticed her, took a few quick steps, put his arms out, stopped her and led her back to the car. He opened the door and indicated for her to get in.

"Sit in the car, Ann," he said, "It's all legal. They have the papers."

"Who does?" she shouted.

"The FBI team currently searching your house for electronic documents, CD's, computers and anything else they think may have a bearing on this case."

"What case?" she asked.

"Any information which Smith may have shared with me," I said. "Is that right, Jack?"

"Yes, John."

Ann and Jack sat down and closed the doors.

"Who authorized it? Do we know?"

"Christopher Miller."

"Miller! But he knows I don't have anything like that here, or anywhere."

"I agree. He didn't tell me anything about it, and that's not like him. Let me call him. And stay in the car." He ordered.

Ann took a deep breath and said, "OK...if you ask nicely."

"That is me asking nicely, but I'll say it again. Ann, please stay in the car. Let them take what they want. They'll give you a list and you'll get it all back in a few days, but stay here for the time being. Now let me call Miller."

We could only hear one side of the phone conversation. Initially, Jack seemed as upset as we were to have this home invasion sprung upon us, but then he seemed mollified and surprised as the call went on. He hung up, looked at his watch, and turned to us.

"Miller apologizes and says he will explain all in a few days. He says he owes you dinner, and you pick the restaurant."

"Good."

"He also said he talked to Shanty. He wants Shanty to deny any collusion between the FBI and him to catch Smith, so John, you have no knowledge of that either. And, John, if anyone asks, you fell, hurt yourself, and ended up in the hospital. Keep the rest of the story vague and don't mention anything about being chased. OK?"

"OK, I suppose."

"And I'm booked on the next flight to DC, which leaves SeaTac in just under one hour. I have to go."

"You won't make it in time. It'll take you longer than that to drive there."

"Are you going to leave us at the side of the road here?" Ann asked.

"No, they've nearly got all they want. Another ten minutes and they'll be out of there."

"And we're supposed to get a list?"

"Yes, they keep a catalog of everything they've taken. They'll also put it all back where it came from if they don't find anything." He spoke hurriedly and added, "We have to get going. I'm not driving."

I asked, "What do you mean? You're 'not driving'."

"The chopper will be at Manchester Laboratories in five minutes. Do you know where that is?"

"Yes."

"Get me there and please look after my car while I'm away."

We drove him there and stood in the cold November wind watching the helicopter take off. Maybe because that's what you're supposed to do. At least that's what they do in the movies, but I think neither of us really wanted to get back to the house and deal with the FBI. However, we had no choice.

The FBI agents were waiting for us in their van. The woman got out and politely handed a sheet of paper to us with the list of what she said they had taken. Fortunately, there was no small print at the bottom and nothing to sign.

Ann was no longer as upset by the home invasion, but it was unsettling having to walk around the house noticing clean shapes surrounded by dust on the desks where our computers and screens had been. Our CD collection had gone too, along with the miscellaneous memory sticks which had littered my desk. It was also obvious the whole house had been searched – there was a general feeling of disarray. Drawers and doors had not been completely closed. The few pieces of artwork we had on the walls were not quite straight. The refrigerator and freezer were not packed like they had been, and around some of the heavier pieces of furniture were pressure lines in the carpet showing where they had been moved. Nothing seemed damaged, apart from the sense of safety we normally had in our home. It may seem a cliché, but we felt violated. Our feelings of anger had been replaced by depression and frustration. We had a choice.

"Shall we clean this place up now or later?" Ann asked.

"Now," I replied. "Let's put some music on and go for it."

"They took our CD's."

"KZOK then?"

"OK."

I tuned the radio to Seattle's classical rock station KZOK at 102.5. They were playing Deep Purple's "Smoke on the Water". Somehow it seemed appropriate. I turned it up louder than was good for us, and we took our home back. We tidied, we cleaned, we replaced, we danced, we kissed. After an hour we took a break for lunch, and less than another hour later it was done. We'd restored our castle to its rightful owners and now we no longer had to battle intruders on the ramparts. Well, maybe it wasn't that much of a feat, but at least we felt we'd been able to fight back.

By the time we finished I'd had enough KZOK for a while. I turned off the radio, relished the quiet, and found myself feeling totally drained. We agreed it was time for an afternoon nap. I'd been thinking about how tired I was, but Ann had lost just as much, or more, sleep worrying and caring about me at the hospital, so we went to bed.

Holding each other it seemed we weren't quite as tired as we thought we were, but fifteen minutes later we were both asleep.

We woke to darkness and the wind spattering rain drops on the window. The two hours of sleep had a remarkable rejuvenating effect on both of us. I made tea and we were contemplating our dinner plans when the phone rang. Ann answered it.

She called out to me, "It's someone called Alice. She wonders if you would like to go to Shanty's house for dinner. She says he's having people over for dinner around 6:00, and then going to his campaign headquarters when the polls close to wait for the results. Do we want to go? What shall I tell her?"

I nodded and mouthed a quiet "OK?"

Ann nodded back and said into the phone, "John and I would love to come. We'll see you around 6:00." She replaced the handset.

I said, "Of course that's only going to give me about ninety minutes to get ready. I may not be able to make it."

"Oh, dear. Why don't I call back and tell them to postpone the dinner until nine. Would that be enough time?"

"It'll be close, but I think I could make it by then."

"Well, get moving!"

I got moving, and with barely eighty minutes to go I was ready. I spent the rest of the time catching up on mail, emails, The Economist, and was thinking of taking another nap when Ann said it was time to go.

She drove and we arrived shortly after six.

24

The door was opened by Alice who gave a little squeal and ran at me with a hug.

"You're OK! Will told us you'd been hurt and ended up in hospital, but you're OK?"

"I'm fine, " I said, a little taken aback by the greeting. "Um...this is my wife, Ann. Ann this is Alice, William Shanty's right-hand man, or person. Actually, what is your title?"

"Girl Friday."

"No?" I said. "I thought we couldn't use terms like that."

"You're correct. I'm Will's campaign manager."

Ann rolled her eyes in apology for my social ineptness, gave Alice a brief, female-type hug and said, "He is getting better, but, as you can see, he still needs some training." They nodded, knowingly.

The door bell rang; Alice excused herself and left us. As we hung our coats, I murmured my thanks into Ann's ear. We turned and moved into the magnificent main room of Shanty's house.

There were about twenty-five people present. Most I recognized from the campaign, but there were a few strange faces. Shanty spotted us and broke off his conversation with a balding, obese, middle-aged white male in an expensive grey suit, to come forward and greet us.

"Ann, John, I am so pleased you could make it. I heard you had some bad luck, John, it's great to see you up and about. Ann, you look magnificent as always." He meant it. In the months we had been together I knew when he didn't mean it. For an outsider it was hard to see the difference, but the transformation was not quite complete, and maybe would never be. He might be lucky and never fully metamorphose into a total politician. We exchanged hand-shakes and brief hugs. In a low voice he said he would like to talk to me privately sometime during the evening. He turned and introduced me to the balding, obese, grey-suit who had followed him.

"John, I would like you to meet Gulliver Huntsman from the national Republican Party. He's here to see what happens this evening."

He turned to Gulliver Huntsman and said, "John is my..." He turned to me, winked, and asked, "What would you call yourself, John?"

"I think driver, or chauffeur, would be apt, Mr. Shanty," I said, as politely as a servant could.

Shanty smiled.

Gulliver extended his hand to mine, delivered a fraction of a smile, turned away to look at Shanty and continued his previous conversation as if I had never existed. Clearly, being civil to drivers did not figure high on his social niceties list. I was grateful it didn't.

Ann and I drifted around the room, exchanging pleasantries. His other two drivers, Dick and Harry were picking at an hors d'oeuvre offering. Their wives were nearby chatting. Ann joined the wives and I joined the pickers at the crab and lobster tray.

"What happened, John?" Harry asked.

"Well, it's a long story," I started, popping a small crab delicacy into my mouth.

"We like stories," said Dick quietly, "especially ones which don't seem to make sense."

"What do you mean?"

"Well, it's strange. First I get this call on, I think it was Saturday evening, and it's from Ann and she

doesn't know where you are. She called Harry too."
Harry nodded. "Then Monday I get this call from Harry, who tells me Ann is asking if we can retrieve your car from Olympic View Loop Road in Silverdale. You know, the place where my boat was moored. Well, we go up there and find your car, all beaten up, full of food, but no you. I also go and check on my boat, and it's not there either. It's all a bit of a puzzle, but on Tuesday I get a call from the sheriff in Jefferson County. My boat apparently slipped its moorings in the storm and ended up in Mats Mats Bay. I ask the sheriff how this could have happened. How did a sailboat, dragging its anchor, with no one on board, find itself battling against a storm, navigate through Hood Canal Bridge and slip through the Scylla and Charybdis of the entrance into Mats Mats Bay? He said it must have been a miracle."

I was about to say something, but Dick stopped me and carried on.

"Furthermore, we get here and find out you were in some form of accident in Silverdale, spent a couple of days in the hospital 'for observation', but you are OK now. Is that it?"

"Yes. I'm OK now."

Harry asked, "So how do you get injured in Silverdale and at the same time leave a battered car five miles away?"

I couldn't resist it.

"It's a miracle?"

Dick opened his mouth, hesitated, smiled, shook his head, and gave me a hug.

"If I hadn't known you all these years I'd have thought you were keeping something back from me," he said.

"I am keeping something back, but I promise I'll tell all when I can. It'll take a while to explain it all, and I'm still not certain about all that went on."

"But you're OK now?" asked Harry.

"Yeah. I think I'm fully recovered," I said.

"Good you can buy the beer."

"Deal."

Dick added, "And the pizza."

"Deal." It was the least I could do. "Was your boat insured?"

"Yes, but I've been through thick and thin with her. I hate to lose her."

"Does the insurance pay out if the boat is lost because of a storm and potentially inadequate mooring? Would it pay more if the boat had been... stolen?"

"Why do you ask?" said Dick.

"It would seem a more logical way for a boat to get from that mooring to Mats Mats Bay."

"Oh, I don't know. Only a total moron would've taken out a boat in that storm, so the insurance company may not find that scenario any more credible, and it probably pays the same both ways."

I was saved from further barbs by Ann, accompanied by Dick's and Harry's wives coming to join us. We were all going to sit at the same table.

It seemed dinner, a catered buffet, was ready.

The meal passed pleasantly and uneventfully. Shanty stood and gave a short speech thanking everyone present for the work they had put in to help him get elected. He hoped they had been successful - they would find out soon. He invited everyone present to relax for another half hour and then accompany him to his campaign headquarters to wait for the results. He sat down to cheers and applause. He caught my eye and with a slight nod of his head indicated he was ready for our private conversation. He stood and headed for his study. I excused myself from my companions and followed him.

I closed the study door behind me. We chose not to sit at his desk, but in easy chairs near the window..

"John, are you really OK?" he began.

"I am now, but it could have been a little tricky."

"Miller called me. He said you'd been in the hospital. What happened?"

"You mean what happened from when I left you at the school?"

"Yes."

"In a nutshell, I presume. You have to get going soon."

"Yes."

As briefly as possible I told him about the flight from Silverdale, my time on the boat, the beaching of the boat, and my stay in the hospital. I brought him up to speed on the events earlier that day when the body had been brought to shore and tentatively identified. I also told him of my house being searched, my computer being taken and Jack's leaving for Washington. He remained silent during this. I finished with, "Well that's enough about me. What about you? Are you ready to win, or would you secretly like to lose and get your life back again?"

"I want to win. I have come to that conclusion, and I also realize I am in the right party. That man I introduced you to, Gulliver Huntsman, is a total jerk in my opinion, and probably I'm not the only one who thinks that about him. In some ways that might push me away from the party, but I decided, no; I am going to do my best to change things. The party may not like it, but I hope my constituency does. We'll find out later tonight, and then let's see what happens after that.

"But, John, to use your words; that's enough about me. You could have been killed. You were lucky. Do you know what happened to Smith?"

"No. He disappeared. CCTV showed him leaving the hospital, but there was no trace of him after that."

"When Miller called me he said it would be better for everyone if no one mentioned our efforts to snare Smith, and to not mention any potential deal we may have made with him."

I said, "I was asked that in hospital and admitted to complete ignorance about anything. I have no reason to discuss this with anyone. Also, and I'm sure you've thought about it; it may not look good for your political career. Colluding with the FBI may not win you many friends. I don't necessarily thing that's wrong, but you'd be a target for all sorts of malicious press coverage."

"You're right. Part of me wants to say 'to hell with politics' but the other part of me says I have to be realistic about this."

"So 'mums' the word?"

"'Mums' the word...and thank you again...look, I have to get going. Destiny awaits. Are you coming to Shelton?"

"No. You're going to have to find another driver now. Ann is going to drive us back home for an early night. I still feel exhausted."

We stood. He approached and gave me a big hug.

"Thank you, John, for everything. I don't think I would have made it without you to talk to."

"Oh, yes, you would. I have faith in you, " I replied.

"Is there anything I can do for you?" he asked.

"Can't think of anything."

"Well, I am a billionaire. I'm sure you could think of something."

"If you must put it that way... I'll think about it."

"Thanks, John."

He shook my hand and left to rejoin his party. I waited another minute before leaving and rejoining Ann and my friends.

Ann asked, "Everything OK?"

I nodded and said, "Let's go home."

25

He won. By midnight on Tuesday Shanty had received 51% of the vote, Chris Hall, 46%. Not all the postal votes had been counted, but his opponent conceded and the final tally showed Shanty extending his lead a little.

In his televised acceptance speech he again thanked all those who had supported him, and announced he was going to take a short vacation before he settled into the role to which he had been elected.

"Where do you think he's going?" Ann asked me. It was the Thursday morning after the election.

"Central America," I replied with a pencil hovering over a five-star Sudoku.

"How do you know that?"

"He has a Guatemalan girlfriend," I replied. I erased the '9' I had just written.

"So, he's off to Guatemala?"

"Maybe, or maybe they're meeting somewhere." I should stick to three-star Sudokus.

"So, he's going to get laid?" Ann asked.

"I suppose..."

That wasn't an Ann-like comment, but it got my attention. I looked up. Ann took the pencil from me.

"Good. Now I have your attention."

"Oh, yes...he has a Guatemalan girlfriend."

"Do you know anything else about her?"

"I think she's an academic...you know, a professor of something."

"Anything else?"

"No, can't think of anything. I don't think they're engaged or anything."

"Well, you don't know much do you?" said Ann.

"That's not true. I know she's about six foot four, and about three hundred pounds; three hundred and five when she doesn't shave, but that's about it."

Ann laughed and gave me a short poke in the ribs.

"What else aren't you telling me?" she asked.

"Well, I don't know. I'm not sure what else I should tell you about. What do you want to know?"

"I don't know until you tell me."

"Oh...I think it's going to come out in little chunks then. I have never met his girlfriend, and he only mentioned her once, and that was on the ferry. I think he wanted her kept out of the election lime-light."

"Good for him. Anything else?"

"Um...his father was a jerk."

"Oh."

"Yes."

"Should I give you back your pencil and leave you to your Sudoku? What do you think?"

"Yes... well, no. I'm sorry. I'm still feeling exhausted. I think it's a let-down from the last week and maybe before that too. I think I'm still trying to piece it all together. I don't seem to be able to concentrate properly, and the other night, when I introduced you to Alice, I couldn't remember her job title. I'm not sure if that's because of the hospitalization or everything else."

Ann said, "I think it's probably both. You may not have banged your head, but you have some memory loss and you weren't coherent for a few hours after you were in the hospital. You need to take it easy."

"So, I probably shouldn't try any Sudoku for a while then. I need to rest my brain, just like a head injury?"

"Yes. You doctors haven't a clue how to look after yourselves. You don't have any insight."

"You're probably right there. I will turn off my brain immediately... 'Sometimes I just sits and thinks and sometimes I just sits'. I will just sit."

"That's the idea. Who said that?"

"I don't know. I could look it up."

"No, you don't. You rest. No screen time until you are better."

And so I rested my brain. Ann treated me like a concussion victim and prevented any attempts to restart my overloaded head. I slept for at least twelve hours every day and resisted turning on the computer. Of course, since the computer wasn't there that was easy, but I was surprised how many times I ended up at the computer desk before remembering it was elsewhere. Ann took away my phone and turned it off. She kept me away from all written materials and didn't ask me any more questions about Shanty's love-life.

It worked. By Sunday I was sleeping a normal eight hours and was allowed a two-star Sudoku, which I quickly and correctly completed. On Monday I was given back my cell-phone. Harry turned up with my renovated Subaru that evening, but I was not allowed to drive it. Tuesday I was allowed to read "Time", Wednesday, "The Economist", and we discussed the articles in both. I must have passed the test, and by Thursday she considered me well enough to pronounce cured.

It was on Thursday evening we had a brief call from Jack. He told us we would be getting our computers back the next day and, surprise, nothing of any criminal or political value had been found in them. He asked us if we would like to go to dinner the next day. We accepted.

We chose "The Lighthouse Restaurant" in Port Orchard. It had reopened and we thought we might as well check it out before it closed again, and then reopened in yet another gastronomic form. It was the sort of restaurant which was just a little too big, or just a little too up-market, for its surrounding population. It looked like it should succeed, but it hadn't. Maybe this time would be different. It was local, and that, more than any culinary concerns, was the main attraction.

I drove Jack's Explorer and Ann took her Camry. We parked in the drizzle and climbed the stairs to the lobby where Jack and Miller were waiting for us.

We were seated in a distant booth by a window. I noticed the adjoining booth had a "reserved" sign on its table, but only four of the other tables and booths were occupied. For a Friday night this did not auger well for the survival of the current owners. We could make out the lights of Puget Sound Navy Shipyard through the gloom and the water streaming down the glass.

We exchanged the usual pleasantries and ordered. The food arrived promptly, the server left us alone, and Miller began.

"I would first like to apologize for the search of your home and the examination of your computers. I didn't think it would reveal anything. In fact I would have been very surprised if it had, but at the time it seemed the best thing to do."

"Why?" I asked.

"I wanted the focus of our investigation to remain here, on the west coast."

"What investigation? You mean the people who shot at me?"

"Indirectly," he paused. "John, you know a lot about what Smith was up to, but not all. Ann, I assume

John has told you some of what was going on, but not all."

Ann said, "I don't know what I don't know though."

"That applies to me too,' I said.

Miller said, "True. In a nutshell Jack, Shanty, and I were involved in setting a trap to catch Smith. I had been approached by a senator in DC and he told me about how he'd been compromised. He thought he was not the only one in Congress who was in the same situation. He came with a priest and I took his visit to be some sort of confession. Now I'm not so sure. The priest was the one you saw hauled out of the water last week in Port Townsend. Who he is, how he came to be in my office, or out here, I don't know, and may never know. Jack says when we looked at the body in Port Townsend you thought one of the others there may have recognized who it was?"

"Yes, Agent White."

"White?"

"He means Assistant Director Agnelli," interpreted Jack. "He labeled Agnelli and Griswold as 'White' and 'Black' because he couldn't remember their names when he was in hospital."

"Is that correct?" Miller asked.

"Yes. That's what I told Jack."

"I had to confirm it," said Miller and continued. "The next thing I have to ask is have you heard from Smith, or do you have any idea where Smith is?"

"No on both counts," I replied.

"What's this all about?" asked Ann, a little annoyed. "You know John doesn't have any relationship with Smith."

"I know, but I was asked to quiz John again about it. Someone is very concerned to find out where Smith is. Or, more likely, is very concerned to know what Smith has."

"I thought Smith left some CD's at the hospital in Port Townsend for you," I said.

"He did, or he left some CD's for someone. The CD's were examined and viewed by Agnelli and Griswold, but neither Jack nor I have seen them yet. Based on our conversation with Smith I can guess what they contain."

I thought about this, and then asked, "Do you want to see what's on them?"

"Yes...I think so. I'd like to know what politicians have been compromised by Smith, and how it was done, and I'd like to know who took advantage of it."

"But you seem to be implying you may not get to see them," I said.

"Agnelli told me the CD's are being reviewed by a committee in DC and they are figuring out what to do about them."

"You mean they're unlikely to see the light of day?" I asked.

"I think that's a distinct possibility."

Jack said, "In which case not having any idea of what is on those CD's is probably a good thing, John."

"I agree, but does everyone know I haven't a clue what's on them?"

"They will," replied Miller.

"I don't get it," I said. "You know I don't have any association with Smith."

"I agree, but you were the last person to spend any time with him, and so it's natural that you fall under some cloud of suspicion. And, that's what I am apologizing for. I am checking you out fully. I am turning the spotlight on you, would be another way of putting it, so I can keep the focus off DC."

"John is your fall guy?" a surprised Ann asked.

"No, no. He'll come out of this squeaky clean. It's just that I want it to look like we are focusing our attention here, in the Pacific Northwest, instead of DC."

"You haven't really told us why though, have you?" she persisted.

"I'm concerned this investigation will go nowhere and the material in the CD's will never be released."

"Why?" she asked.

Miller sighed and said, "I sent Jack back to DC last week for a couple of reasons. The main one was I wanted him to review the security tapes from when I met with Senator Preston and his priest. They were interesting. There is a clear recording of Preston entering the building and going through security, but there wasn't one of the priest. I made the assumption at the time they'd come together, and never checked. There was no reason to, but the conclusion I've come to is he was already in the building. I have also wondered if he was an FBI employee, but his finger-prints don't show up on any of our files. He could have been with another federal office, but again, we can find no record of him. Of course, it's possible his record has been removed, but we should have had some trace of that too. It remains a mystery how he came to be in the FBI building.

"The other concern is that Smith may have thought he could hand over what he had, and the FBI would act on it. That may not happen. It would be a difficult thing to do, you know, for the FBI to release the information in the tapes. They are probably highly politically charged and the Bureau has got its fingers burned before, so that would be a good reason for them not to be released. I wondered about releasing them to the press, but that has all sorts of ramifications, especially if it ever got out that we handed them over.

"Of course, not handing them over is dangerous too. They could be very potent political tools and in the wrong hands could still be used for blackmail."

Ann asked, "What's this got to do with us?"

"Smith may contact John again, and we'd like to know about it if he does."

I thought about that for a few seconds before saying, "Are you sure?"

"Am I sure about what, John?" Miller asked.

"That you want me to tell the FBI if Smith contacts me."

"Why wouldn't I be?"

Again I hesitated before replying, "From what you have told me I think you and Jack would like to know, but you may not want anyone else in the Bureau to know."

"I wouldn't say that."

"Wouldn't, or can't say that?" I asked.

It was Miller's turn to hesitate. "You know the answer to that, John," he smiled.

I think I knew the answer, but I wasn't going to say anything. I concentrated on my cioppino, which was getting cold, and thought a little more about what had been discussed.

Ann had finished her fish and asked, "Don't you think it's possible he could contact Shanty?"

Jack replied this time, "It's possible, but unlikely. It's more likely he would contact John."

"Isn't it also true you'd prefer not to be seen taking the computers from a member of Congress?" she asked.

"If I said that didn't come into our considerations I'd be lying, but Shanty has no particular love for Smith.

If he is going to contact anyone, and I think that's a big 'if', it's likely to be John," Jack said.

Ann added, "I hope there isn't going to be any more intrusion into our lives. This has been a big hassle. Our house was searched and our computers taken. What next?"

"That's basically it."

"That's not quite true, is it?" I asked.

"What do you mean?" Miller replied with a question.

"Our computers were returned this morning. If I were to run a security search would I find anything?"

"No."

"If you were to run a security search would you find anything?"

His hesitation was his answer.

"So, you'll be monitoring my computer, and I assume our phones? Anything else?"

"That's it," Miller said. "I'm sorry, John. I wasn't going to tell you to spare you the worry of knowing what we were doing. You've been through enough already."

I said, "I think I would rather know. But really, you don't want him to contact me, or at least by email or phone, because it's not you, personally, who will be monitoring them, it's the FBI. Is that right?"

Miller looked me in the eyes and said, "John, all I can say is if, or when, he contacts you, I trust you will do the right thing."

We were all quiet for a minute or two after that, concentrating on finishing the last of our entrees, until Ann said.

"If I'd known this whole thing was so convoluted and mysterious I would have had the lobster."

"I didn't see it on the menu," I said smiling.

"It wasn't. We can make up for it with dessert. Instead of one dessert and two spoons, as we normally do, let's make it two desserts and two spoons."

Miller laughed, relaxed a little and said, "I think we should have liqueurs too. It's the least I can do."

"It was the least he could do," Ann said.

We were on our way home and neither of us was happy. I felt we were, at best, doing our civic duty; at worst we were victims of the system. It didn't seem right we were under surveillance. I could see the rationale behind Miller subjecting us to this scrutiny, but I didn't have to like it.

I also knew what I had to do if Smith contacted me again.

I tried to make light of it. "Well, we have a complete dessert sitting on the seat behind us," I said.

"John, let's be serious. What are we going to do about this? I don't want my phone tapped and my computer hacked by the FBI. Do you?"

"Certainly not, but what can we do? If we kick up a fuss they'll just think they're justified in watching us. All I can think of is we'll have to just wait it out. Whoever is keeping an eye on us is going to get very bored very quickly."

We were both quiet until we were nearly home when Ann said, "I suppose this means I can't visit my porn sites and your cross-dressing sites are definitely off limits."

"Now, who's not being serious?"

"Well, me, I suppose...you're right. We have to try to roll with the punches. It won't get me anywhere otherwise. And, like you said, we still have that untouched chocolate decadence sitting behind us."

"Is it calling to you?"

"Sort of. I knew we'd never eat it in the restaurant, but we deserved it, didn't we?"

"Oh, yes, we deserved it, and more. What are you going to do with it?"

"I think we should just lick at it," Ann said.

I pulled into the driveway.

"Lick at it?"

"Where do you think we could put it so we can lick at it?" she said, raising an eyebrow.

I smiled, brought the car to a stop in the garage, gave her a kiss and said, "Oh, I'm sure we'll find a few places."

We did.

26

Life went on, and most of the time we didn't pay any attention to the fact we were being watched. How long they continued watching I wasn't sure. Jack later told me they gave up in mid-December.

We had a quiet Thanksgiving, spent at a neighbor's, and for Christmas both children came home with their partners. We had a little snow in January and on a bright day drove to Hurricane Ridge for an afternoon of snow-shoeing. But it can get quite dismal in the Pacific Northwest with rain, fog and cold winds. By early February we were ready to get away to somewhere where there was sunlight and warmth. Mail, which would normally go straight to recycling, was opened in the morning if it had words like 'cruise' or 'sun' on its cover. Ann was reading one of these to me.

"Apparently we have to call now to take advantage of this amazing offer. Oh, it says there are age and marital requirements too."

"We can always claim we're not married if that would help."

"And we can say we're twenty-nine too. Ah, it seems we have to attend a ninety minute presentation, and there is a $75 fulfillment service fee, a fulfillment fee of $99... an activation fee of $100, and let's not forget, the non-refundable processing fee of $100. Then there's all the taxes and gratuities. That's what...about $350 or more. I'm glad we were identified by the cruise line. Doesn't it warm the cockles of your heart?"

"I haven't heard that expression for a long time, but it would be nice to have warm cockles at this time of year," I said.

"So, where would you like to go?"

"Where is that offer for?"

"A cruise in the Caribbean."

"That would be OK, or we can always go back to Puerto Vallarta."

"Let's make a decision this evening then, when you get back from Costco," Ann said as the amazing offer she had been reading floated into the recycling bin.

Sometimes, shopping in a Costco warehouse was something we did together. Sometimes, it was sort of fun. However, we'd both been barricaded in against the weather for the last few days, and Ann had decided she needed to finish her book in time for her book-club meeting the next night. The shopping expedition became my responsibility and we thought the break would be good for both of us. I was pulling a couple of bread loaves in to my cart when I heard, "Hey, doc, howya doing." I spun around and said.

"Oh, shit."

"Doc, that's what you said to me last time. I'm beginning to think there's something about me."

It was Smith, smiling and looking like he was my best buddy of all time. He even gave me a hug. I just stood there.

"Well, isn't it good to see me?" he asked.

I recovered and said, "I think so. I'm not sure."

"Not sure? I am disappointed. Do you want any help with your shopping?" he asked.

"What?"

"We can shop and talk, can't we?"

"Yes, but maybe we shouldn't be seen together. What do you think?"

"Are the Feds watching you?" he asked quietly.

"I don't know. They have been."

"Well, they didn't follow you here. I thought by now they'd have given up, but maybe you're right?"

"How do you know they didn't follow me here?"

"Because I did."

"Jesus! Why'd you do that?"

"Think about it. It's that face blindness I have. I have to get around it in lots of ways."

"But that means you were waiting for me to leave my house. You were watching my house in fact." I was pissed off.

"I wasn't there long, and if you hadn't appeared I was going to risk it and just knock on your door. But then you appear in your Subaru. I see you got it fixed."

"Yeah. It's as good as new now. I still don't like you watching me, or my family."

"I don't really have a choice, and this will be the last time. Why don't you finish your shopping and I'll see you in your car. It'll be just like old times won't it?"

He walked off leaving me perplexed and angry. I noticed he didn't seem in any hurry and he helped himself to a sample of buttered bread as he ambled away. His face showed a light sun-tan, so wherever he'd been since we last met, it wasn't around here.

Fortunately, I had a list and stuck to it, because it would have been difficult to concentrate otherwise. Fifteen minutes later I had emptied my purchases into the back of my Subaru Forester. I opened the door to sit in the driver's seat and as I did so, the passenger door opened and Smith sat down.

"Let's go to another parking area," he said.

I started the car and drove to the edge of the Costco parking lot, backed in against a low bank, and turned off the engine.

"So, you're not sure you're pleased to see me?" he asked. He was scanning the parking lot, not looking at me.

"I know I should be, and I know you saved my life, but if I hadn't met you my life wouldn't have been threatened in the first place."

"Yeah, I suppose that's true."

"So, thank you for saving my life. I couldn't have survived without you."

He was apparently satisfied we were not being watched, and looked at me. "Doc, it's a mutual thing. I couldn't have survived without you either, and I meant to thank you too. You know, you did a pretty good job sailing that boat."

"You seemed to know what you were doing too. Is that where you got the sun tan?"

"Doc, do you really want to know where I've been since we last met?"

"Yes, I'm curious."

"Are you sure? Promise you won't tell?"

"I'm used to keeping secrets."

"OK then. After I left you at the hospital I walked to the Boat Haven marina and spent a few days warming up on my sailboat there. Yeah, I know how to sail. Nobody bothered me. It was November, after all. Then I went somewhere warm and waited. You know what I waited for?"

"I can guess."

"Yeah?"

"For the information you left on those CD's to become public knowledge."

"Right. So what happened?"

"I don't know what was on those CD's, and as far as I know, Christopher Miller and Jack Straw, the two FBI agents you met, didn't get to look at them either.

They guessed what was on them, like I did, but it was their superiors who saw what was on them. They were apparently reviewed by a committee at the FBI. Obviously, they decided that whatever was on them wouldn't see the light of day."

"Who told you about that?"

"Miller."

"Huh," he paused for a few seconds. "Why did the FBI keep an eye on you?"

"They thought, sooner or later, you and I would be in contact."

"So, they thought you might be working with me somehow?"

"Yes." I thought about telling him that Miller had wanted to focus attention on me, but that seemed unnecessary.

He asked, "So, now I've contacted you what are you supposed to do?"

"I am supposed to 'do the right thing'."

"Does that mean you tell them I've been in contact with you?"

"Maybe. What do you suggest?"

"I want to leave this life behind and not have to worry about looking over my shoulder any more. I want the information on those CD's to be available to the public. As soon as it becomes public knowledge it no longer has any political or blackmail value. Well, at least I hope so."

"What are you thinking of?" I asked.

"What I have needs to be aired in public," he said, nodding his head emphatically. "When that's happened I am going to destroy any evidence linking me with it and never think about it again."

"So, why don't you give it to the press?"

"Good idea, and don't think I haven't thought about it. How do you think I should do it?"

"Me? You want me to tell you what to do?"

"Yeah. Humor me. I've had a few ideas. Let's see what you'd do."

"Well, I'd make copies and mail them to newspapers."

"Which newspapers?"

"You mean you haven't thought of any?"

"No, I have, but let's see if we agree."

"Well, OK...let me think...one west coast, say the LA Times, then The New York Times, Washington Post, maybe Miami Herald." I was warming to this. "Then, I think you should include a few international newspapers too...send copies to Der Spiegel in Germany, The Guardian in Britain, and Le Monde in Paris."

"Why include foreign newspapers?" he asked.

"Just in case the US papers get cold feet and don't publish anything. I'm sure you've thought about this too."

"Oh, I have. One of my concerns is getting it to a newspaper without it being traced back to me. How would you get around that?"

"I suppose you'd have to mail it. You couldn't take it to each of these papers and put it in their in-box. You'd be spotted on CCTV cameras. You couldn't FedEx or UPS it either – you have to give your name and address for that. You'd have to send it through the Post Office. For the foreign newspapers you may have to provide a customs form, so you would have to provide a false name and address for that. But, otherwise, you could just mail it."

"You mean go into any post office and mail it?" he wondered.

"Why go into a post office? Why not just stick it in a mail box somewhere?"

"OK, but how would you guarantee it couldn't be traced back to you?"

"Well, you'd have to avoid having fingerprints or DNA on the CD's and the packaging. So, you have to handle everything with gloves. Probably you shouldn't lick the envelopes and you would have to use address labels instead of writing the address."

"Sounds good. Where would you mail it?"

"You mean what town, or part of the country?"

"Yeah."

"I suppose you mail it from somewhere other than where you are, or you mail it from multiple sites. The trouble with multiple sites is you have to travel between them and travel can be monitored. You could ask friends to mail them, but that would increase the number of people who know something about what you are up to. You could mail them from a large city. Maybe that might be harder to trace. You've thought this through. What would you do?"

"I've thought it over and come to the same conclusions. I have four CD's I want to share with the world. I only left three in the hospital in Port Townsend, and I wasn't sure what to do with the fourth."

He hesitated, so I asked, "What's on the fourth?"

"The fourth is the one I am most concerned about. I didn't just randomly choose where I should concentrate my talents. I had meetings with people who were paying me and I managed to video and record a few of those. It wasn't easy because most of the time I was visiting them on their turf. As you know I have difficulty recognizing faces, so I'm not sure if the fourth one is any use at all, but it may be. I can recognize my own face, so I took off any parts where I could be seen."

"Why don't you just mail it with the others?"

"Do you want to look at it?"

"Certainly not," I replied, shaking my head. "I don't want to know who, or what, is on any of these CD's."

"I'm sure you're right," he said.

"I also think you should send a copy of the CD's to Miller at the FBI. He'd know what to do with them, especially the fourth one you're concerned about."

"Good idea," he said. He seemed distracted, gathered his thoughts, looked at me and said, "After this meeting I think it better you and I never see each other again. Do you agree?"

"Yes. I suppose that's right," I nodded.

"For many reasons I think we'll agree it's best," he said quietly, and continued, "However, one of those reasons is I have to have surgery. It's surgery for cancer, and I need to get it done soon. I think you'd understand that."

I was surprised and said, "Sorry to hear that. I hope it's fixable."

"I hope so too, but who knows?"

I nodded.

He said, "So, I hope it will help you understand what I'm about to do."

I looked across at him. He reached into his inside-jacket pocket, handed me a package, and said, "It's all there doc. There are four CD's. You'll know what to do. Just do the right thing. Thanks."

He opened the car door and walked away without another word.

I never saw him again.

27

"He just walked away," I repeated to Ann.

"The ass-hole," she said. "Why couldn't he take responsibility for them?" She pointed at the package on our dining room table. I'd opened the envelope and pulled out four CD's each inserted in a sealed freezer bag. I also found five, one-hundred dollar bills in another envelope labeled "for expenses". The groceries I'd bought remained untouched in my car.

"He said he needed surgery for cancer."

"Which, of course, we can't prove."

"Of course," I said.

"What are you going to do with them?"

"I thought about it on the way home and I suppose it's time to 'do the right thing'?"

"And that is?"

"Plan B."

"Plan B?"

"Plan A was for him to mail the CD's out of his life. Plan B is for us to do the same for our lives. I think that's what we should do, but first we're going to book a trip to somewhere warm. That flyer you got this morning," I started rummaging in the recycle bin, "Oh, here it is. Yes, why don't you call and find out what we have to do and if we can take the cruise in about a week. I'll empty the car while you do that and then we can go over Plan B."

> Plan B went something like this.
> We made a list:
> *Plan B*
> *Packet of 100 blank CD's*

Mailers for CD's - individual and for 4?
Labels for mailing.
Printer ink cartridge.
Plastic bags
Plastic gloves
Plastic sheet
Customs forms from Post Office (4)
Stamps?

The next morning we both went to Staples and entered at different times. Ann bought the CD's and the ink cartridges. I bought the CD mailers (two sizes) and mailing labels. We paid using cash, not using Smith's hundreds – they might be remembered.

We bought the plastic stuff at The Dollar Store.

We went to the US Post Office at lunch time, when it was busy, and Ann picked up the customs forms. They were obtained without interaction with the Post Office staff.

We went home, brewed a pot of decaffeinated coffee and figured out our next steps.

They continued like this:

Plan B/1

The customs forms (CN 22's) were numbered so the Post Office may know where they originated. However, same form said, or at least we thought it did, that we could send individual CD's overseas without the form.

John went back in to town, used the automatic mailer in the Post Office and sent himself four CD's so he knew what it would cost for domestic mailing.

Ann went to Staples to buy another sixteen CD mailers.

The cost of mailing four CD's domestically was less than three regular first-class stamps.

The cost of mailing a CD internationally was not known. Assume it was two international stamps?

Plan B/2

John went back to Post Office and sent a single copy of a music CD to friend in Devon, England. It cost less than two regular international stamps. He will have to explain to friend in England at later date why she received unsolicited CD. Bumped into two ex-patients.

Now realized we were one CD mailer short. John went to Office Depot and bought two mailers, just to be safe.

Ann went to main Post Office for roll of 100 domestic first-class mail stamps and 20 international stamps, then to smaller Post Office for 12 more. They only had 8, so had to go to even smaller Post Office for last 4.

Plan B/3

Ann disconnected her computer from the internet. John left his computer attached since not sure if still being monitored. He played an online computer game from AARP. While John was losing at this game Ann, using sterile technique (gloves, mask, plastic sheeting) started to make eight copies of each of the CD's. John took over from her half-way, finished the CD copying and put them in individual plastic bags. He then put them in mailers of four for domestic mailing, and singly for international mailing. When he'd finished he found he had two CD mailers left over and Ann was winning the online game.

Debate over whether it was safe to look up newspaper addresses on the internet if computers were being monitored. Decided to risk it and obtained the addresses of the domestic and international newspapers, and the FBI in DC.

Printed address labels.

Printed small labels with 935 Pennsylvania Ave, DC, 20535 as the return address. Affixed all labels and postage stamps while still wearing plastic gloves. When finished placed all items to be mailed in large plastic bag.

The hardest part was waiting to mail them. We assumed it would take at least five days for them to reach Europe. On Tuesday we drove around Tacoma and posted them in twos and threes in different mail boxes. On Friday we did the same with the rest of the CD's on our way to SeaTac airport. We caught a red-eye flight to Detroit and on to Miami. By 4:00 pm on Saturday we were catching up on our sleep, waiting for our Norwegian Cruise Line ship to leave the dock and head for The Bahamas.

This was our postponed, or second, honeymoon.

28

We weren't sure if, or when, any news story would break, and initially we weren't sure if we wanted to know. We made no extra effort to follow news stories (we'd pledged a screen-free vacation), but as the days went by we wondered if we had "done the right thing" after all.

It was near the end of our ten-day cruise, when we were walking down a dusty street in St. John's, Antigua that I stopped at a corner newsagent and browsed the two-day-old selection of European papers. I could see nothing in the German and French newspapers, but on the second page of The Guardian there was a small sub-heading which read, "US congressmen sex scandals."

I paid for a copy, and this is what it said.

Three current US Congressmen are among those identified in photographs received by this newspaper in the last week. The photos apparently show the congressmen in compromising sexual situations. Our correspondent in Washington, DC, USA confirmed that The Washington Post had received similar information. A spokesperson for the Post said they delayed publication until the photographs could be authenticated. The photos were accompanied by details of where and when they were taken. Other information was included with the photos which this newspaper is still authenticating.

For some Caribbean reason there was no Washington Post available. The article in the Guardian was all I could find. It seemed like the newspaper was signaling, "we have them too", to the world, but wasn't quite sure what to do with them.

Seventy-two hours later they did know what to do with them, and so did all the other newspapers we'd sent the information to. The story made front page news as reporters confronted those they could identify. Active and retired congressmen, senators, and governors were questioned, and in the spirit of creative disingenuousness, practiced universally by politicians, denied everything. It didn't last. By the end of the second week of "Buttgate", as the scandal was called, the first resignation and the first, "will not stand for re-election" statements were announced.

At the end of the third week four more political careers were finished and the content of the CD's made it to the web.

Ann and I spent a half-hour looking at the video clips and photos posted on the web and could understand why it was called "Buttgate". It could have been called "Buttboobandballgate" but the predominant visual effect was of white, saggy, fat, congressional backsides. These somehow grabbed your attention from the more nubile bodies seen with them. It was not pleasant to watch. Altogether there were less than forty minutes of "Buttgate" on the web, so not all the information had been released. We wondered what could be missing. A few days later we found out.

One representative, from a state which will remain anonymous, stood tall in congress and expressed his full moral indignation that his colleagues could be discovered in such circumstances. He demanded the FBI investigate.

The copies of his financial transgressions were posted on the internet that evening.

The FBI, which had been silent until now, gave its opinion.

The Director held a news conference and, as is usual during these events, was flanked by minions whose job was to look serious and obsequious at the same time. I noticed Christopher Miller standing behind the Director's right shoulder. The Director said that he had also received the same information, but because of delays from having it screened, it took a week longer to reach his office. The origin of the CD's was not known, but the FBI was looking into it. From their initial investigations it seemed the information in the CD's had been used to attempt to blackmail members of Congress, but he couldn't say more than that at the moment. He asked for questions. There were two I thought interesting. One reporter asked what blackmail payment was being looked at. Was it money or something else? The director said investigations were still ongoing. The other question, from The Washington Post reporter, was whether there was involvement of any other government institution. The Director replied that at this time there was none noted. I noticed Christopher Miller maintained a perfect poker face during the questioning. The news conference ended, like most, with many questions incompletely answered.

The next day it all changed. What was probably the fourth CD was released on the internet. This was different. It had no butt/boob/ball interest and was a compilation of hidden-camera recordings of parts of meetings. Smith's back was occasionally seen, and I recognized his voice, but there was no one else I could identify until almost the last clip. It was about forty-five seconds long and there were three people discussing how to compromise the representative from the anonymous state. One of the three I thought I recognized. The sound quality was poor, and the video unfocussed, but I was pretty sure it was "White" – the FBI man I'd met in Port Townsend.

An announcement from the FBI the next day stated that one of their senior management had been asked to resign and investigations into criminal acts were ongoing.

As the online postings were viewed more people on CD 4 were identified. Most seemed to have two things in common. They were rich, and they all wore dark jackets with dark ties.

The press had their proverbial field-day. Usually newsworthy items, like exposing which northern-club baseball player had not turned up for spring training in Arizona, didn't even make the first page.

One news anchorman claimed, "The scandal was bigger than Watergate and all the other gates put together." He may have been right.

Congress made the most of it too. Some representatives and senators who found they were not on the CD's put together committees to investigate and report (in due time) on their colleagues' transgressions. The FBI proceeded to arrest and indict one of their own.

Lobbyists held back on visiting, cajoling, and "enhancing" until they could be sure their usual congressional targets were clean, or maybe not too dirty.

For a while it seemed the country was paralyzed by the scandal, but the White House had come through apparently unscathed. The President made the most of this and acted...presidentially. He directed, he appeared on television, he appointed and, for once, the country and the press appreciated it.

During all this Ann and I wondered if we had done the right thing. With every prurient revelation we became a little sadder in the knowledge of the fallibilities of our elected representatives. They seemed human, or less than human. We realized the hopes we had for them being different was misplaced, and there were probably no more transgressors in Congress than in any other similar group of people. It's just we expected better.

For a while we also hesitated to answer the door when anyone knocked, but there was no SWAT team raid at 3:00 am, and no black Suburban following us to the grocery store.

I think we did the right thing.

29

Spring led into summer and baseball players resumed their status on the front page of newspapers while the ongoing committees, investigations, and interviews of "Buttgate" were relegated to the interior.

In Port Orchard, Washington State, life went on and I did my best to forget about the events of last winter. I weeded the yard, watered the vegetable garden, and bought my crabbing license so I could accompany a friend on his crabbing expeditions. The Dungeness crabs were tasty, but if we just got out on the water it was enough for me. I loved the way Puget Sound changed with the tides, the seasons, and the weather.

Dick decided against resurrecting his ship-wrecked Luders 33 from Mats-Mats bay, so it had been patched up, refloated, and towed to a sloop graveyard somewhere. With the insurance pay-out, and money he had earned working for Shanty (as well as driving he had been paid for his legal skills) he bought a 1975, thirty-five foot, Hallberg-Rassy sloop. Hallberg-Rassy was, and still is, the Rolls-Royce of sailboats. He thought he'd got it for a steal, and from his perspective maybe he had. I thought it may have been a Rolls-Royce, but it was a middle-aged Rolls-Royce. It would need a lot of TLC, which Dick was ready to lavish on it.

I suspected sanding, pulling, and wrenching would play an important part in my future relationship with the boat, which he had named, Roho 2.

One Friday in late July Dick invited Ann and me to join him on an evening cruise, with dinner and wine, on his Hallberg-Rassy. We had to be there at 6:00 pm.

Ann stepped aboard first and, as soon as I followed her, Harry cast off both bow and stern lines, stepped aboard and Dick steered us out of the marina. We started to sit in the cockpit, but Dick shooed us below into the mahogany-trimmed cabin with our bottle of wine. Harry followed us closely.

"Please welcome Dr. and Mrs. John Beaton," Harry announced over our shoulders.

There were three other occupants of the cabin who stood and moved to allow us room to sit down. William Shanty, Christopher Miller, and Jack Straw smiled and shook our hands. It was great to see them all again, and judging from the smiles and handshakes our feelings were reciprocated. We sat, and Miller spoke first.

"Here's what I promised you a while back," he said to Ann, and with a flourish he swept away the cloth over the table to reveal a lobster dinner with wine, salads, and all the fixings.

Ann thanked him and accepted the glass of Pinot Grigio he offered her. I accepted one too. I noted he looked a lot more relaxed, had a sun-tan, was dressed casually, and had a little less around his middle.

"Chris, you're looking good. Have you lost weight?" I asked.

He seemed pleased I noticed and replied, "Yup. I retired at the end of April and have been living on a boat in a marina in Portland since then. I'm selling my place in DC and moving as far away as I can; well as far away as I can and still be civilized. I think I may have found heaven."

Jack commented, "He's even met a hot lady marina-occupant too. Isn't that right Chris?"

"Early days yet. Just good friends," Chris replied with a smile.

"That's not what I understood," Jack said. "He said she is... well, I'm not going to say what he said in front of Ann. And, of course now he's retired I can say things like this about him. I don't have to be tactful around him anymore."

"You were tactful before?" Chris said and helped himself to salad.

I turned to Shanty, "Will, I haven't been following your career. I've done my best to ignore all news for the last few months, and you may not want to talk about it, but what about your love-life? Is it still Guatemalan?"

"It is, and you and Ann will get an invitation to the wedding in October. It'll be a quiet affair."

"That's great. I'm very pleased for both of you," I said.

Ann asked, "What does she think about your being the new representative for District 12?"

"We discussed this. Maria is not going to be the politician's wife, stand next to me, smile sweetly and look adoringly at me. There are some in the party who would like to pigeon-hole her like that. She is going to have her own career and will be spending the next three years teaching at the University of Washington. In some ways we'd like to model our marriage on yours and John's. I spent enough time in the car with him this year to know about what goes on in your lives. You have your own careers and you respect one another. We're going to do the same."

"Thank you. To marriage," I said, and we all raised our glasses.

Ann said, "Jack, I've never asked. Are you married?"

"Yes. Twelve years, two children, ages five and eight, one dog, no cats – Charlotte is allergic."

"Charlotte is your...?"

"My wife. Lucy and Aaron are my children."

We continued to munch and exchange chit-chat until the "Death by Chocolate" dessert silenced us for a few minutes. Once again Ann and I did not share one dish and two spoons.

With the meal over we cleared the table. Miller left to take the ample remains of the meal to Dick and Harry in the cockpit, and then returned to his seat.

"I checked with Dick and Harry and invited them to come down here, but they said John would fill them in later. Is that OK John?"

"Sure," I replied, a little apprehensive about what was coming.

"I'll start," Miller said, "and, as usual, none of this conversation ever happened if anyone asks you in the future. We're just old friends having dinner and an evening sail. Everyone agree?"

We all nodded.

"John, the first questions are did Smith contact you, and did you distribute the CD's or did he?"

Sometimes you just have to trust someone. I hesitated then replied, "Yes, and yes I did."

"What happened?"

"He cornered me in Costco again. He basically manipulated me into taking the CD's from him and distributing them. He's pretty good at that."

"Where'd he been?"

"He said he'd stayed on a boat in Port Townsend for a few days until the fuss there settled down, then went somewhere else?"

"Somewhere else?"

"He didn't say, but he had a sun-tan, so it wasn't around here in the winter."

"Did you keep any of the CD's he gave you?"

"No, and I didn't look at them before copying them. I decided I didn't want to know what was on them."

"So, you sent them to...?"

I named the newspapers.

"All of them wrote articles about the CD's?"

"I believe so. My plan worked it seems. My turn for questions. I sent you a set too. Is there any way you could trace them back to me?"

"No, and I made sure of that. I made sure there were plenty of fingerprints, tea stains and stray DNA on them after I copied and distributed them through the FBI. There's no way they can be traced to anywhere other than Tacoma, where they were posted, so don't worry there."

"But didn't they have the same information on them as the CD's you got hold of in Port Townsend?"

"Well, that was a piece of luck. I never saw the CD's in Port Townsend, although I think there were only three, not four, and when these arrived on my desk I had no way of knowing if they were the same, so I made sure at least the three were distributed far and wide through the Bureau. You see, the CD's from Port Townsend never saw the light of day. I don't know what happened to them, but I was told a committee had decided to not do anything for the time being. This sounded suspicious, but because I really couldn't do anything about it I had to let it go. I never found out how Preston, and the man we know as Father Riley, met up in the DC office, so I was stymied. Then the newspapers got the story, but they only paid attention to the lurid details. They didn't say anything about the fourth CD. I hadn't paid much attention to the details on that CD. I'd given it to a colleague to work on, and we both spent an hour or two looking and listening to the CD. And there it was, a shot of the man you apparently called White. It isn't perfectly clear, but I'm sure it's him. You saw it too?"

I nodded.

Miller continued, "Unfortunately, the audio is poor quality too. There was only one thing to do. I called up Jack."

Jack said, "I have friends in low places, and untraceable low places, and for a slight consideration my friends agreed to post the fourth CD on line. For some reason the newspapers had hesitated to do this. I don't know if that was because pressure was applied. I hope not, but you never know. I like to believe they were holding back and still studying the CD."

"So that's it then?" I asked, "There will be no more repercussions?"

"Director Agnelli, your Mr. White, has been indicted as you know. I don't know if he'll be convicted, but he won't have a job with the Bureau again. There may be a few others who will fall with him, but I don't know, and to tell you the truth, I don't care anymore. I gave my three month notice on January 2nd and am learning to love life again. However, there is one problem I haven't figured out. Do you know what that is?" He asked me. "I've discussed it with Jack."

I hesitated, "I'm going to guess, but is it why Preston came to see you in the first place?"

"Exactly," Miller replied, "and I still don't know. We have a couple of theories, and a couple of strokes of luck. It seems Preston was not being completely honest. I was not the first person he turned to at the FBI. After we'd seen Agnelli on the CD I asked my tech person to go over the CCTV in the building with me the day Preston came to see me. By mistake we started looking at the recordings two weeks before Preston visited me, and there he was, large as life coming into the building. Any visitors we have get recorded, so we should have been able to see who he visited that day, but the records of Preston's first visit seem to have been "mislaid". We were working on finding them again. So, when Preston visited me he may have thought Father Riley was there to help him, but we don't know for sure. We can speculate, but we really don't know what the good Father was doing there, especially since we still don't know who he was or who he was working for. Jack has some other ideas." He nodded at Jack.

Jack began, "There's the fact that no one in the White House was implicated on any of those CD's. Maybe someone there was in charge, but it's unlikely. However, since the White House occupants change more frequently than most members of Congress, we'll give them the benefit of the doubt. The other theory we have is something Smith said about how he'd thought the people directing him had changed. So, one idea is it's likely Chris here was set up to try to find Smith, or more likely, what Smith had."

"You mean Preston, the priest, and Agnelli colluded to get Chris to start an investigation?" Shanty asked.

"We think it's possible," he shrugged. "It's also likely Preston was a pawn and didn't realize what was going on, but it's going to be hard to prove," Jack replied. "The other factor is Chris covered his tracks well and made it hard, or impossible, to trace what he was doing. It's also possible he would have been the fall guy if an investigation of Congress's voting patterns became public knowledge. Whether they, and we are not sure who "they" are, were intending to expose the politicians Smith had worked on, so they would be disgraced, or whether they would have used Smith's information for their own purposes is unknown. Of course, maybe there's another rival group blackmailing politicians. Who knows? In the end we just haven't figured it all out, and it's likely we never will. We just have to expect nothing in politics, or DC, is ever black or white. It's all shades of gray."

Miller said, "Then I asked myself are these politicians any worse than the rest of the population, or did they just get found out? If others in Congress accept money for their election campaigns in return for unspecified favors aren't they equally culpable? You can drive yourself mad thinking like this, and so I've come to the acceptance that we, all of us here, have made some difference to the course of democracy, but we can't fix it all. I'm going to leave the rest to my colleagues at the FBI. They work hard and I wish them well. From my point of view all I can do is to stay retired, but remember that, and to paraphrase Jefferson, "the price of democracy is eternal vigilance". Please, I ask you, let's toast to that."

We all raised our glasses and toasted.

I'd spent enough time below, it was a beautiful evening and I wanted to get on deck again, so I stood with my glass and climbed the companionway steps. Dick was still at the tiller and I noticed we were getting close to the marina in Bremerton.

"They want to catch the 9:05 ferry back to Seattle," he said.

Ann had followed me to the cockpit and Shanty, Miller and Jack appeared too. The ferry was still unloading cars, so it would be another fifteen minutes before it left. Dick sailed the boat close, and slow enough, to the breakwater that Jack and Miller could step off.

We said our good-byes and Dick headed away and back to Port Orchard. I could see his relationship with his Hallberg-Rassy was developing, and he was enjoying the sailing.

I didn't want to go below again. I wanted to enjoy the evening sun setting over the Olympic Mountains. I sat in the cockpit with Shanty opposite, and Ann next to me. Dick relaxed at the wheel in the light breeze while Harry unwound on the foredeck with a beer.

"Will, you didn't say much down there," I said.

"You're right, John, but there wasn't much to say. I've been in DC for about six months now, and there are those who want to get things done, and there are those who think it's their role to make sure nothing gets done, and nothing gets spent. I agree with Chris, there's no black and white; it's all shades of gray. You do what you can do and hope others do the same. Sometimes it's all plain sailing; sometimes you hit a wall you know you'll never move. I'll do my best and I hope it's good enough."

"What do you think is going to be the issue closest to your heart, the one you want to work on more than anything?" Ann asked.

I looked at her. She hadn't said much during dinner either, but was leaning forward and very attentive to what Shanty was saying now.

"There are so many, but I've seen how people live, or scrape-by, in Guatemala and Bangladesh and a host of other countries, and the poor are basically the same everywhere. Until we improve their lives we can't claim to be any more civilized than they are. So, poverty is one issue I feel strongly about, and the other is global warming. I don't think most of my party has a clue what the science is saying about it, and if America doesn't do anything about it no one else will. I've been wondering how I can support responding to it." He looked at Ann directly, sat back, and added, "The way you're looking at me, Ann, I suspect you have an idea or two."

Ann laughed and said, "You're right, and if I had to pick two things to work on, I would have chosen the same. So what are you going to do about it?"

Shanty started, "I...Ann, tell me what you want me to do."

"Am I that obvious?" Ann asked.

"I'm afraid so," he replied.

"Well, I was thinking. John said you had offered to give him something for his services, and he said he hadn't a clue about what to ask for, so I'm going to ask instead. Is that OK, John?" She asked and looked at me.

I replied, "That's fine with me." I wondered where she was going with this.

"Well, you don't need the salary do you Will? You have plenty of money. Had you thought about not accepting it?"

"I had thought about it, but I also thought it would be a gesture which wouldn't mean much. But you have other ideas?"

"I agree if you just didn't accept it no one would really notice, and it might give you a holier-than-thou reputation. Instead give your salary to an anti-poverty group and a climate change awareness organization."

"Do you have names in mind for these groups?" he asked Ann.

"Yes, but I want you to choose, not me."

"My party isn't exactly known for championing these issues," Shanty added.

"I know, and I think I know you. That's one more reason to do it, don't you think?"

Shanty chuckled, "Ann, I think you have a great point there. I'll talk it over with Maria and I'll let you know. No, I won't let you know. You and John need to pay more attention to my career and find out for yourselves. If people like you don't, who will? Deal?"

"Deal."

"But I haven't promised anything yet, " Shanty emphasized.

I added, "Will, I think you have, but we can pretend a little longer. It's your money, but I like the idea and I think it will increase your credibility. It will also establish your, I hate to say, moral credentials. You may also find some lobbyists you would rather not talk to avoiding you, and others approaching you. The alternative was to ask you to buy me a new Hallberg-Rassy, but that would make Dick here incredibly jealous."

Dick had been listening to the conversation, while standing at the wheel and steering, said.

"Please don't buy him a Hallberg-Rassy. He wouldn't have a clue what to do with it, and I need him for working on this one."

Shanty laughed and said, "I promise I won't buy him a sailboat of any sort."

We were approaching the entrance to the Port Orchard Marina. I stood to help take down the main sail, but Dick told me to sit.

He said, "This evening's cruise is courtesy of Dick and Harry cruises. Thank you for sailing with us."

He started the motor, headed into the light breeze, and pulled in the Genoa with the roller furling. Harry lowered the main-sail and five minutes later we glided into the mooring.

Harry secured the mooring lines and Dick stopped the motor. Ann, Shanty and I said our goodbyes, stepped off Roho 2, and walked along the marina deck to our cars.

Ann and I both hugged Shanty and promised we would spend more time with him in the future. We watched him drive away, and then took a few more minutes to enjoy the remains of the sunset before we sat in my Subaru.

"Let's go home," Ann said.

30

He didn't say anything at the small, private wedding, nor did we ask, but at the beginning of November Shanty made national news when he said he was donating his salary to two organizations. Half was to go to RESULTS, a lobbying group for the poor, and half was to his foundation which he was directing to support studies on climate change. Ann was pleased.

In the middle of November I received a postcard with a picture of a bland hotel in Phoenix on one side. On the other It read:

"It's been a year since our voyage and I've been good. Even thought of getting married, but that requires interaction with government. Liked the stories in the news. Hope the right, or maybe wrong, people, got nailed. By the way the cancer surgery was successful. I have a 1" scar on my neck from where they removed the skin cancer and I have promised SP 30 will be part of my life from now on. Live long and prosper. S."

I smiled, showed the card to Ann, and then ran it through the shredder.

After all, that's what he would do.

END